Nessun Dorma

C000161709

D J Peat

First published in 2023 by Blossom Spring Publishing
Nessun Dorma Copyright © 2023 D J Peat
ISBN 978-1-7393514-0-3
E: admin@blossomspringpublishing.com
W: www.blossomspringpublishing.com

For Cerys and Siân

Prologue

Mam

The last shards of moonlight were as vibrant as memories. Through the murkiness, he shovelled debris at breakneck speed. The wind rhythmically breathed a kiss of life. Even with misted eyes, I recognised the formation of trees that scratched and wrestled in silhouette. Unable to move, my insides twisted. I tried to scream but he'd stuffed my mouth until I'd gagged. The restraint was too strong... too tight, squeezing my stoved skull and leaving a steamroller headache. Ripped tights and a missing shoe chilled my left foot. If I escaped, the best dry cleaner wouldn't be able to remove the stains. *Never be a victim*, my family had always told me, but above, the man's frame blocked out everything. How would I survive? My heartbeat a train, I tried to focus.

My promotion had provided extra pocket money for the boys. I'd felt woozy delight at becoming Head of Commercial Property; my specialism was putting clients at ease.

I'd had only one appointment today.

Where were my clipboard and keys?

How had I ended up here?

Earlier, I'd been on the industrial estate to meet Mr. Patel, who saw me as central to his expansion plans.

Nothing.

No memory.

Between standing on the warehouse's forecourt, where the pit used to stand, to becoming the lead in a living nightmare, there was just a void.

The whooshing spade was the only sound for miles. The world had stalled; all movement belonged to him.

Suddenly, he jumped into the ditch, feet splayed either side of my shoulders. Fear froze my bones. His face was covered. Our gasps fused: low, hoarse, and rasping. Sweat clung to him like decaying fish, some of which drizzled over me. Sturdy hands neared my throat. In desperation I swallowed, hoping against hope to displace the gloved hand, but it was nothing more than a pathetic reaction. I didn't want to be prey. I didn't want to be a newspaper headline or tomorrow's chip-paper. Another inch and my doom would be sealed. He ruptured the necklace ornamenting my grandmother's ring and scrambled away. A car door slammed.

Anxious air filled my nostrils. Tears catapulted, knowing the earth would gulp me into an organic feast. Above, the dirt no longer fell, but he was back leaning against the spade. He cast no shadow. Panic made my body vibrate. Trying to propel myself upwards was wasted. On my thighs I sensed the now dry crustiness of his bodily fluid.

I grew faint.

Paler.

Otherworldly.

Then he was pressed against me again, gripping my throat with deadlock force.

The final memory was a shard of soothing moonbeams. Yet, the light was fading, and the wind struggled to exhale. I floated and dissipated into a cocoon. Curled into the foetal position, a hazy image formed of my husband and boys. There was a guise of humour – it was Friday the thirteenth, and Good Friday. Ironic, dark, pitiful humour. But that happy flashback bathed me. My husband, my beautiful boys – three peas in a pod, blessed... I'd been truly blessed.

How would they cope without me... without their mother?

Chapter 1: Missing

DC Carter

I rolled over. Blinding sun basked through pale curtains. 'Neil, Neil – that pager is going fifty-to-the-dozen!' my mam's voice called from downstairs. I tried to reply, but my mouth was drier than a dusty flipflop, my saliva turned to glue. My feet fought to move the duvet, but my legs were too heavy. Aching knees were reminders that I was no longer young.

I reached out and accidentally knocked over a picture of my kids – Sammy and Caz – in their school uniforms. Volunteering to work the weekend shift was sensible, as they were in Tenerife with Jane and her fancy man with his fancy car, fancy shoes, and fancy job. And I was back at my mam's, killing time before I'd see them again. I re-straightened the frame.

Shoving myself out of bed, my feet landed on last night's pizza. I skidded, scattering cans, falling on a mound of clothes that reeked of cigarette smoke. Eyeballing an empty whisky bottle, a black-and-white striped pizza box, and a bucket for emergencies, I vowed to give up... well, until the next time.

'Neil? It's still going, love. I've stuck on some bacon and eggs.'

I opened the window, and whirring lawnmower blades cut through the air. In the bathroom, following a painful, yellow pee, I splashed water onto my face and brushed my teeth, which felt slack, like pushing an open door. Thankfully, enough drool formed to croak: 'Breakfast would be lovely; I'll be down in a minute.' Gagging after sniffing my armpits, I gave them a quick once over. An ample splash of Kouros would cure all ills. I brushed what was left of my hair; there were more strands on the brush. The follicles were weaker than my chances of promotion. Yesterday's shirt would do another day and my tie, which I'd shoved into my blazer pocket, was still knotted. My trousers dug into the chaffing on my waist left by last night's jeans. The fitness regime remained on the back burner.

On entering the kitchen, the pager sprung like a starved creature. I sat at the kitchen table and viewed the newspaper's back page. My eyes regained focus on news of Newcastle's game against Wolves. I pulled on my reliable loafers, soled and heeled on at least three occasions; I loved the softness of old leather. Mam scraped the fry-up onto my plate. Pulling bread from a Sunblest bag, I could feel her disappointment was deep-rooted. Carrying a sausage on a fork, I made my way to the telephone.

'Hello DI, sorry, DC Carter here,' I said. 'You paged me.'

*

Soon after, I was at the dismantled pit. It was already afternoon. I was glad that they were able to do something with the old place. Keeping the iron-gates was a masterstroke – that and cleaning up the war memorial. Monkey Island Industrial Estate had a grand entrance, which was different from many of the soulless retail parks that had been spat out around the country. *Enterprise Zones for entrepreneurs*, they'd called them, but it was just the usual cronies who were taking advantage of low rent.

As a copper, The Miners' Strike had changed me. Back in '84, the area had been a political battlefield. Six years on there wasn't even a commemorative plaque. Sergeant Irving had been my gaffer back then; he had encouraged me to become a detective. I had become disheartened by how the police were viewed as the enemy – but, like many others, I had taken advantage of the unbelievable overtime rates.

The forecourt was a greyish-white concrete, waiting to be drenched with tarmac. The huge tin-shed warehouses looked like a strong wind would send them crashing. Thoughts of The Great Storm from three years ago weren't good. That had been a missing person case, too, and my first big failure. A football hooligan on the run for three attempted murders had just vanished, as if the storm had sucked him up and dumped him in another universe. Everything fell apart later. But, due to my holidaying superiors, there was a chance to redeem myself by locating this missing person.

I pulled in. A male and female officer were waiting. 'Morning sir,' she said. They must've thought I hadn't noticed them sniggering when I parked my Ford Cortina.

'Morning. It's Smyth and James, isn't it?'

'Yes, sir,' replied Smyth, who was about seven foot tall and so thin the veins in his forehead were evident. 'Isn't this unorthodox?'

Here we go. 'Look, son.' I adjusted my waistband after breathing-in to compete, but even a toothpick would've felt plump next to Slimline-Smyth. I stuck out my backside and rested my arm on the cop car's roof. 'It's Easter Saturday. I want to work out if we've got a case and the best way to do that is to have all the players here. Have you scanned the area?'

'Sorry, sir,' James intervened with a moonbeam smile. It'd take more than that to disarm me. 'We found nothing – except her car – and we were under the impression that DI Quick would be leading the enquiry.'

Looking across at the green Ford Fiesta, my nostrils flared, but I managed to hold the anger. 'He's a nine-to-fiver, girl – off for the weekend. If needs be, I'll contact him – if that's okay with you?' I growled. Their heads bowed; they'd remembered their place.

For me, it was all about the job. The young 'uns at the station called me the Clichéd-Cop. I understood. My wife had divorced me for being married to the job. Bells Whisky was delivered to my mam's like others received milk. Being a loner, a smoker, and a fast-food addict, my waistband had increased an inch every sixth months since my emotional breakdown, which had almost ended in disaster. So, they had a point. But how dare they? Clichéd-Cop. What did they know? I was worth fifty DI Quicks and I'd prove it.

If I lived long enough.

Killer

I kept seeing the eyesore of pylons from the night before. They had been like aliens willing me on: *Welcome to the '90s, your first of the decade*, they had said. Being the only witnesses, I'm sure they had celebrated my metamorphosis. A first operation on home turf. When I'd started, I'd gone further afield, but the wooden-tops were so gormless that I had planned an event on my own plot. This godforsaken hole deserved it. Reading up on others like me, they often talked about the pleasure they got from seeing their victim's loved ones. I couldn't wait; I knew the family well.

When I find the right one, everything begins to brew and brew and brew until the only thing in my head is a fog of sounds – hissing and drumming – and the dream of touching their big, scared eyes.

Nothing can beat it.

Surfing the adrenalin rush, I knew from experience that I'd have a few days before it'd drain, and then I'd be immersed in gloom.

No one could hear me in the lock-up. I turned on the radio and dug dirt from under my fingernails. Thatcher was adamant that any Poll Tax protestors would feel the full weight of the law. Madonna – at number one with 'Vogue' – replaced her. Imagining bundling one of those blonde bombshells into the van, I felt the same invincibility as when I had sapped that lady's last breath. Whirling in the whirlwind was wonderful, but there were jobs to do, tyres to change, and a swimming pool amount of bleach to administer.

A sack which housed her belongings was in the van, and, pressed against my heart, the ring that had adorned her neck. I always keep a memento of my last operation.

Swapping the ornate bracelet to the ring had been purifying. I touched my new possession; the energy was enough to blow the pylons from the grid and I sang along with the song.

I had been privileged to feel this alive on a handful of occasions and cherished it.

DC Carter

'Mr. Patel, Mr. Gallagher – thank you for agreeing to meet me.' I called across the forecourt. They were both dressed in golfing clothing: slacks, polos, and V-neck jumpers. With a blinding reflection, Gallagher's Jaguar had been polished to within an inch of its life. He'd parked next to Mrs. McCarthy's Fiesta. I strode over to greet them, hooking on the noose-of-a-tie and sliding on my sunglasses. Not only did they provide protection from the sun, but they also made me look like Clint Eastwood. Between the buildings, the two uniforms were giving the place a further inspection. Their faces had been a picture when I had sent them packing. 'So, Mr. Patel,' I said with a no-nonsense handshake. 'What time did you arrange to meet Mrs. McCarthy?'

'Two-thirty – I know it was a bank holiday, but she agreed. I'd been in Yorkshire with family, and it was the only convenient time,' he replied, worry-lines creasing his brow.

'And you agreed?'

'Yes.' Guilt poured from Gallagher like wine: he was alabaster. 'As Mr. Patel is such a loyal customer, she said that she didn't mind.'

'Is this usual practice for an estate agent?'

'No, she'd usually check in with the office.' I could tell by Gallagher's expression that he felt this on a human level, not just as Mrs. McCarthy's employer. 'As it was a bank holiday, she paged to say that she'd arrived and all was well.' He held up the small, plastic device which showed that the message came through at 14:17. 'We were at Seahouses for the night. I thought nothing more of it.'

'What time did you arrive, Mr. Patel?'

'A little later. I stopped to talk to an old friend on the terraces, so about twenty-to.' He looked at his watch – people often do that when they speak about time. 'When she wasn't here, I drove to Gallagher's Estate Agents, but it was closed. I thought she must've got mixed up, so I left. I didn't want to get her into trouble. When I saw Gallagher at the golf club, we chatted, and, well, you know the rest. We called you.'

I scratched my chin and some dead skin fell, which I tried to wipe from my blazer without them noticing. Their faces showed that I'd failed. Beneath Gallagher's wheels, something poked out from under the lengthy body. Was it a skid-mark?

I commanded him to pull back, and he climbed in. Once he'd reversed, it was apparent that a black tyre-streak – about two-foot-long – had stained the forecourt. I went down on one knee, which almost ripped my trousers, they were so tight. I cursed Smyth and James. How could they have missed it? In a swift movement, I hauled off my sunglasses and scanned the area, spotting warehouse cameras. 'Are those things switched on?' Adrenaline flowed; there was a case brewing.

Gallagher followed my eye-line. 'Not yet. The place won't open until July. We're completing the paperwork on the final properties.'

Damn. A twenty-five-minute window, a skid-mark, and a missing person. I'd have to contact Quick. 'Have you any idea of her husband and boys' location? My bobbies went round earlier but there was no answer.'

'At the football – playing away, I think. Newcastle fans.'

'Wolves.' I remembered from the paper. I staggered to my feet. 'You've been more than helpful. We'll be in touch for a written statement.'

They looked troubled as they drove away. Time is

always of the essence, and they'd made mistakes. But they weren't to blame. They were just victims of circumstance. Not half as much as Mrs. McCarthy had been, though.

I was thinking abduction, and lit a cigarette. 'Smyth. James. Come here, you useless idiots.' Trampling over the forecourt like Bambi chasing a giraffe, they looked sick. 'Get the camera. How could you have missed this?' James continued to the cop car and, almost snapping, Smyth inspected the stained concrete.

'Oh, no,' he gulped.

'What is it now?'

'There's a shoe.'

Isaac

'It was a good header,' I said.

'They should've been one up before that. How did they miss that effort early-doors? It was practically an open-goal,' Dad replied. Whilst queueing for drinks, shouts of 'The Blaydon Races' and other raucous songs filled the air.

'Are yer sure they used to be a big club?' Carl – my brother – inquired. I understood why. Behind the goal, much of the terracing had been removed and the old ground, like many of these clubs, needed rebuilding.

'When I was a lad...' Dad begun. We jeered whenever he uttered those words. He smiled. 'Wolves were massive – not just in the Midlands, but in the country and in Europe; an enormous club.'

'Easter Saturday – you'd think there'd be more people here, the atmosphere's terrible,' I said. Too old for Easter eggs, Dad had bought us tickets for an away match. Although it was expensive, we tried to attend a few games each season when we weren't playing ourselves. 'Where's Dan?' In what looked like a prison-courtyard, groups of men were sporadically gathered. My other brother was talking to some student types with Beatle-haircuts. Music had surpassed his love of football.

Over the tinny Tannoy, the Happy Mondays' new song 'Step On' blared. Carl moved to the groove. 'Ooh, Dan, do yer want a Bovril?' he yelled. Dan reacted with the V-sign. When we were becoming more independent a few years earlier, Dan and Carl had lined up for half-time snacks. Dan had thought that Bovril was like other hot drinks and required milk and sugar. He had dropped in the condiments and circled with a plastic spoon. Watching with a mix of merriment and disbelief, Carl could hardly contain himself. He had waited in anticipation for Dan to taste it. Whenever he retold the tale, the distance in which the spray propelled expanded. Carl made the cup sound bath-sized, pebble-dashing the whole Gallowgate.

'Get 'em a tea, Da'.'

'Okay, son,' Dad replied, handing over a fiver. 'You two queue whilst I go for a slash.' Carl and I watched Dad disappear as Dan twanged an air-guitar.

Travelling down in the bank holiday traffic – the day before – had been great. A night in a B&B and a drive into Birmingham in the morning had felt like a real break. Dan and Carl had complained about how I always secured the front seat. Being twenty-seven minutes older than Carl and a football match older than Dan, I milked my position as the eldest triplet – more than Dan milked Bovril! The real reason was twofold: firstly, my brothers were sleepyheads. Secondly, I didn't like change and needed everything in its place, therefore I only slept in bed which meant Dad liked me up front. Being from a large family meant that he hated being alone. We had taken turns playing tapes. As usual, I had organised a rota.

The Sierra Cosworth's sound system was a million miles from the football ground's Tannoy: sophisticated, sleek, and multi-layered. Being a Beatles fan did not mean that Dad hadn't kept up with trends. He loved The Stone Roses' album. Mam, who was working, was exclusively a Bowie fan and listened to nothing else. Likewise, being faithful to his chosen one, Carl was U2 through-and-through; even listening to another band caused him to question the time-spent. Eclectic and electric, Dan loved discovering anything new or old.

Carl and I were chatting when we froze. At first, I had to register what was being said. The croaky tinman's words ground through the Tannoy, but Carl's grip, creasing my jacket, told me to listen intently to the repeated message. 'Could Mr. Simon McCarthy make his way to the nearest Steward?'

Dad burst from the toilet, adjusting his fly.

Why did they want Dad?

Carl

Dad spoke to the police. They told us that Mam was missing. It was enough to make uz want to smash all other cars off the road, but Dad was as sensible as ever. Why did he drive so safely? If ah had a Sierra Cosworth, me feet would be through the floorboard – like some modern-day Fred Flintstone – breaking speed-of-sound records. Crappy cars, with smiles in the windows, overtook us. There weren't too many smiles in our car and under the circumstances we should've been ripping up the tarmac.

When we had left the ground's crumbling structure, we'd listened to the end of the match, but there were no cheers when we won one-nil. Then the radio was off; the atmosphere in the car was deathly. It must've driven Isaac mad as he'd spent ages explaining the rota. 'We'll be no good to her if we're in a ditch somewhere outside of Halifax,' were the only words Dad uttered on the journey-to-hell, and that was when we'd groaned about being overtaken by rust-buckets. Pretending to sleep, ah saw him turn towards Isaac on more than one occasion. They'd give each other silent glances, whilst Dan – who'd taken off his shoes – was also feigning sleep. Isaac was so bloody responsible he'd often stay up at night and talk to Mam and Dad about adult-stuff: mortgages, politics, and stuff like that. Dan and I would be in our rooms with our music and mags.

Strange thoughts consumed uz. Something must've happened, she wouldn't just do a moonlight-flit, she was me Mam. Then again, me mate Davey's mam had buggered off. When we were little, we'd go around there and butter wouldn't melt. She had a smile for everyone and was dead kind – always had a chocolate biscuit for uz. Then she disappeared with a vacuum-cleaner salesman from Cockermouth. There were also rumours about her being a centrefold in a dirty mag. Ah could've been knocked down with a feather. She had been me first real crush – her and Betty Rubble from *The Flintstones*. Nah – me Mam wouldn't do that. She was happy and had just got that promotion at work. She loved Dad, her family, and her job. If a writer was making up a happy character, it'd be Mam. She was a bundle of sunshine wrapped in silver paper.

No happiness came from me thoughts because the alternatives were unbearable. She wouldn't have run off with another bloke, but what if someone had taken her? Me head dug deeply into the pillow, but ah couldn't stop thinking about killers from around the country. Ah wished the details from me A-level Criminology course hadn't filled me head – loved reading about it, shocking, though. Ah suppose it meant that ah was a good student because ad memorised it all. Leaving Wolverhampton, ah remembered a forty-six-year-old who was born there and was brutally murdered in London about a hundred years ago and one of Jack the Ripper's victims. Colin Pitchfork, caught by DNA, sprung to mind at Leicester. For killing girls, he was locked up for life. Nottingham, and John Bainbridge was another who should never see the light of day again. Then the long drive through Yorkshire: Peter Sutcliffe. *Die. Die. Die.* Those words scared me when ah was little; I'd never heard anything like it on TV before. The killer, hidden in a blanket like the wolf from 'Little Red Riding Hood', had the crowd baying for blood. Ah wish he'd been lynched. Ah used to have nightmares about his dark beard, driving a lorry. Having grown, ah would've loved the chance to kick seven-colours out of him. Nearly home and thoughts of that Mackem idiot who'd pretended to be the Yorkshire

Ripper, and the even stupider police who'd believed it. They had called him Geordie Jack when he wasn't even a Geordie! Ah wondered if he'd ever be caught.

Me pillow was wet. Thoughts of how that Mackem's stupid game had caused more deaths wasn't the reason. We were approaching the unknown. What would hit us when we got back? Ah hadn't cried since ah was eleven and felt embarrassed. Dan's bare foot rested on mine. If anyone had touched me Mam, ad do worse than any of those that I'd been thinking about had done to their victims.

They'd be worse than dead.

Someone was going to get seriously hurt.

Dad

Thoughts wouldn't stick. The air freshener was pine-fresh like cut trees, which made me think of weekending in the Lake District with Donna before we were married. The hum of the engine – like the purr of a big cat – made me think of taking the kids to Edinburgh Zoo when they were bairns. Even flashing lights on the motorway made me think of bonfire nights. *Oh, Donna, where are you?* I kept thinking. No music was a change; it would've only caused distractions. Songs were stronger than smells for memories.

Isaac looked concerned. His Harrington was fastened to the neck, and he continuously rubbed the creased sleeve. A Stone Roses badge – like a chaotic Jackson Pollock's design – reflected, which was ironic because disorder was what he hated most. I could feel him willing me to stay focused, but my life was suspended in cruise control. What had the policeman said, his voice husk as if he'd spent Good Friday in the pub? *'We're afraid to say that we believe your wife is missing. Could you return at the earliest opportunity?'* If I hadn't known better, I may've thought it was a hoax.

Occasionally, there were groans from the back. I knew that I'd been plodding along but I wondered what we'd return to. But I also wanted to face reality, whatever that would be. The Tyne Tunnel's mouth was dark, and it dared us inside like an animal's jaws. Slowing before being swallowed, my hand shook as I changed gear. The movement created further shuffling from the back. Dan and Carl leaned forward. Heading towards the curve of its throat, I swore that Carl was snuffling. That couldn't be right. He was the toughest of the lot. My midfield dynamo on the football pitch.

'Nearly back, lads, it'll be alright,' I croaked, reassuring myself as much as them.

'Aye, she's probably gone to bloody Suzie's caravan and there'll be a message when we get in. It'll be a load of bull,' Carl remarked.

'I was thinking the same thing,' Dan continued. But it was easy to tell when he was lying as the inflection in his voice changed. Isaac's eyes were fixed ahead, not engaging in the *'She's Okay'* game. We all knew that things were far from fine.

'She would've done her job before heading off,' Carl added.

'You're on the money,' I lied. Why hadn't I asked the police more questions, like why they thought she was missing? Why was it so important to call me in the middle of a football match? When I had approached the nearest Steward, the other supporters had teased, thinking that my wife had given birth. Back by eight-thirty was all I had said before chucking down the phone.

Conversing the lie was done on autopilot. Inside, the options circled like smoke rings before vanishing. Had she run off with someone else? There'd been no signs. In fact, we were closer than ever. Suicide? Not Donna, she was sunshine and didn't hide behind shades; she was no-nonsense glorious technicolour. Then the unthinkable, to what the conversation with the police implied. Abduction, mur… no, hold on a minute… no way.

Before long we turned onto our street and the conversation stopped. Fear is about not knowing. Something else took over… trepidation, foreboding, alarm…

Blue lights flashed.

Dan

If the neighbours' curtains had been closed, they would've been twitching. Lyrics kept forming but couldn't conceal my mushy insides. I felt sick. What if she was dead? I knew that once we went inside, that'd be it. I'd have to feel everything she had. Possibilities threatened to send me to sedation. I separated my toes on the metal under Isaac's seat until the skin ripped. That helped ease the internal pain. I shouted, 'I'm not going in.'

'We've got to, Dan,' Dad crooned, and the others got out. Slouched into my seat, I sulked – *the situation was grave, it was time to be brave.* More lyrics: stressful situations are good for writing. Gathered next to a police car were a crumpled detective with a cocked hip, a freakishly tall copper, and a stripper-gram. Behind them were imminent clouds. Carl's face was at my window, gurning like mad, making his cheekbones more prominent. We'd inherited them from Mam; they were high and protruding but our other features were slightly different. Carl's were finer and mine more filled. Isaac had rosier cheeks, but we were from the same pod, of that there was no doubt.

'Get out man, yer freak!' Carl yelled with venom. 'Don't be pathetic.'

Dad herded my brothers with finesse. 'Come on, son.' I could barely hear him. I edged down the window. 'We're like the three musketeers and I'm an ageing D'Artagnan. We stick together. All for one and one for all. United we stand, divided we fall.' But a perpetual force – unbending and true – was waiting. My life had already changed, but to which degree? What if I couldn't take the pain? I split my feet again, which helped.

'I'm scared,' I said, but my words sounded hollow.

'We all are, son.' His eyes were hound-dog heavy. 'The police will help. We've got to hear what they've got to say. It should be okay.' He was lying, like we'd done in the car. Isaac hadn't participated. Even when there was trouble, he'd never complain or explain. Part of his obsessive-compulsion, I thought.

I opened the door and my heart missed beats like a rookie drummer. Wild Bill – our neighbour – looked as if he were being blitzed in a thunderstorm as his television flickered. Isaac was talking to the lanky cop and Carl squeezed a smile from the stripper-gram. Dad and I approached the detective. Skin greyer than moon-dust, he couldn't hide his scooting eyes that were livelier than Carl's after he'd sniffed that white powder. 'Hello – I'm DC Carter, we spoke on the phone.' He shook Dad's hand. 'Should we go inside, avoid prying eyes?'

'If your light wasn't flashing and you hadn't brought Lurch and Morticia Addams, we might be less conspicuous.' Oh no, Dad was nervous. He rarely snapped. Like The Beatles crossing Abbey Road, we followed each other down the pathway with purpose – me, barefoot, à la Paul McCartney.

Isaac

Spaced out on the stairs, we listened to Dad and the detective. The spindly copper had stayed outside; perhaps he was too tall to be indoors. At the foot of the stairs, the policewoman loitered as if she had no ears. There wasn't even a glimmer of emotion when voices spun from the front room: she was stone.

'Sorry to ask, Mr. McCarthy.'

'Call me Simon.'

'Simon, when did you last see your wife?'

I was at the top. Carl was in the middle, head-in-hands. On the first stair, Dan's feet were on the banister; they looked like they'd been bleeding. If any went on the wood, I'd volunteer to clean up. I needed something to do. The detective, whose overbearing aftershave had infected the house, had orchestrated the set-up.

'Friday lunchtime, yesterday. That's when we set off. I'd dug up some veg for Easter Sunday. She was nipping to work and said she might visit her sister, Suzie. I called three times yesterday and this morning. The messages are probably on the answering-machine. I thought they might have gone to the caravan for the night with their parents.'

'Weren't you worried?' asked the detective.

'I thought it was a bit strange, but she'd mentioned the caravan, so I put two-and-two together. I came up with five.'

'Let's give the caravan site a ring.'

Dad and the scruffy detective made the call from the kitchen. It'd take a while because the site manager would have to locate Aunt Suzie. So, I skimmed through my wallet. I wished I had a picture of Mam, but I did find an HMV voucher from Christmas. Of course, Dan and Carl had spent theirs as if it risked burning a hole in their pockets. On Christmas mornings we had sat like this. Dan dreaming, Carl pensive, and me ready to pacify things in case Dad became angry about an early start. We had sworn that poor behaviour wouldn't spoil the festivities. The biggest crime was unwrapping a gift without Mam being present. There was no way I would've allowed that to happen. Presents had to be opened in order. Dad was obsessed by ingratitude, and ensuring that Mam was able to, '*see our little faces,*' was non-negotiable. Christmas had always been her favourite time of the year.

Before I could process the information, the police were whispering in the hallway. Even she flinched; maybe it was the sting from the detective's fragrance. Dan's eyes widened, making his eyelashes look like spiders' legs.

I continued to think about Christmas time. Each year there had been the usual big presents: skateboards, BMXs, a Commodore 64, Walkmans, and Ghetto Blasters. But my parents had a sense of fun, which made them buy a "jokey" present to test our powers of gratitude. One year they had bought Carl a Cabbage Patch Kid. His volcanic personality had blown for less. So, seeing as it was the first present opened, no-one was surprised to see him empurpled. A collection of jazz-tapes had stilled Dan. The only music he despised was jazz, especially acid jazz which left him cold. When I had wanted a chemistry set, they'd bought a Girls' World beautician's head. It had ended up in our old primary school. They had once purchased Sunderland shirts, which we refused to try on. Mam had to take them to a charity shop in that very town. Last year we had all received belts, our initials emblazoned on the buckles. When we stood in the correct order it said CID: Carl, Isaac, and Dan. Carl had been impressed to be first for once, not twenty-seven minutes behind. We were photographed like an advert for a teenage cop-show.

I wondered whether I had spent my last Christmas with Mam.

Dad came out of the kitchen. 'She's not there, lads. Aunt Suzie hasn't heard from her.' The irony of a genuine CID officer receiving a plastic bag from an overgrown stick-insect wasn't lost on me. Across the bag, there was a shadowed word: "EVIDENCE". We all scampered into the front room. The uniforms failed to block us, despite Mr. Tickle and Little Miss Icy's best efforts.

Dad rubbed his eyes.

'Is this your wife's shoe?' asked the detective.

Someone had decided to turn me inside out. They'd taken her. Secured in that bag was one of the shoes that she'd bought to celebrate her promotion.

It had a broken heel.

Chapter 2: Search

Dan

That night was terrible. I thought of long, joyous summers when we were kids: *Not yet teenage vagabonds, running through the corn / the sun painting shadows, through a burning dawn.* The trio. Who would've thought those memories could be ripped apart?

If it wasn't childhood, it was thoughts of Mam screaming. Confusion transformed into neon horror: *We'll find you soon / By the light of the moon.* Oh, I was a better lyricist than that – soon and moon? At least it wasn't spoon, but the tunes kept coming. Pupils dilated or contracted when I fiddled with my bedside lamp. *The deluge and the misery pulsate like a heartbeat, ripping through my chest / The refuge and the tragedy vibrates like a wasp-sting, stopping me from rest.* Pain. If only I could've switched off. Maybe I should've kept a pen and paper next to my bed.

We all met on the landing, our bladders in-tune, like our suffering. Dad blew his nose from inside the bathroom, which sounded like a trumpet; Carl was itching his six-pack, trying to hide wet-eyes; Isaac looked pale and zombie-like; I shuffled from foot-to-foot, wondering if any of us had slept.

'Hey, lads,' Dad said, visibly surprised to find a welcoming-committee lingering outside the bathroom. 'It's not a party. Get some sleep, we'll find her.' Carl nipped in first, which upset Isaac who'd arrived before him. Sticky sweat clung to Dad. Even his hair was soaked. When he playfully jabbed my bare shoulders, I swore that pain was emitting from his every pore. Appearing stoic must've been difficult through hollow eyes.

Downstairs I stared into space and liquid sun poured in like orange juice. Easter Sunday – the resurrection; I begged for nothing more for Mam. Whether my eyes were open or closed didn't matter, the images remained the same. I promised to be mature and accept the pain.

The house felt strange. Music had always weaved through the brickwork. Sometimes it was a battle-of-the-bands; speakers from different rooms would try to outdo each other. Silence was lonely. A clicking clock, a buzz from the fridge and a throaty-grunt from a cat – eyeing birds – were my only company: *Silence ain't golden / it's deathly n' broken.*

Later, Dad and I walked to the shop.

'When I was a lad-' I half-heartedly jeered, '-everything was closed on Easter Sunday.'

Inside the local, which only opened for a few hours, we collected necessities: toilet roll, beer, and cleaning products.

Eyes stalked us from the aisles. Wild Bill, our neighbour – known as the local madman – was one to avoid. Living alone, his only relationship was a destructive one with drink. Since his wife had left with the children, he'd become grizzlier than his beard. Apparently he'd beat her, and she'd left when he'd turned on the kids. I'd written a song about him; it had a kind'o punk vibe: *Wild-man Bill beats up his wife / The prick abuses all good life / With a beer, spirits and dozens of cigs / If I had a chance – I'd feed him t'the pigs.* Loitering at the till, last night's indulgence had stained Bill's shirt, which stretched over flab. A smell that would make a rat turn up its nose encased him.

'Saw the police at your door. Word is your wife's gone missing.'

Behind the counter, the shopkeeper – who'd obviously

watched several westerns – ducked down.

'Howay, Bill, I'm with me lad.'

Bill showed us a clean pair of heels, but muddy footprints splattered polished tiles. Outside, he lurked with the newspapers tucked under his arm, peering at adverts. The shopkeeper guzzled us in. Her aching eyes resembled a woman in a power ballad; except the sense of hopelessness was for real. As we left, Bill stopped Dad. Black nails dug into his shoulder.

Something fizzed.

'I know what you've done. I saw yer. Cut to the chase – the police will – I know yer lying!' Bill bellowed.

DC Carter

Bloody DI Quick. Where did he get that hair? It was like one of those Mr. Whippy ice-creams, wave after wave of creamy blondness, like Barry Manilow in a hurricane. When he had been on the beat, my old boss – Sergeant Irving – advised him to get it cut. A joke went around about him working in a butcher's: *A woman walks in and says to Butcher Quick – Do you have a sheep's head? No, it's just the way I comb my hair.*

We were certainly the thin-blue-line that Easter, nobody else had ventured in. Inside his office, University degrees (notice the plural) were uniformly staged above the desk alongside pictures with local celebrities, prominent politicians, and policemen well above his rank; the gallery was pure theatre. The message: connected, on-the-rise, self-assured, personable. But funnily, in none of those images did he don a brown nose. How he'd got so far through life without anyone catching him with his hooter up someone's backside was beyond me. As he coughed and cleared his lungs, I thought that he also used his tongue and was a licker as well as a sniffer.

'Howay, Gov.'

Sat perpendicular to his desk – he thought that they provided a barrier – he discarded a snotty tissue, which joined the others in the bin. With legs crossed, he tried to have the presence of Al Pacino by resting his face on his hand, but he only succeeded in having the allure of 'av no-idea-oh. 'We must respond. It's often the closest person, in this case: the husband. We have a report from a neighbour that he was digging the garden on Friday morning, for Christ's sake. We can't ignore that.'

I wished I could smoke. Stroking the filmy box in my pocket was of scant consolation. Temptation grew. I wanted to flick lighter flames into his face to wake him. But he wouldn't be able to smell the coffee or that throat-itching hairspray. My only pleasure was that he had a cold, which made him look more ferret faced. 'We can when the message is from an alcoholic wife-beater. They have a vegetable patch, that's what he was doing.'

He pulled a haughty look, as if I should be grateful for access to his superior mind. 'Look, Carter.' He was younger than me, how dare he call me Carter? An absurd characteristic of my Clichéd-Cop status was that people thought that I was jealous at being usurped by this fast-tracked, rule-book-obsessed buffoon. True, I was worried about the force if he were the future, but being green-eyed about his filing-system and computer printouts was ridiculous. I was nicking criminals before he'd had his first demi-wave. 'I was on a conference with Interpol. April '88, just after the ferry strike. Thought we weren't going to make it.' I might've guessed that he'd been on a course. 'Fabulous, an area just outside of Bruges. The moules-frites were out of this world, and the scenery was to die for. Anyhow, a leading French detective gave a talk about how criminals – especially killers – often appear to be feasible. Of course he would tell you that he was digging vegetables. Perhaps, just perhaps, his readiness to disclose this could, just could, mean that she is buried in the back garden.'

My breath shallowed. It took everything I had not to laugh. Had he read the notes? Had he taken time to consider what he was saying? 'With all due respect, sir, by the same token the informant could be applying similar tactics by throwing doubt onto another party. There are three seventeen-year-old youths – triplets, no less – in the house. What you're suggesting is that they were complicit in their mother's murder. That they allowed their father to bury her in the garden and stage an abduction by leaving the car and paging a fake message to her boss from the retail park. I've read some lousy crime books with worse plots, but that couldn't have happened.'

Showing as much intuition as a fly on a spider's web, he itched his cheek, pretending to ponder. 'I have listened to your points, Carter. But the modern-day policeman must think sideways as well as forwards. This is the best lead we have.'

Obviously, another line from a course which had no relevance to our case. 'Sir, if you take this action then you're labelling the family as suspects.' I swallowed nausea. 'Remember who the victims are here.'

His face became stern. 'I think you'll find the missing woman is the victim.' If he really believed he could see the big picture, then his illusion was more deep-rooted than I'd imagined. 'Anyhow, Carter, I have something I wish to discuss.' My eyes tapered. 'The two uniforms have made a complaint. Is it true that you used sexism, calling James a "girl" and labelling her and Smyth "idiots"? I'm sure you'll agree that sounds a lot like mental health oppression. It is 1990, not 1975, and an episode with your namesake from *The Sweeney*.'

Hell's fire stung the back of my eyes. What a sly way to mention my breakdown. 'They'd almost missed key evidence, sir, and you're picking up on a couple of emotional remarks?'

'Apologise, and we'll leave it at that. Keep emotion out of it and be professional.'

Where was the force going? Where was the case going? If we followed his course of action, then we'd become a laughingstock.

Carl

Ah had to get out. Ah wasn't going to be a victim who'd be given a free pass at school: 'Don't say this to him, don't say that. Don't you know his mother's missing?'

They could do one. But ah couldn't stop the tears. They spiralled and left wet patches like a waterlogged football pitch. Cabin fever had infected the house. Dad's tension rose to the size of a mountain about that drunk from next door. Vicious thoughts about what ad do if he said owt about Mam manifested into weird fantasies. Ad rip his insides out. Ah knew he had something to do with it.

Instead, ah got on me bike. Aimlessly ah circled the dead streets. Even thinking the word "dead" made me tears multiply. Sundays were bad, but Easter Sundays were the worst. Some noises, as a family got out of a car, made uz bolt. If am honest, the last time that ad really cried was at junior school.

*

We had started the cycling proficiency course. After seeing BMX bandits at the pictures, ah knew that ah was an expert. One activity had been slaloming between halved tennis balls. A girl called Scabby Mary, who was always falling and had permanent bruises and cut knees, had borrowed a bike. Later she had been adopted and moved away. Shame it hadn't happened earlier, then ah wouldn't have had to suffer the gruesome accident...

As ah had weaved at breakneck speed, with the skill of an Olympic skier, thinking me brothers would call uz The Weaver, the wind had made a beautiful *whoosh* through me spokes. But ah had to hold back. All week, Old Scabby, who had holes in her plimsoles, had been too scared to brake. As usual, adults had fussed around her because she was a victim. If it had been anyone else, they would've been asked to sit out. But not Mary. She had problems, so the same rules didn't apply.

She had raked up so much tarmac that the caretaker had to fill the holes every night. She also left rubbery marks and a burning smell, not too different from a barbecue. Anyhow, like a flapping trout's mouth, her sole had come away; her feet were cut open and she lay in a crumpled mess with her knickers showing. *Whoosh, whoosh, whoosh* – ah had to slam on the brakes to avoid running into her. Luckily Dad had used a tin of WD40 and had tightened every nut until me bike was as finely tuned as a Formula One car. Another *whoosh*. This time it was me back brake; it slithered trying to find friction. Yet it was only momentary, because me front brakes had locked like a Rottweiler's jaws. Propelled forward, me life had moved in slow motion. Ah could hear the miners on the picket line talking about the irony of a hot summer. The waft of ginger cake had spun from the school kitchen. Yellow, with a hint of green, had reminded uz of our team's football top as Scabby Mary's teeth became me focus. Her mouth opened wider, and she had yelled, 'NO!' Me pelvis had involuntarily skewed into a forward motion, and ah anticipated the connection before it happened. Me bits and bob had moved faster than the rest of me body. The chrome clamp, which attached me bike to the handlebar, stuck out. Impact. The pain had been enough to make one of those toady MPs on the telly tell the truth.

Yes, Mary had avoided another assault, but as ah corkscrewed on the hot tarmac, it had been no consolation. Seeing tennis balls cut in half had only created panic at what was going on with me ballbag. Ah had sensed burning, moisture, residue, and dark matter; the only thing to do was give in to tears. Whilst the wheels on the upended bike whooshed and circled, ah vowed never to cry again.

*

Ah found meself in the farmer's field and couldn't believe how much me life had changed. One minute we had been enjoying the match and now me Mam was missing. Ah never thought ad feel pain worse than the day me scrotum split. But there was no comparison: this was crueller. Like that day, a gut-twisting agony consumed uz. Shakily, ah leant me bike against the tree and emptied me stomach. Ah knocked the handlebars and the bike crashed to the ground. Ah couldn't fight my tears from dousing the tree.

Scabby Mary and me Mam's face were indistinguishable. Victims. Ad never really thought about Mary in years. At the time she was just a strange character, who was in and out of class. She'd obviously been abused and put through so much. How could someone do that to a little girl? How could someone take me Mam?

Ah had to find out who'd kidnapped her and payback the hurt. That was a fight ah could have. Ah wouldn't be a victim but would be happy to create one. They deserved it.

DI Quick

The rooms in GHQ's Victorian building were far from soundproof. When I reach Chief Super, I'd work with the best interior designers: chrome, glass, and wide-open spaces were the future. Training on the continent was a godsend; the fulfilment of my meteoric rise to DI, which everyone agreed was well-deserved. I saw how the glass-walled offices in Northern Europe created an openness, where culpability was not concealed. It was a juxtaposition. Here, everything was closed off, but the walls were so worn that they practically invited leaks. Whilst on the continent, everything was open but insulated for privacy and confidentiality.

Sweep-it-under-the-carpet culture had allowed clichés like Carter to stay on the force. In other countries his transgressions would've been exposed, and he'd have been asked to leave for bringing the force into disrepute. A mushroom complexion and a suit designed for a smaller man; he didn't have the slickness of a detective. DC Carter's days were numbered. If we were going to work together, I wouldn't have time to mollycoddle him. Having the DCI as SIO was great news. He'd give me the room to pursue Carter's extraction.

The Chief Super's room was galling. David Attenborough could've been hiding amongst the plants. There were so many, it was like a jungle. Pictures of wildlife and angling achievements made the place too personal. Even stood at his desk with the door closed – and the radio informing us that the prison riots were approaching an end – the boom of his stride was uncurtailed. I felt irritated by the lack of secrecy.

DC Carter half turned to greet our superior. He placed an envelope on the desk.

'Sit, sit. Don't stand on ceremony for me,' the Chief Super said.

No matter how often I'd met the Chief Super, I never got over his size. He was a goliath of a man – there was no wonder there were dents in the ceiling.

'Thank you, sir,' I said.

'Okay, okay,' he replied. His gravelly voice was the personification of an American whiskey. Dressed in civvies, he filled a watering can and addressed us. 'With both the DCI and DSI away, you're lucky that I've come in to sort out my plants. As SIO, the DCI will set up an incident room at your Nick. Back on Wednesday, he said on the phone. The legals were less than impressed with being disturbed on Easter Monday but owed me a favour.' Somehow, I didn't writhe with disappointment. Nepotism was part of the old-school network that I found most detrimental. 'Anyhow,' he said pouring water onto greenery, 'I've read your notes and, publicly, I'll support you. However, do you think they fully substantiate a warrant?'

'Sir, I realise that we can ill-afford any mishaps and need to provide the best yield from our actions.'

He sniffed a plant. 'I'm just concerned that the report came from someone known to us, and not for positive reasons. A wife-beater?'

I patted my hair, which was held perfectly in place. 'I believe it is one-hundred percent worth following up, and doing it properly will send a message throughout the Island.'

'And Carter. You have no reticence?' A hair tickled my forehead.

'No, sir, I support the DI.'

Bemused by Carter's loyalty, the opportunity to weaken him surfaced. After all, he was a cliché. 'To be fair to DC Carter,' I began, 'he had many reservations, which he communicated with passion on handover.' He must've been breathing in, as suddenly his gut barrelled.

The Chief Super cut Carter down with a glance. 'Come on. You're the Major Incident Team, and if this does become a murder case, I want you as my top DI and DC. I need no bull,' he growled. 'Is that clear, Carter?'

'Sorry, sir. I explained to the DI that it may cause problems with the family. We don't want to isolate them. Yet, when he explained the importance of this action, I was duty bound to support him.'

The Chief Super placed down the watering can and stretched his shovel-like hands. 'Right. I believe that everyone's ready downstairs?' his voice echoed.

'Yes, sir.'

'Go ahead – swiftly and smartly – but the family are untouchable. There's three seventeen-year-old lads, isn't there? No matter how they react, I want them to be treated with kid gloves. Understood?'

'Yes, sir.'

The Chief Super picked up a pointing stick and stood in front of our area map. Jabbing with a rat-a-tat, I crossed my legs; surely a computerised image would've been more productive. 'Okay, they live in the private houses on the Island. The shoe was found here, on the site of the old pit.' He began to tap again. 'I always think the peninsular that the locals call Monkey Island is the shape of a scrotum.' Carter's gut wobbled, whilst I remained expressionless; the Chief Super's vulgarity was beneath me. 'The answers are on the Island, do we agree? There's only one way in and out.'

'Yes, sir,' we said in unison.

DC Carter became greyer. The shadow of his past spread over him. Cases on the Island had never ended well for Carter: firstly, he'd failed to locate the missing football hooligan; secondly, the Dead-Babies, which had catapulted him towards breakdown. Filmed on the television, he'd cried, 'The answers are on the Island.' Gracelessly, the Chief Super's audacity to paraphrase those words cemented Carter's feet firmly on the pathway marked exit.

Killer

Strangeways. The radio continued to broadcast views about the prison riots. Who cared? Loony lefties ranting about the intolerable conditions which had made the situation inevitable. Stuff 'em. If they were stupid enough to get caught, then that's their lookout. If I ever went inside, I'd keep my head down and look for opportunities. I wouldn't embarrass myself like those mugs.

Six in the morning and I still couldn't sleep; it'd been three nights. I knew the pattern. It was like a drug. Images and hallucinations became sharper and sharper: my special handful of naked ladies dancing; the voice from deep inside my balls controlling them; and then I'd delve into my metal cabinet that I called Aladdin's Cave, where I'd flick through my scrapbook and cuttings. I loved validation through the press. Not that I needed them to pin on a badge, but I loved their perspective on my operations. They made the fantasy real. I was shocked that there'd been nothing about my latest. With the news finished and the music blaring 'Snap' by The Power, I'd have to wait another hour to see if there'd be an announcement. I kept telling myself that it was Easter weekend, but it was also 1990. Surely things moved quicker. They must've known there was a missing woman.

Soon I'd sleep and fall into blackness. A lesser person might be intimidated because they didn't possess the necessary mindset. Carrying out operations of my peerless magnitude had its consequences. The low after the high was like being trapped in a nightmare. It's a natural consequence, not a manufactured one, like those fools at Strangeways. The first sign of wilting euphoria was a twitch to the cheek. I raised my hand, as if there'd been a mosquito attack.

With my new lady being so close, I thought about walking through the cobwebby curtain to where she lay. Was it too soon? I'd never had one nearby. I pacified myself by touching her ring whilst recalling our moments together in the van and the lock-up's freezer.

Every summer, I'd take a trip and visit my *ladies*.

This one was within walking distance, which caused a stir.

I wondered how her family were getting on.

Isaac

None of us were sleeping. The last time I'd looked at the clock it'd been 4:37, and I hadn't slept a wink. But, to help self-regulate, Mam and I had decided that lists to ten or cataloguing things from A-Z would help. I had organised an A-Z of footballers; the last I could remember was Ian Wright of Crystal Palace but must've drifted off because I was woken by footsteps and chitter-chatter. It was 7:03, but I hated waking when the minutes weren't a multiple of ten. A chorus of voices reached crescendo, bickering about where to begin. I wiped sleep from my eyes, my brain up to eighty percent. I was sensitive of my whereabouts. It pleased me that my CDs were in alphabetical order and I touched the third from last, which was always half-a-centimetre further out than the rest. When I squeezed last night's towel that was hung dead centre on the radiator and now dry, the sound of clanging metal and bossy verbs made me dizzy. Maybe I was still dreaming about the prison riots that had filled the screen for days. I shouted for Dad but there was no response. Negating the need for stairs, I flew to the kitchen. A cinematic scene from ET was being reconstructed in the back garden. Men dressed in plastic suits were milling around like it was a public convenience, armed with radios and intent. Had the aliens landed?

Outside, I found Dad slumped against the fence with a piece of paper in hand.

'What's going on?' They were trampling over my garden. My brain was now in overdrive and there was a lump in my throat.

'They've only got a bloody warrant.'

'What for?'

Dad didn't answer. He gave room for my thoughts to catch up, then the pique turned to rage. 'They've got to be bloody joking.' All energy seemed to have syphoned from Dad as if he'd accepted the order with acquiesce.

More spades were brought in. With military levels of devastation, they'd ruined my straight lines and colour-coordinated strip. It'd taken me ages to develop so that in summer it'd look like a paint chart. Over the neighbouring fence, Wild Bill stood with – judging by the white, polyester suit – the lead policeman, who sniffled into a handkerchief. Bill's eyes were a kaleidoscope of colour and his tongue slipped like a worm from that matted beard.

'Please stop,' I said to the nearest policeman with SOCO on his breast-pocket.

'Sorry, son. We're only doing our job.'

'You're making a mess.'

'We'll put it back as best we can.'

The garden wasn't my main concern, but as he'd mentioned it, reform would be impossible. It'd taken years to develop, and they'd destroyed it. One of my favourite sounds had always been the slice of a spade into crisp, resistant mud. No longer. My eyeballs prickled. Some of the police were sieving soil – for what? What did they expect to find?

Breathlessly, I looked to Dad, but he was a statue. The police took on a strange guise and were identical to an advert about safe sex that I'd seen in a magazine, showing condom-covered cocks.

My brothers arrived at the mayhem and Dan sat with Dad. But not Carl. Clad in a pair of second skin boxer shorts, every sinew and ripple of his vexation was evident. I felt his blood reach boiling point. Hurdling the fence in one swoop, he shoved Wild Bill and went for his throat. Bill – no stranger to violence – swung a punch, but Carl was too wily. He banged a quick one-two onto the wife-beater's face. A policeman that looked like a girthy-penis was negotiating our fence, whilst the one with Bill – thinner but longer – had stupidly stood between the warring parties. Struck with blows from both sides, the lengthy policeman shrivelled flaccidly onto the grass. Bill and Carl turned their attention to each other, but my brother was too cunning for the fat man. He headbutted him solidly on the nose. Down Bill went like a sack of spuds. If I hadn't known better, I would've thought the stout policeman was deliberately fumbling in his pursuit of Carl. Placing a gloved hand on his shoulder, Carl – although tetchy – backed off. Helping his colleague from the floor, the chunky one brushed the thinner's blooded suit, whose hood slipped to reveal locks of blond hair.

'Arrest him!' he yelled. 'Assaulting a police officer!'

'Think about public relations, sir,' The girthy-penis said to the lengthy one. 'He's untouchable – how did you think he'd react? His mother's missing.' On removing his hood, DC Carter revealed himself as the wider one and he had a strange smirk upon his face.

Aunt Suzie

By the time we arrived, the police had packed up and gone. Surprisingly, paramedics were aiding the lunatic from next door and another man. The neighbour filled me with dread, as he looked like the Yorkshire Ripper. The other casualty was softer. His hair fell in bouncy waves. Whether he had a severe cold or a burst nose was difficult to judge. Fussy neighbours and a gaggle of girls with puckered mouths parted waters so we could park.

We'd kept away on Easter Sunday, but left the caravan when Simon called the site-manager about the warrant. Of course, we hadn't slept. Since we had found out that she was missing, our eyes had been pinned open. Rattling around in the tin box, Mam found pictures of Donna and me when we were younger. Dad polished his shoes, his collection of silver coins, and even Monopoly pieces. I spent so much time sucking my teeth, I thought they'd be enamel-free. Occasionally, one of us would break. Babbling and overwhelmed, the others would cajole and hug until the fear abated. How we'd arrived at the house unscathed was beyond me. I just wanted to be with the boys. True, Donna was my sister and Simon's wife, but she was the boys' mother.

What were they going through?

On entering the kitchen, Simon stood with an overweight man who was dressed in a shirt and tie; there were perspiration rings around the armpits. His lower-half was covered in a plastic covering, the top-half had been unzipped and hung behind him like a deflated parachute.

'DC Carter – you must be Suzie?' He introduced himself before moving onto my parents, who, after embracing Simon, slumped wordlessly at the table.

Unable to conceal my emotion, I grimaced. 'What on earth are you playing at? Simon and the boys – it's ludicrous. How could you think…' My words dissolved into chaos.

The detective held up his hand. 'I know. I've apologised to Mr. McCar- sorry, to Simon. I've reassured him it is about eliminating the family from our enquiries. I fully realise that we could've gone about things in a better fashion...'

'You can bloody well say that again.'

'However, it was just procedure – we never thought, in a million years, that they were involved in Donna's disappearance. Now we can focus all our efforts on finding your sister.' Although his skin was in desperate need of Vitamin C, he had genuine eyes. However, I wasn't ready to let him off the hook.

I realised what was missing and went to flick on the radio. Simon grasped my wrist. 'No music, Suzie.' In this house those words were almost sacrilegious.

'Well, Mr. Carter,' I said, viewing Isaac in the garden, 'if the police have upset my nephews, you'll be for the high-jump.' The bedraggled detective nodded.

Isaac was shaking. The police had wreaked havoc with his garden, but he didn't sob. Fixated on the boggy plots, I knew that he'd restore order. Donna had worried endlessly about his OCD. With the mess being more disorganised than my thoughts, I hoped he wouldn't spiral out of control. 'You don't have to do it today, Isaac.'

'I must get the angles right.' He swirled the wood like a martial arts expert. 'There must be ninety-degree angles. I'll have to dig deeper to make sure that my memory's right about what's growing where.' I squeezed his thigh, but he was in a zone. A default position of being self-absorbed was a dangerous place to be.

Disdainfully, I scowled at the tea-drinking Carter as I headed through the kitchen, and he gave me a look like he needed something stronger. But at least he hadn't run away like the rest. 'Are the boys in their rooms?'

'Yeah,' Simon replied.

'Suzie, you need to know…' I kept walking, as Carter wiped spurts of spilled tea from his shirt.

Despite being born on the same day, with the same upbringing, opportunities, and experiences, the boys were like chalk, cheese, and something unrelated to both. How they'd react to my sister's disappearance was in the stars. What did connect them was their love for their Mam.

Upstairs in the loft rooms, the silence had thickened into a deafening abyss. Dan was slouched over his guitar but didn't strum a string. 'Where's Mam?' he asked. I'm embarrassed to state that I choked; the silence grabbed my throat. I had never been so brittle. 'It's okay.' He put down the guitar and came to me. 'Shhhh, it's too weird for words, I'm sure it's not real. It can't be.' I clung to him. 'How are you feeling? What's the pain like? I feel like there's crushed glass inside my head,' he said, gently. Only later did I feel guilty. Being strong was my job, but his readiness to absorb my pain was heart-breaking. I thought he'd be in pieces, but he simply wanted to know how I felt.

Finally, I arrived at Carl's room. Even before entering, I heard the surprising sounds of muffled cries. How could that be? Carl was the toughest by far. He never backed down, even as a baby. On the boys' first birthday we had stopped for a pub lunch and had ordered cream cakes. When I had tried to take his from the highchair – as a piece of mischief – he shrieked with the might of a hurricane before wrapping his arms around the cake and sinking his face into it.

I stayed with him longest. He explained why there

were paramedics. He talked about Yin-Yang, revenge, and victims; his thoughts were as cluttered as mine. He kept saying that he'd find out who'd taken his Mam and that he'd punish them. He asked whether I thought Wild Bill was involved. The not knowing had smashed him into pieces.

Carter was washing up when I arrived downstairs; the smell of his aftershave almost knocked me over. Sheepishly, he asked, 'How were the boys?' My Dad, who'd fought on the beaches in Normandy, was broken. He had always said that we had to be survivors and never victims. I couldn't help but think that it was a household of victims, and I longed that we'd all get through.

'Hard to say, detective. Did Bill from next door prompt this?'

'He can't say,' Simon answered.

'Well, in view of community cohesion and to stop any further violence, has the bearded fool got an alibi?'

Carter undid his tie. 'I shouldn't really be reporting this, but you're right. I don't want the lads doing our job and getting into trouble. Mr. Wilde was in the pub until two and was seen at the fish and chip shop soon after, so he's not a suspect. We will conduct many interviews, which we'll cross-reference for validation.'

Isaac

Due to the morning's activities, I'd locked the gate. It would've been nonsensical to allow the police to re-enter. I fancied being a forensic scientist and swore that I'd never leave a site in such a pitiful state. They should've put things right, but it was my garden, and only I knew how it should look.

Usually, nothing would be able to move me from my task. But when the police returned with an Alsatian with the healthiest coat, I went inside. Playfully avoiding its long, floppy tongue, Carl hugged it and swizzled the dog's collar. Assigned to track Mam's scent, the handler – a woman about Mam's age with a fluffiness about her skin – told us that the dogs could track scent in the air from, what she called, the *cone* that flows downwind.

I worried about hairs on the carpet. Dad and I had spent Sunday piecing the place together: washing, scrubbing, hoovering, ironing, and polishing. So, it'd be an aimless task; the only scent the dog – Hendrix – would pick up would be washing powder.

Dan rubbed noses with Hendrix, Jimi being one of his guitar heroes. Apparently, this phase of dog was named after musicians: Page, Prince, Lennon, Bo-Diddley, Townsend, Rogers, and Chuck Berry. Dan's actions disgusted me. Dogs basically spent most of their life licking their balls and sniffing backsides. I offered him a box of wipes and promised never to sit within two feet of him ever again.

We congregated at the retail park where Mam had gone missing. A torrent of people arrived with canes, clad in wellies. Half of our sixth form were there, as well as the football team, the staff from the pizzeria, the chippy and other shops, and neighbours and folk from the terraces. I'd seen events like this on the television and thought, for the people who turned up, it was more about themselves than the family. Yet, the foreboding on people's faces hid any voyeurism. Luckily, Dan had brought the wipes and Carl blew into them.

'Just keep your head down,' said Dan.

'It'll be over soon,' I replied. Carl tried to speak, but it sounded like his throat had contracted.

'We won't find anything because there's nothing to find,' Dan continued. I disagreed but kept my thoughts intact. Whatever Carl thought was welded in his chest, the convulsions guttural.

I was impressed by the police's organisation. They'd briefed everyone on *'dos and don'ts'* and provided a formation in which to hike. I settled for a three-sweep manoeuvre with my stick: right, left, right – every five seconds, and if we stopped, I'd rest on it, on the right-hand side. The dog and handler went first; next, a dozen police with sticks traipsed behind covering every centimetre in methodical fashion; then it was us – the family, Auntie Suzie and our grandparents, and the ever-present Carter – scanning every blade of grass, nettle and stone; finally, the volunteers, who were visibly anxious about what they might find. I couldn't help but think that my garden should've been treated with the same meticulous care. We headed around the Island: the allotments, terraces, the gut, ginnels, the farmer's fields, teenage wasteland, suspension bridge and the expansive fields where people walked dogs. There wasn't a murmur. We were never going to hear anything; people may as well have been yakking.

The search brought more despair, which I thought would leave Carl traumatised. He'd spat out so much phlegm; he must've realised that his girlfriend, Zoë, was there. Leaving deposits for the volunteers to avoid, he seemed to be crying on the inside, so as not to upset her.

At one point, my brothers and I huddled. 'We'll have to work out who's done this,' Carl puffed.

'That's down to the police,' Dan responded.

'You must have your suspicions.'

'Not really.'

'We'll talk later,' I rebuked, not wanting prying ears to hear.

Of course, the mission was fruitless and there was nothing but public torment. The dog never did pick up a scent. But at least it didn't run into the laundrette. Gratitude was expressed to all for their efforts and the police offered their apologies and promised to find Mam.

I wasn't so sure.

Whilst we were looking, I noticed that we were being tracked by television cameras. Okay, they kept a respectful distance, but had we asked to become public property? I hated the fact that we'd end up as tomorrow's chip paper, or a sensitive anecdote – even a joke – when people were at work the next day.

We returned to our house; it was no longer a home without Mam and the morning's violation. I should've stayed in the garden because things needed to be organised.

Like Carl said, I had to work out who'd done this.

Dad

At sunrise everything was quiet, but everything was wrong. I hadn't a clue what to do. I couldn't stand the long, isolated wait until breakfast, which seemed longer each night. Stillness burned. I imagined the boys smothering their heads into pillows or staring at walls. We all suspected that Donna was dead, but couldn't voice it. The pain just ate away. The house was always filled with music and life, but once she'd gone, the rooms were silent. Music signalled happiness, individuality, and choice; now there was simply grief and despondency.

What could I say to the boys?

I watched how they struggled. But, like living on separate planets, I didn't know how to reach them. As a parent you want to make everything alright. How could I tell them that nothing would be right, ever again?

Wandering aimlessly was far from therapeutic. The morning had slayed the night, leaving a red sky. The newsagent's billboard displayed the legend: 'Local Woman Missing – Presumed Murdered'. Passing our favourite pubs on the Island, I remembered pushing the buggies, and the perfect pride that had swept over her when she showed off our triplets. Even the smell of the allotments reminded me of our courting days: we had hidden away, just the two of us, discovering one another. Once we had found an abandoned shopping trolley. Spontaneously, I'd coaxed her into the cage. Rapturous laughter had erupted from her as she twisted precariously. Her back had been pinned down and she had kicked madly. My face had looked down on her, our smiles wider than the ocean. Suddenly, a darkness struck, and I thought that her last seconds could've been the same: trapped, and instead of me dreamily gazing at her with a heart filled with love, someone had murderously stared at her with unimaginable hate. Slumped over the suspension bridge, I looked for my reflection in the water, but there was nothing except kohl blackness.

*

Echoed voices – swiftly followed by heartfelt apologies – filled the vastness. Word was out. I trudged over the factory floor, where my colleagues were as robotic as the machinery. Some fixed their eyes on me, others held their caps, whilst more still played with their faces. Whirring technology transported parts with efficiency. Even one of Isaac's goal kicks wouldn't have crossed the huge space that was as clean as a surgeon's theatre. A heavy clank and buzz made most return to their tasks. Co-workers on my line gave uneasy microscopic nods. What could they say? Foreman Bob approached. 'Sure you should be here, kidda?' he asked, with two friendly pats on my shoulder. 'None of us can imagine what you're going through.' A ghostly look haunted his face; I'd seen the same expression in the mirror that morning.

'Best I'm here. Try to keep things as normal as possible,' I said. Although I knew the whole world had flipped, I couldn't curl into a ball. Absurd as it seemed, being at work was the best thing. Rambling through the internal wilderness was too savage.

'Top Brass said that if you arrived you were to go straight to him.'

'I just want to get on with this.'

'I know, Mac, but he was insistent. It'll be part of their culture.'

Upstairs, as I traipsed through the offices, people froze and drew breath like they'd seen a ghost. The staff stood as one when I rapped on the boss's door.

'Enter.'

He bowed deeply for several seconds. When he

returned to attention, his eyes were steely and brow wrinkled, which caused a twitch in his right cheek. The Japanese flag – with the company's logo adorning the red spot – and the most intricate bonsai trees were efficiently organised behind his head; a neater office would be difficult to find. Wearing overalls like the workforce, he led from the front, knowing every job on the production line. I was lucky to work here and had been amazed by the structured working practices. They, in turn, had been impressed by our endeavour and diligence. 'Please, sit.'

'Thank you, Mr. Tanako.' He waited until I was comfortable before he sat. A computer, booklet, and gold pen sat on the desk between us.

'I have had a message from Mr. Takahashi in Tokyo, who says his thoughts are with you.'

I bowed. 'Thank you, Mr. Tanako. Please send back my regards.'

'I watched in horror on the television news last night. When I saw you walking with your sons and the newsreader informed the world of what they believe has happened. Well… horror is the only word.'

'Thank you, Mr. Tanako.'

'I am impressed but embarrassed by your efforts to work today. As a company, we would not expect such a thing. Building cars can wait for another day.'

'With respect, Mr. Tanako,' I could see by the tilt of his head that he was unused to being interrupted, 'with your permission, I would like to remain at work. Whilst there is a glimmer of hope that Donna – my wife – is still alive, I would like to be here. It is best for my boys to see some sanity during this time.'

He ran a finger over his lips, before tapping the computer. 'Your boys attend Island Comprehensive?'

'No, Mr. Tanako. They completed their GCSEs there, but now attend Hillside Moss Grammar for their A levels

50

– there were more options there.' I wouldn't have liked to be the administrator who hadn't updated the document. Humiliated, he looked like he wanted to hide under the desk.

'I am so sorry not to be abreast of that development.'

'Mr. Tanako, there are over five-thousand employees here. You cannot be expected to know the schooling of all their children.' His eyes showed some light, but I was sure that he wouldn't forgive himself – and certainly not the administrator.

'Thank you for your understanding, McCarthy-san. What are they studying, may I ask?'

'Isaac's the scientist: Chemistry, Physics, and Biology. Carl is doing PE, Politics, and Criminology. Dan is studying Music, English, and Art. They'll complete their exams next Summer.'

'A wide range. They must be very intelligent and make you proud.'

'They're all very different, despite being triplets. They make us very proud.' I wondered whether it was still 'us' or just 'me'.

'You have been truly blessed. If there is anything that we can do for them during this time, please do not hesitate to ask.'

'Thank you, Mr. Tanako.'

Despite my boys' intelligence, I worried about their ability to manage. I hoped they were stronger than me, as I kept thinking of taking my own life. I'd have to fight for the boys' sake. If we'd had no children, I'd be dangling from a rope. I had to keep busy and stay alive. I couldn't be selfish.

But the pain was unimaginable.

Chapter 3: Football

Chief Super

Twelve days since the incident at the McCarthy residence and we were no further forward. I had spoken with the SIO about team dynamics. My nous told me that this was a dream team, but only if Quick and Carter worked to their strengths. Heaven help us if they worked to their weaknesses. Quick had brought in Pearson to be his DS in the control room. I knew that including Carter in the meeting would show Quick how highly I still rated our ballooning friend.

DC Carter – the Clichéd-Cop, the wooden-tops called him. Poor bugger. After the debacle with the Dead-Babies case, when the sentimental-fool became a gibbering wreck, there was a strong argument for him to be dismissed. I had to fight dispassionately on his behalf. Crying on the television, whimpering around the terraces, and disturbing the peace with frantic drinking sessions, he had fallen apart. That's when the cliché had really begun, losing his wife, the alcohol, the cigarettes and weight-gain. The story is old, but it goes on. At tribunal, he had been demoted two-ranks. I pleaded for one drop to DS, but the decision was made.

He had been an exceptional DI and should've been going up the ranks. Some fools care too much. He had lead teams, dealt with corruption and the most damaged victims with expertise. He got results. Yet his career was as misshapen as that belt-breaking waistline. Having timeout for counselling had helped, but the paranoia almost ate him. Carter had thought it was like TV when the killer tries to destroy the detective. We had told him that it was a literary device, and it didn't happen in real life. Yes, violent criminals threatened retribution and many detectives' houses were rigged with alarms, but in my experience they simply gathered dust. We were just doing a job, and someone else would merely step-in. Criminals knew that and a pre-meditated attack against an officer would mean life. Despite our reassurances, Carter's mind had spun out-of-control. In hindsight, we were lucky that – with his old Sarge's help – we had got him back.

Brown-noser Quick had brought in his own DS and a dozen-sized-team were onboard, with double again on standby. Not only did Quick like to have his nose where the sun don't shine, but he obviously liked the feeling of a nose up his own jacksy. DS Pearson was another brown-noser. I could smell it on her (which wasn't easy with Carter's aftershave and Quick's hairspray). She fussed, showing me pictures of her horse. Every interaction made me dream of retirement. Respect was missing from the new breed. I had voted for Maggie as it was best for the force, and Quick and co' had been dubbed "Thatcher's coppers". They'd ruthlessly cut your throat to protect their careers. But, despite Quick being a ponce, he had his strengths. Understanding forensics, DNA, and criminal motivation, he spoke about coordination, networking, algorithms, and national databases, and, like Carter, he got results. Carter could thicken the soup of Quick's wishy-washy course-filled modern-ology. They were both outstanding coppers, and I wanted the best of both worlds, the old and the new.

'I've spoken to the DCI – as SIO – and told him that I'll keep an eye on the case.' There wasn't a flicker from any of them. 'How's your nose?' The bruising around Quick's eyes and crooked hooter was concerning. Populated by hay-fever, the constant sniffing must've been excruciating.

'Fine, sir, I'll take some annual leave to have it straightened. Other than that, it's perfectly fine.' Thirty years on the force told me that he was lying.

'Sooner rather than later, DI Quick. That's an order.'

'Thank you for your concern, sir.' Word around the station was that he was aggrieved by the decision not to arrest the McCarthy boy. But if he waved warrants like Bertie Big-Balls then there would be consequences. That area was more Carter's expertise.

'Right, I hear that we have bugger-all, zilch, not a Scooby-bloody-Doo.' I stood up and my shadow spread over them. Nothing on their courses would show them how to intimidate. Pearson squirmed like she was in the saddle.

'Sir, I've been liaising with other forces, getting our computers in-line, seeing whether there are similar disappearances.' Quick wriggled. 'We are currently wading through the monumental response.'

'Sir,' Pearson was on her feet, trotting around. 'There's been nothing from forensics, and there's nothing unique about the skid mark, apart from it being from a van. The search of the area, including the family home and the old pit, have been eliminated; they're baron in terms of evidence.'

'Thank you, please sit.' She was giving me motion sickness. 'Carter?'

'I've built bridges with the family. The DCs have taken statements from William Wilde – the neighbour – Mr. Patel, and all at the Estate Agents,' he listed. 'I've been door-to-door with the other DCs, taken accounts, the usual donkeywork. Seems like a typical Good Friday affair. Men having a lunchtime pint, families eating fish and relaxing with a film. Unfortunately, nobody noticed anything unusual, no speeding cars – sorry, vans. It's a mystery. The DVLA have provided a list of van owners on the Island, and we'll alibi them this week. The DCI is doing a great job handling the media.'

Quick nodded, but the flick of his hair showed that he thought it was his responsibility, not Carter's, to comment on the DCI. I agreed, that was Quick's strength. Despite the friction, I was convinced they'd make it work.

The DCI allowed his teams to work the case. He was great at knowing which leads to follow, but this case was quieter than a church mouse. They were always the worst; the quieter the case, the more investigation hours. I continued to stand. 'Right, we need to plan. Quick, I'm coming to your Nick. I've asked the DCI to meet us there. Pull everyone in. Let's go back to the beginning, make sure we haven't missed a thing. That poor family.'

I don't think Quick had given them a second thought. Maybe he'd dreamt of locking up the McCarthy boy, but he looked more concerned about me coming to his station. Carter had welled up, which wasn't a good sign.

Dan

I was fast. Always had been. I'd catapulted past so many defenders that I was used to their threats and bullying, none of which worked. I'd refuse to engage and enjoyed taking them to places that they didn't want to go, showing jet-heels. Being a centre forward allowed me to do that. Carl was the midfield enforcer, and Isaac was our captain and centre half, the organiser. Although he hated the mud and sweat, he loved to rake out studs and polish boots afterward until they were fit for a king. Funnily, neither Carl nor I complained. There are perks to having a brother with an obsession for cleanliness. I once wrote some words: *Shine, you shine like a king / but here is the thing - you / I want to shine like spring - too.* Many songs are written about inanimate objects and people assume they're about the heart.

During the week, we had a visitor and, unfortunately, eloquence wasn't something that Coach Taylor had in abundance. However, he had come around our house when most had stayed away. He had crookedly parked up. The strapline on the side of his van stated 'Forget Chips -Try a Stottie' which had made my stomach rumble; but in the absence of appetite, I strangely enjoyed the hunger pains.

The forthcoming semi-final was on the coach's mind. He had been coaching at Hill Hotspur for years and had switched to us a few summers ago. The gridlock inside his head, as he perched on the sofa with a milky coffee, was evident. On one hand, he was sincere and fought back tears when he had told us how sorry he was to hear about Mam. He couldn't take his eyes off her picture on the sideboard as he rambled about how she'd arranged the purchase of his food business' new premises on the

Island; she'd apparently softened the deal with a half-price lock-up. He must've seen how uncomfortable we were – especially Carl – and had been glad to stop uttering. On the other hand, losing three players from his team-sheet was unthinkable. Clumsily, he had tried to unlock the dilemma. 'I don't expect you to play. Unless you want to. Then one-hundred percent: you're in. It'll be great and might stop you from thinking about… not that you'll ever stop thinking… I mean in the grand scheme of things, the match is a speck of dust in the desert or something…'

'We understand,' Dad said, which had stopped Coach Taylor's clumsy metaphors. 'If the lads are up for it, they're in.'

'Aye.'

I couldn't speak for the others, but I wanted to play. Going through the megamix of negative emotions, I knew that football would only provide more nothingness. But knowing Mam would want us to play was the overwhelming thought. Wallowing in my room was the toughest. Mam's disappearance was nothing compared to when I thought about how she might've died. It terrified me. Visions ranged from an accident to her being tortured, skinned alive. Simmering beneath the surface were thousands of gruesome thoughts. All linked to pain. I wanted to know how Mam felt when she was taken. I had to peel back my toenails to stop the thoughts. Scribbling down lyrics was distracting, but everything remained disconnected, like jigsaw pieces in a box.

*

We decided to play. Yet the game was passing me by. A nondescript Saturday morning. A few clouds in a warm sky. Goalless at half time, both teams cancelling each other out. Half-heartedly I'd made runs, but they were thwarted by an organised opposition. Cumbersome and, despite his foxy appearance, crafty as a ten-ton truck, the lad marking me was educated in the dark arts of the centre-half: studding my heels, digging in my ribs, and standing on my toes. His pointy face was enhanced by pointed ginger-sideburns, like a cockney spiv. The big difference was the whispered verbal assaults: *Your Mam's better off dead with you as a son; Do you think she was raped?; They'll probably never find her body.* His painful words were nothing. I'd already magnified everything his pea-sized brain could produce by a thousand at three in the morning.

My manoeuvrability foiled his attentions, but when Carl swerved a pass in my direction, I drilled both feet into the turf. Simply, I could've spun away and left the foul-mouthed fool in a haze. But no. I waited. Coach Taylor caught my attention. I was thinking about how he had looked at Mam's picture and how he always brought a seat in which she could sit. Without exception, he celebrated with her first when we scored, grabbing her and swinging her around. Was it him? Did he have anything to do with Mam's disappearance?

Like the dog-handler said about dogs sensing information that flows on the *cone* down wind, I detected the foxy boy gliding through the air and braced.

I wanted to feel pain.

Everything contracted as two feet, twelve studs, and thirteen stone collided against the back of my knees.

Facedown.

I grimaced.

The pain was fabulous.

Excruciating.

Just what I wanted.

No, what I needed.

The agony was the best release since Mam went missing. *Tasting mud in my mouth, I was suffocating /*

But memories of you are far from fading. Lyrics faltered as Carl reached the scene, and the foxy boy joined me in the turf.

Carl

Ah took a sharp breath. Feet splayed over the player's shoulders, ah could smell the fear. With blood frothing from his mouth, he went for me balls like a rabid fox. Since the incident with Gazza and Vinny Jones, ball grabbing had become part of the game. Aggression and anguish had spliced simultaneously over their faces; it was one of the greatest sporting photographs. Anyhow, there was no way this ginger-haired chancer was going to crush mine. Ah banged him back into the floor. God, it felt good when me knuckles bust his nose. Am not sure if it was as pleasing as watching Wild Bill go down, though. Anyhow, it happened in a milli-second before the mêlée.

*

Me reputation for being hard had been blown out of proportion. Being one of the lads with a sense for larkiness was as far as it went. Until the day of the loose cricket ball. Ah was in my first year at the comp, and the year above had some lovely lasses. Although Tabitha was only thirteen, she had massive breasts and was shaped like an hourglass, more of a woman than a girl. Her pretty mate, Penny, had sublime eyes. They were wearing PE kits: gym skirts with socks over the knees. Uneasily, watching them from behind, an involuntary erection had stalked. Ah wasn't a weirdo, it just happened at that age. Prodding like a cartoon bone, it had tried to penetrate me trousers. From nowhere a cricket ball had looped in slow motion, like someone was conducting an experiment with me balls as bails; it connected with the tip of me erection.

Raw excruciating pangs.

Pain.

Livid.

From next to the food place, a skinhead, two years older, had sent a sloppy wave and shouted, 'Sorry!' Me preoccupation with the girls had vanished. With me pulsating and aching balls, he had become me new focus. Me eyesight was like one of those American TV programmes where they search through binoculars and blur the peripheral vision. He had said something about a missed catch. Stupidly, he had held out his hands which made a bigger target. Although he was over half-a-foot bigger, he'd never stood a chance. Wading in, ah produced a myriad of punches with such precision and accuracy that they had created me legend.

A massive lad called Big Eddie from the year above had picked uz up, pinned me arms, and told uz to stop. As a weird forfeit, everyone in the vicinity had spat on the skinhead and me. Ad only told Zoë – me brothers didn't even know – about what had triggered me transformation into a Pitbull. From then on, with the skinhead being a tough lad, everyone knew that ah could go mental.

*

With Dan and the would-be ball-grabber face down, and Isaac's reluctance to get involved – his hands were open, looking at Dad – the other lads sprang into action. Some were peacekeepers, others were happy to shove, and the more hot-headed piled in. Ah took a fist to the ear and winded a lad with a swift boot to his gut before punching another. Parents and spectators supported the officials to segregate the players; both sides pointed fingers and promised retribution. Ah noticed Wild Bill by the goalpost, doubtlessly half-cut from the night before. He often watched the football. In the past he had probably been eyeing Mam. Dad had mentioned his alibi, but I didn't believe a word.

Me ears were ringing, but when the ref raised a red card, ah understood. So, it was done. It'd be a tale to tell like the Bovril story. Maybe ad turn it into a comedy routine to impress the lads, who'd magnify their own discretions. That's how things worked. What ah didn't want was for people to say it was because of Mam. It wasn't. It was down to the fox-face.

Dad

Maybe I shouldn't have allowed them to play. Yet, more than anyone, Carl had dragged the canaries to the semis. Swashbuckling in midfield, a vision in yellow and green, he'd been the star player through the muddy fields of winter, providing hope. But hope had been hoovered quicker than Isaac cleaned on a Sunday. With death's hands pulling them down, I thought that they deserved a chance. We'd become oil paintings, framed in time, defined by what'd happened. Functioning was difficult but not due to fear, like John Lennon had said. Superseding everything was a sense of guilt: *if I smile, it'll look like I'm not thinking about her; if I enjoy a piece of music, it'll sound like I'm not thinking about her; if I so much as breathe in the wrong direction, it'll feel like I'm not thinking about her.*

Suffocating.

No, the boys had earned it. As I had been at work they had gone to school, which must've been torture. But they said it had gone as well as they'd expected, although people had been quieter around them. I wasn't sure whether any learning had taken place, but the facade of normality was essential. If we stopped pretending that Donna was alive, then everyone else would.

When we had arrived at the park, the car next to us had been blaring David Bowie's 'Ashes to Ashes'. Scowling, Carl had run to the newly built changing rooms. The old ones had been so dilapidated that they'd had to be pulled down. Donna had worked tirelessly with Coach Taylor and the other mothers to raise money for the state of the art facilities. He had picked her up for meetings in his van, and they had completed the Great North Run as a fundraiser. Carl had rested against the metal panel displaying the team's badge – a canary and monkey standing either side of a mine's wheelhouse. Fuming fury had billowed from him. When he was little, Donna used to say that he was a comical bull, like when steam is banished from flared nostrils. Isaac and Dan could read him like a book and knew that hearing their Mam's favourite singer had sparked something. Carl muttered something unmentionable under his breath.

'Hey!' With everything else, I hadn't spoken to him about his language. 'The song was on the radio; you can't blame them.' He had looked ready to fight the world. Perhaps that's when I should've stopped him from playing.

*

Pandemonium.

All match there'd been a frosty atmosphere on the side-lines. Coach Taylor and Foreman Bob from work, whose son played, had stood either side of me like bookends. The mass brawl had been quickly quarantined, and I was glad that they'd held me back. I couldn't condone Carl's sending off, but Donna and I had brought up the boys to watch out for one another. Two of their lads were dismissed: the fox-like villain and the one who'd punched Carl. Unfortunately, Dan had to be substituted. Isaac's instructions created a new formation. He was in his element, scientifically positioning people to scotch the opposition. In contrast, Coach Taylor looked bemused and distracted.

The bloodstained foxy lad was restrained, and Carl laughed.

'Howay, son, no more. You don't want to extend your ban.'

'He could've broken Dan's legs!'

I looked skyward. 'Calm it.'

'What was he saying?' Carl asked Dan. 'He was like

Whispering Smith all day.'

'His tongue's too long. Talking about Mam.'

Pincered. Foreman Bob, Coach Taylor, and I captured Carl. Mind, it took the strength of three grown men to hold him. Like a pulsating steam-engine, he would've blown if we hadn't. The foxy lad wasn't any better. His Dad had him gripped in a headlock. 'If you've got something to say about me Mam, then say it to me face, you pointy faced, ball-grabber.'

'Have a go if you think you're hard enough!' the foxy lad screamed. I wish he hadn't. Carl fought to slither through our hands. A parent near the foxy lad said something to his dad. All colour drained, and he surprisingly shoved his son to the floor. Avoiding stares, he traipsed towards us. 'I apologise if my son said anything about your wife, your mother,' he said pitifully. I nodded, Dan hobbled and shook his hand, but Carl was unsettled.

'We don't want your sympathy. Sympathy's pointless.'

The man held up his hands in surrender. Carl's body wilted; he'd burned his fuel. We let go.

Kindly, Coach Carter offered Dan the camping stool that had been previously reserved for Donna. Carl slumped on the grass, viewing his knuckles. Thankfully, the game was within its final throes. Despite the persistent effort, it'd been a chess-like game, but once the drama faded ardent encouragement returned. Jostling for position, Isaac sneaked into the box for a last minute corner. Rising above all others he made the sweetest contact and the ball bristled into the top corner. Legging from his teammates' muddy embrace, Isaac approached with unusual abandon. He jumped onto his brothers. They curled together. A forcefield of feelings radiated from them, and, as I watched their elation, my mouth curled upwards… the guilt would come later.

Killer

After the match, I walked through the park. Lines of cars were selling rubbish. When had car boot sales become a thing? Would this be Thatcher's legacy? The dream of entrepreneurship dissolved into a teacup of tat. Neighbours were ripping each other off, including some old miners. Apparently, one of their lamps could sell for sixty quid. People tussled, dreaming they'd find something from the Ming Dynasty, but went home with a scratched Kajagoogoo LP.

When they write about people who've done what I do, they etch an image of a friendless psychopath who lives in solitude. I was different. Many operators fall before their first strike because they don't have the right stuff. True, a fortnight after an operation and I was at the bottom of my cycle; the downer was excruciating. Looking at album covers from Mud and Slade was a new low. Digging for resolve was insufferable, and I was sexlessly frustrated. The next part, which I enjoyed most, would happen soon. With my silent companions walking alongside me, I'd find an equilibrium. Then the planning would begin.

'I've got some Northern Soul and Motown, mate,' the boot-boy said, thinking he was Arthur Daley.

I flashed him a granite grin. 'No, thanks.'

I was different. I was different because I was always around people. I didn't sit around waiting for someone to rake up my mistakes, wallowing in a suicidal state of regret. Nobody had a clue about my secret life. I was even visible on the day she'd gone missing – a trick of light, smoke, and mirrors. Since then, I'd been up close and personable with the lady's family. I'd participated in their stupid staged search, which would've been successful if only the police had widened the net.

At the football, I had tasted blood when the fight kicked off. But I'd enjoyed the new game more. My lady's broken family's lives were going down the plughole. I deliberated: which one would destroy themself first? Having a lady close to home had its perks, and I thanked those who'd gone before me for the advice.

I'd be watching.

I'd learned that life always worsened for my chosen few.

Isaac

Shrilling across the pitch to avoid my teammates' grubby hands had worked. I had wanted to be with my daft brothers; but what had they been playing at? When we were little, we'd roll around. Two of us would gang up on another, our limbs wrapped like a mutant insect.

Anti-climatically, I had cleaned our boots on the back steps and mixed salt into cold water to remove the blood from Carl's top. The repetitive tasks had been calming, but I should've stretched after the game because my legs were jelly as I walked to work.

Sunbeams pleasantly dodged clouds, but the rays on a warm wind couldn't make me forget. Everywhere there was a song or smell which let me know that Mam was dead. Of that I had no doubt. Even though we pretended she was alive. When I crossed Teenage Wasteland, scooter-riding teens gestured with raised fists. Half-heartedly, I returned a wave, but bathing in celebration wasn't my thing. Don't get me wrong, I was no killjoy, but I wanted isolation. The exuberance had been too much, so I dashed by our old primary school on Brass Band Road.

Halfway along I was accosted. The stilted looks since Mam had disappeared had been from a distance, but three elderly women had other ideas. Laden with shopping bags and teary eyes, they'd formed a barrier. My anxiety prickled, resulting in a feeble smile. Mam had brought me up properly, so despite every bodily fibre telling me to run, I headed headlong into their wallowing.

'Eeeh triplet, how are you?' I opened my mouth, but, before answering, spindly fingers walked over my arm.

'It's a silly question. None of us can imagine. She was… is a fine woman, your mother.' Now, they were all touching and crooning sympathetic noises. Being mobbed by the footballers would've been better than their feather-light strokes. Though I was about to dissolve, they hadn't finished their script.

'We just don't know what to say.' Why would anyone stop someone to say they had nothing to say? Madness. My skin crawled.

'Thank you,' I managed to grunt without hyperventilating. 'I'll let Dad know you were asking after us.' I hurdled their bags and my knees creaked. I made a list about soft landings.

*

Turning the corner to Geordie Pizza, I'd reached a bed of feathers in my list, which helped to regulate breathing. I wiped the air as if I'd walked through a spider's web. My part-time job had been a tonic. I'd come up with the slogan '*Cheaper Than Chips*' and arrived early for shifts to organise boxes, replenish fridges, sort toppings, grate cheese, clean ovens, wipe surfaces, and stack menus. Of course, I was a strong advocate for Dad's principle of keeping to a routine.

The owner – Stefano – had been brilliant. Preventing the onslaught of customer's prying eyes, I was no longer on serving duties. That was my job, but he'd provided a new role: a trainee pizza-chef. The methodology was fascinating, and he'd said that if all his employees were as whole-hearted there'd be Geordie Pizzas everywhere! Being invited to Stefano's family home and being offered extra shifts had been a great help. He had watched the match with his son, and I wondered what they'd made of Carl's exhibition.

Rumours that Stefano was an Italian POW during World War Two, detained in Northumberland, were true. Staying on afterwards, he'd become a miner and was amazed at how he'd been accepted. His son and daughters – whose husbands were also Italian – were successful restaurateurs with a variety of establishments around the North East. On retiring from the pit, they had helped Stefano open the takeaway pizzeria. He'd wanted to maintain contact with the people who'd made him feel at home.

I headed by the fleet of scooters and opened the back gates. Some scattered pizza boxes had littered the ginnel that accommodated a series of lock-ups owned by Coach Taylor, the pizzeria, and others. Why couldn't people clean up after themselves? As I picked up the last box, loud music pounded through a lock-up door. Back inside, I disinfected my hands for forty-seven seconds. The cyclical choke of the coffee machine was more comforting than the clanging sound from the lock-up.

Sophia – Stefano's granddaughter – was cooling an espresso with gentle blows, and I focused on her lips. A white-toothed smile widened her mocha eyes. When someone dies, the rage is enough to split your soul in two. But seeing Sophia calmed and sequenced my heartbeat. Learning the trade, she'd spent time in the family's fine restaurants, in the solid medium ones, the cheap-and-cheerful ones, and, of course, the take-away.

Looking like a star of the silver screen – Natalie Wood or Audrey Hepburn – many scooter boys gave her pervy glances. To me, she was more important. She was foreign. Not her Italian heritage, but how alien she was from my world. Attending private school and living on the Hill meant that she was separate from the day-to-day reminders. I savoured our moments together. She was private, confidential… special. My favourite part of the day – and the only thing that I looked forward to – was when, after a shift, we'd sit on the back step. She'd sip coffee and I'd clean – sometimes our knees would touch.

'How have you been?' she asked. 'There's time to

talk.'

I hung my head. 'Thanks, but it's okay.' I only spoke about Mam if I wanted.

She put down the cup, walked over, and took my hands. I breathed in her sweetness. I didn't mind her touching me and sponging away the isolation. In fact, my jelly-legs wobbled.

Chapter 4: Girls

Killer

Subjects present themselves and are never chosen. Amongst the beige, they're another species: larger than life, multi-coloured, bursting with sounds and smells. They standout like a sun in a moon-filled sky. Once a lady appears, I become consumed with the operation. Not allowing their glow to reflect in my eyes is hugely difficult. After tracking and building chemistry, everything aligns. Timing is essential and the key is concealment.

The last one was no exception. She assisted in the search for extra premises, wearing a neckerchief and blue suit. I'd known her for a while and had fought my instincts, but when contact was made with a limp handshake, and she had presented the first beaming smile, I could've eaten her there and then. However, the chase was important. I needed to know everything about her. She had shone like the others. I'd had no choice; the skin-on-skin had hit me like a thunderbolt. That first touch of flesh and I had already imagined stuffing that neckerchief down her throat. Whenever I had looked at my hands, I could feel her. Nothing else had mattered. I had studied her secretly, and we had several meetings. I had picked up her mannerisms and taste. She loved David Bowie and I cherished how she had fiddled with the ring around her neck, which was now mine. I remembered the nail varnish's vertical strokes and the sound of her car's engine. I knew what she sang when washing-up, and mimicked how she viewed the pager with religious zeal; I knew her inside out. I had been that close. More importantly, I had observed that she'd arrive fifteen minutes early for appointments. Details like that were a godsend. A year in the planning had provided distance, as I understood that the police would look at her clients in reverse and probably wouldn't go back further than six months.

Then it was time to fill the hole. Once I had her as my first burial, I cherished every swish of the blade, removing the ring before our final contact.

Dan

Unable to form a wavelength at the Comp, my hopes were raised when we had joined Hillside Moss Grammar. I was dizzy with wonder when I had entered the music rooms: brass, wind and percussion instruments were professionally organised around guitars and synthesisers. They even had a mixing desk behind glass. I had been rebuffed by my new classmates for suggesting that we form a rock group. They were into an acid-jazz fusion to titillate the opposite sex. Undeterred, I had looked through the music press and found a band from Sunderland who needed a guitarist. Rollicking through a riff-crazed concoction at my audition, going from T-Rex, The Who, The Jam, and to The Kinks, the retro band had snapped off my hands.

Fraternise. That was the name of the group. It had begun as an insult from Carl. When he had heard that I'd joined up with lads from Sunderland, the brevity of his disgust had been farcical. 'We're black n' white – they're red n' white – the two should never meet. They're Mackems – different from Geordies. Don't be an idiot.' We were just into music. Anyhow, he had managed to shoehorn all prejudice into a couple of sentences. 'You're fraternising with the enemy – you're a fraterniser, like those turncoats who sucked up to the Nazis during the war. We built better ships than them, had better coal mines, and now we've got the better… shopping centres!' Grandad had told us that when anyone brought an argument down to the level of the Nazis, then they'd lost. Carl must've realised and had stormed off.

Incapable of concealing Carl's onslaught, I had told my new bandmates who'd taken no offence; on the contrary, they'd loved it. Rolled Up Jeans had been the name unfurled at the original gig, but they weren't attached to it. Pete – the drummer – insisted that we rename ourselves Fraternising with the Enemy, which was shortened to Fraternise. Once I had written *Fraternise / There's no surprise / Inside your eyes / You knew I'd come / Not just for fun / The dark and sun, that's fraternise* there was no turning back.

*

We rehearsed above Pete's parents' pub. When I entered, they thought I'd filled my pants, but the soreness from the foxy boy's foul had made travelling worthwhile. The guitar had caught my legs and the spasms caused suffering; the throbbing torment had brought me closer to Mam.

It was our first run-through since Mam had disappeared. If it'd been one of their mothers, I wouldn't have known what to say either. They asked one inept question after another and looked glummer and glummer. I saved their blushes by demanding that we begin. No music at home was appropriate, but that now meant that I frantically grabbed the guitar. Rehearsal was filled with energetic, extraneous noise and blew away the awkwardness.

Suffice to say, afterwards we mellowed in the evening sun. Unexpectedly, a serious-looking Coach Taylor was finishing a pint in the beer garden. Although he stood alone, he said that he'd met some old mate and was heading off. I never knew he had friends in Sunderland. Communication was difficult because I kept thinking about how he had looked at Mam.

After we'd cooled down, we reclined inside. The police had turned a blind eye to underage drinking, and we were joined by friends. Egotist Sean – our singer – wearing leather trousers and a buttoned-up paisley shirt began a conversation about sexual fantasies.

Flirtatiousness soared from the table; the rule was one fetish at a time. But lethargy from sleepless nights crept through me. I thought about Mam and whether Coach Taylor was involved whilst digging my calves into the chair's tough leather. Clueless, my drinking buddies were too consumed by sex to notice my hurt. When I drifted back, I heard anecdotes about threesomes, romps in cinemas, and MILFs, somehow managing to chuckle in the right place.

Then I heard the words. 'Your turn, Dan.'

'What?'

'Your turn, Dan. What's your sexual fantasy?'

With the shirt unbuttoned, Sean had the post-coital glow that I'd seen in magazines. If the truth were known, my sexual fantasy was… to have sex! The expectant faces and hums-and-haws told me that would be insufficient. Silly lyrics sprang to mind: *I spoke to her all night about sex / About positions, hands on desks / Morning came, I dreamt of breasts / When I rolled over, she'd already left!*

Naïvely I plucked up the courage and opened my mouth…

Carl

Lasses sloshed around the McCarthy boys. Hilarious, really. They'd said that we were good-looking, with cheekbones like Nike ticks. A girl who ah had once played with in the park said that we were like houses on an estate; built the same but garnished differently – different doors, different paint, different gardens. Of course, she had been on the cider, and after we had kissed she was sick on me shoes. Ah was furious, but Isaac had offered salvation with a disinfected toothbrush. Despite her drunken behaviour, she had a point.

Ah had never understood me brothers' limited success. Even boffins had tasted more of what was on offer. Yes, we all loved lasses, but the words ah had put in me brothers' ears had been unproductive. Ah loved with passion and knew what ah wanted. What me brothers failed to realise was lasses liked that. Isaac had talked about cleaning products and his favourite scientists. Dan had waxed-lyrical about bizarre B-sides and elongated guitar riffs. But material like that had never made a lass's knickers fall off. Listening was key, ah had told them – then swoop like a peregrine falcon on something the lass had said, showing understanding or humour. That's what ah had done.

Until Zoë.

Ah had cascaded through the lasses in me year group like a kissing whirlwind, a new one each week. Easily bored, ah soon moved on. Womaniser. That's what ah had been labelled. But ah could tell that some whom had cast stones would've liked a bit themselves. After all, nobody got hurt; it was a laugh. Joining a new school had provided a fresh legion. Parties and alcohol had allowed them to be more innovative, and ah was there to facilitate their desires.

That's until the night of the criminal-profiler.

A lecture series arranged by the school and delivered by specialists was designed to broaden our aspirations and knowledge. All on the criminology course had to attend. Exhilarated by the psychologist, who had explained how the CIA had influenced police forces around the world, ah had found her words mind-blowing. Thinking the whole thing was going to be prattle, ah had ended up being inspired by what she described as, 'Profiling for the 21st Century.'

On the way out, ah had negotiated traffic. Not long into the new year, sleety-white streaks in the cars' yellow headlights had shown a turn for the worse. Huddled in the bus stop were a group of girls from the year below. In me first term ah had stuck to sixth form and hadn't paid attention to anyone younger. Following a series of muggings, the school had arranged for extra lighting around the area, which had caused a spotlight effect. And that is where ah had seen Zoë for the first time, like an actress stood centre-stage. Tawny-brown skin had told uz she was mixed-race and – despite the season – a flutter of freckles crossed her nose. For once, dazzling repartee had failed uz and ah sensed a whiff of desperation. Ah had been caught staring and the girls nudged one another. But Zoë also had a fixed stare. Her ski-jacket had been fastened to the neck, and her silky hair was corkscrewed. 'You alright?'

'Not bad,' she replied. Her mates had sniggered and turned away, leaving us facing one another. Pitter-pattering hailstones struck the plastic roof.

'Enjoy the lecture?' Ah sounded like Isaac. Straight away, ah knew it had happened; me knees began to sag, and ah was falling. Ah had racked me brains but had nothing.

'Yes – y'doing Criminology?' The bus had appeared.

'Aye, its why ah joined this sixth form. Class.' Cracking under pressure was new. It was unfortunate that ad laughed when others had described it. Ah had sounded like a right loser. Pulling in, we had stepped back to avoid being splashed by the bus's sludge wheels.

'You're a McCarthy, aren't you?' she had asked, turning to look at me as she paid the driver. In profile she was exceptional. Her voice had a huskiness, and a tiny scrap of melting ice was playing dot-to-dot with her freckles. Forget being a loser, ah had turned into a king-sized-lovefool.

'Aye – how do yer know? Am Carl.' Raucous hoots of laughter had filled the stairwell.

'So, you're the one who thinks he's a magnet for girls?' She had smiled coquettishly as she shimmied away. Ah had wanted to touch her. Not in a weird way, just to measure her skin's temperature and softness. It was sickening. Ah had thought about the profiler and what she would have said about me: *sleep-around, been on longer holidays than his lengthiest relationship, misogynist (probably), patter-merchant, lad, thinks all he must do is smile* – that'd be correct. Zoë had been right: ah had thought that ah was God's gift.

An old woman had stared daggers when ad ricocheted and slipped on the wet floor. A more guileful seduction would be required than me usual grin and deftness for listening. Dan would've come up with some lyrics. Watching the steam rise from wet clothes, ah had sat above the droning engine. Ah didn't mind because her face had filled me head. Through headphones, U2's 'Sweetest Thing' had never sounded so sweet. Ah knew ah had a trick up my sleeve: Mam. Dad would've gone on about, 'When I was a lad…' but that's no use when yer moonstruck.

*

As ah waited for Zoë – our relationship secure – ah kept telling meself that boys don't cry, and realised that ad never hear Mam's advice ever again.

DC Carter

Sometimes the Island was referred to as "Mini-Moscow" and the allotment's sheds were painted red. It was a small town with a mentality to match. On one hand, if you said something about another family, they would be waiting for you when you got home; on the other, secrets were deep routed, and if you committed a crime then it was like people who had their beaks in each other's business found their eyelids had been sewn together.

I'd been brought up on the terraces and it was rare for a resident there to join the force. Pig and Judas references were common, despite most folk being law-abiding. Of course, the Miners' Strike had strained relationships to breaking point. My old Sarge was also raised on the terraces and had moved to the Island's private estate near the McCarthy's and now lived on the Hill. In contrast I had moved in the opposite direction. My marital home had been on the Hill, but my Mam's – and her spare room – was a few streets from the McCarthy residence. Whilst taking statements from Donna's colleagues at the estate agents, I had viewed some terraced houses.

At the heart of the Island was The Monkey Bar. I'd detected that we were the only police who were welcome. Since becoming the Clichéd-Cop, I had an ever-decreasing circle of friends. The pub had provided salvation, which only deepened the self-fulfilling prophecy of being a cliché. Sergeant Irving had been a constant beacon through the most desperate times; he was a good man.

When the Sarge entered two fresh pints of Exhibition adorned the bar, not to mention my demolished empties that embarrassingly clenched onto their suds. I had also created an ashtray that was sprouting too many butts.

'Hey, Neil, that one for me?' he asked as he pulled up a stool. Our bellies meant he had to push back against the bar to find room and his bald head had angrily caught the sun.

'Hey, Sarge. How's the wife and Penny?' I asked whilst he supped the foamy head of beer.

'A-Level revision for Penny, so I'm glad to get out,' he chuckled.

From the dartboard, locals gave him a nod, and a group of older women, with bags under their table, raised their glasses.

'I was surprised to hear from you, I thought it was your weekend with Sammy and Caz,' the Sarge continued, wiping away a foamy moustache.

A weatherworn expression reflected my heart, but I didn't have to hide. 'No, Jane's fancy-man had theatre tickets in London. It's best for the kids, she said, to see the West End. Suppose a bit of culture does no harm.'

'Seeing their dad is best for the girls, Neil.' I supped half-a-pint in one go. 'It's great how you've got on with things, and you're involved in this big case. Looks like you're doing great.'

I had made a prize-fool of myself when I broke down on TV during the Dead-Babies case; it could've been the end. The Sarge had plucked me from the depths and had provided the stability to go on. Gossip-mongering in the force had been comparable to the chitter-chatter on the Island – my colleagues' professionalism had been shocking.

'Just glad to be in the game. That poor family; three lads, triplets, y'know? It's just that pain,-Quick.'

The Sarge rubbed his squeaky head. 'He was always going far. Knew all the answers, which hands to shake-'

'-And which backsides to kiss!'

We laughed as a song by Elton John played on the

juke box.

'Insidious, little blokes like him will end up running the country. But listen, the word is that the Chief Super wants it to work. He thinks you're two sides of the same coin. So, make it happen. Do your stuff. You're a great copper and can handle people.'

I nodded. 'Remember when you took the mick out of Quick's hair at morning briefings?'

We laughed again. A couple of old-miners propping up the bar asked after the Sarge's old-man.

Once they'd gone, he said, 'We used to laugh at crime books and television cop programmes. Now *they're* the real cliché.'

'I know. There's always a couple of suspects who lie about their alibi. My favourite bit is when the maverick cop announces that he can tell the murderer is left-handed, wears Old Spice, and eats a curry every other Thursday. They follow no procedure, despite the novels being crime procedural fiction!'

'Imagine if it was that easy? Remember when we used to read chapters to each other in the canteen? Hilarious. That one about how they caught the serial killer because of the smells from the abattoir.'

'I know. Same as the cop shows on telly. I rarely watch one without saying, 'Ahhrr, come on,' or, 'For F's sake, that'd never happen.' Do you know that a fictional cop has twenty-thousand-percent more chance of being killed in the line of duty than in real life? There are books published every day where an officer dies.'

'Oh, writers love a dead copper; books are littered with them. Sometimes we even kill each other! When a plot becomes difficult, the solution is to see off one of the team. It's as if there's a Harry Roberts in every police station.'

'I'm just glad that a copper only dies on duty every

few years, and it's still shocking enough to be front page news. The only thing writers like more than a dead copper is Stockholm Syndrome. Any potential kidnapper who reads books must think they're the next Mr. Darcy!'

Despite the alcohol, the conversation moved onto the case. 'Did anything unusual happen on Good Friday that I've missed?' I asked.

Scratching his chin, he answered. 'Nothing.'

'The boss agrees. Evidence from interviews and forensics show that. They're bloody sick of me at the estate agents. I reckon one of them will invite me for Christmas dinner.'

'Got time for the DCI; he's hands-off and lets you get on with it,' the Sarge remarked, whilst holding up two fingers – in a good way – to the landlord. 'There were parking problems at the Methodist Church. Obviously, with the influx of special day visitors, the one-way street became overrun. An altercation between two of the congregation had cars grinding bumper-to-bumper. But my PC didn't help.'

'What happened?' I asked as the Sarge paid.

'Daft lad said, 'Come on, let's calm down nobody's been crucified.' One of those Freudian-slips. It caused ructions on holy day. Took me ages to perfect the stone face to discipline him, though. Bloody funny thing to say.'

I laughed and circled my finger around the glass whilst the landlord removed the empties. 'Hope you didn't get *too cross* and helped him *resurrect* things with the community.'

The Sarge shook his head at the pun. 'Queue at the fish shop got out of hand, too. Feeding the bloody five-thousand. Apparently, they were running low on fish and had to fetch some more. The line went around the top of the terrace. Things became heated, and it wasn't just the fish that got battered. Two lads were punched. The chippy crew calmed the mood by walking up the terraces offering free peas, curry sauce, or gravy with each order.'

'Amazing what a bit of moisture can do,' I joked, before taking a gulp.

'That was it. There were a couple of domestics, but it was quiet. What have you got? Anything that us uniforms know nothing about?'

'A bloody mystery. A missing person – presumed dead – a broken high-heel shoe, and a van's skid-mark. Her history is about as interesting as watching golf. She married her first boyfriend, everyone speaks highly of her, she has no enemies, and there's no avenues. We've found nothing despite the massive search. I wish it was a book where we'd uncover a photo from 1968 with all the players smiling, but there are no players. The only positive is that Quick's hair might fall out.'

He chuckled. 'It must be someone who knows her, but… with nothing coming from the interviews, it sounds like a stranger murder,' he pondered. 'But they're rare, just a million times more common in books.' An over-riding sense of grimness filled me as the fourth pint took hold. 'Something will give.'

I wished that I shared his certainty, but real life was no crime novel.

Dan

What on earth was I going to say? Streaking sun reflected from glasses onto my inexperience. Since Mam had gone, I hadn't thought about sex. Especially when Mam could've been… no, I couldn't think of that with others around, so I swallowed the thought. That was a pain I could imagine later. Eyes were on me. Not just my bandmates, but several girls whose low-cut tops seemed to have been unveiled by the wave of a magician's wand – *DAH DAH*! Seriously, I hadn't even noticed their looks or hair colour, never mind their breasts, but my brain was playing catch-up. Neurotransmitters stimulated neurons, rekindling lost desires. Amongst the McCarthy boys, Carl was the only one who'd had success. Rejection had followed me around. Having no trouble getting girls to go out with me, I had no idea how to move onto the next stage. However, unrequited love was great for song writing: *Why did you have to say it was over? / Why did you have to say we were through? / Why was I your lazy stop over? / Why did I fall for you?* I wrote that at a sleepover where zipped-up sleeping bags offered themselves as contraception.

My mouth opened. 'Okay, picture this,' I started, and Sean took a languorous drink, which triggered a series of gulps around the group. 'My sexual fantasy begins in a mansion that is painted white, with hallways big enough to stretch your arms. This is necessary because I am The Crow.'

'You're what, mate?' asked Pete.

'The Crow.' I thought that I'd been rumbled, and he'd realised that I was making it up. My mind flip-flopped possibilities, just like writing a song, and the inflection in my voice rose like an actor in an Australian soap-opera.

'Sounds interesting,' said a girl with piercing blue eyes who put her hand through her hair, getting off on it.

'Anyway, I'm naked and my arms are covered in gigantic, black feathers, like they've been plucked from a pterodactyl, dripping down like Icarus.'

'You're wearing nothing except wings?' asked another girl with her nipples visible through a yellow T-shirt.

'Not exactly, I'm also got on a… erm, err… a plastic beak and a hard.'

'Jesus on a bike!' Sean remarked. All faces leaned towards me, and something rippled around the circle. Interest. They were interested in my story. Any second, I expected them to laugh out loud. But no, there were a series of encouraging nods.

'Anyhow, I make a noise like this: *"WHAAA WHAAA – come to my love nest – WHAAA WHAAA!"*.' Grandiosely, I stood up, spread my arms, and flapped, which attracted attention. Coach Taylor was watching from the bar; I thought he'd gone. Performing always made me feel better and I removed him from my mind; piecing together the farce was electrifying. 'There's a giggly girl wearing a baby-pink pyjama top and white-knickers. She runs away, saying, *"Stay away from me, you horrible beast!"* but she really wants to be caught. Playfully, I chase her upstairs, flapping my wings shrieking, *"WHAAA WHAAA – come to my love nest – WHAAA WHAAA!"* Protesting with a smile, she dashes into a bedroom, and, after negotiating the doorway, I flap in.'

'God, this is a real fantasy,' someone said. These people weren't docile. How were they falling for it? A cloying ending was required to eliminate the strangeness.

'I join her on the bed where she strokes my… beak. We make love and, when we're finished, she snuggles deeply into the feathers, and we fall into the deepest sleep.' Around the table stillness like a photograph changed to elation.

'Better than me getting a BJ from a pair of twins whilst drumming,' joked Pete.

The group dispersed for extra drinks or for the toilet. Some couples became ensconced in public shows of affection. I hobbled from the smoky air to the beer garden, wondering whether there was a song amongst the crow-madness. Coach Taylor left. From wooden benches, people gave me hurried looks. It'd been the same at the football. Our story had filled the press, so we were recognisable. With no prospect of a happy ending, people invented their own grizzly scenarios.

For me, pain and creativity were the only things that had helped.

'That was weird,' Sean said as he joined me, twirling a cigarette. So much for getting away from the nicotine. And, to make it worse, the unmistakable stench of weed clung to his clothes.

'Don't you think it's weirder to start a conversation about sexual fantasies?'

'I don't think *they* mind.' Camouflaged by trees, Jay the bass player was with the girl with piercing blue eyes, squeezing her buttocks. After a drag, he continued, 'You learn a lot about people from raising the level of debate.'

'Ha, ha.'

'Class, what you said, "WHAA, WHAA – come to my love nest." We'll have to get that into a song.'

'It'd be great, wouldn't it?'

He flicked some ash. 'Look, mate, sorry to say this, but has this fantasy got anything to do with your Mam?'

Notoriety wasn't the only thing I had to contend with. People would also use pop-psychology to analyse my actions. 'No, Sean, it hasn't.'

'Sorry, mate.'

To escape, I went to the toilet. As usual, there was a queue outside the ladies. As nimbly as my injuries would allow, I twisted through the girls with an unfortunate limp, but enjoyed the jarring feeling.

'Hey,' I heard, 'you're Dan McCarthy, aren't you?'

Here we go, I thought, *another voyeuristic opinion about my Mam.*

'Yeah, you okay?' I said to a girl I'd never seen before. Behind her, the girl with the protruding nipples was chewing her lip.

'I hear you're The Crow.'

'Eh?'

'The Crow. I'm up for that; it sounds dead romantic,' she purred. Without time to absorb any more information, there was a strange sensation when she pushed me across the wet floor and into a cubicle. She whisked off her baby-pink top and my knees rattled.

Our tongues wrapped together, and soon I experienced a new kind of relief.

Carl

Me Mam had loved Zoë. Ah understood why. When ah had got home after Zoë had accused uz of being a womaniser, Mam had recognised the change. 'You okay?' she had asked. 'How was the lecture?' Due to how ad complained, she must've thought that attending an after-school event had made uz cross.

'Saw a girl at the bus-stop, Mam. She was lush. I wanna go out with her, but ah don't think am good enough.'

'Get those wet things off and I'll put the kettle on.' She had danced into the kitchen humming a David Bowie song. When ah had dried off, she had stopped stirring coffee to run her fingers along me cheekbones. 'No one could think that you're not worth it. My beautiful boy, you'll never break anyone's smile.'

'Pack it in, mother.'

Like she owned a crystal ball, she had told uz:

1. Ah had to be meself.
2. Ah had to persevere and show Zoë that ah was worth it.
3. Ah had to take her out somewhere cool.
4. Ah had to listen (really listen to her, not to just get what ah want).
5. Ah had to give her time and find out if she really was special.
6. Ah had to introduce Zoë to Mam.

Bleary-eyed, ah tried to soothe the ache by capturing Mam's warmth. But it was inside me head. The hands on me face were me own, and her touch faded. Ah composed meself. Stood on Brass Band Road, ah didn't want to be caught snuffling, because word spread like wildfire through the Island.

Next to me, graffitied on the lamppost, was a love heart with *SC + MK, 2geva 4eva 4years 2cum* penned inside. Ah didn't have to write down how ah felt about Zoë. We'd been together for four months and were inseparable. Messed up, star-crossed lovers; that's what we'd called Romeo and Juliet during GCSE lessons. But, with Mam's weird fortune-telling, ah got what Shakespeare meant: *On Hillside Grammar where we lay our scene.*

'Carl!' Zoë yelled along the sun-drenched street, freeing me from my thoughts, and ah felt me throbbing ear from being punched that morning. Ad often lie in Zoë's lap, and she'd stroke me hair. Losing her was not an option. Her parents had wanted her to concentrate on GCSE revision and recommended that we cool things. Acknowledging the seriousness of what was happening in me life, they felt it was too much for her young shoulders. She'd told them straight that she was there for uz whenever ah needed. There was no way ad take advantage but ah didn't want her feeling sorry for uz. But ah needed her to stay with uz because we were solid, so ah had to up me game.

Painting on a devilish grin, ah turned to greet her. Needle eyes arrowed in. Ah was in trouble. Slather and a smile wouldn't do. Wise words from Mam helped uz to win Zoë, and ad handled the seduction solo, but the turbulence in these uncharted waters was alarming. Ah wished Mam was around to help.

Bestowing a kiss was customary before ad pick her up and swirl her around, but she blocked me advance with a chop to the chest. 'I hear you got sent off.' A pacifying stance failed to appease, and she ploughed on. 'Why would I want a troublemaker as a boyfriend? First the fool policeman and that nutter neighbour, now you're fighting at football. Haven't you got enough on your plate without trying to beat everyone up?' Holding up me grazed hands in capitulation provided no defence. Feisty and wild-eyed, she was a bird of prey. Ah retreated from her flailing talons. But ah thought about what she'd said, it had already dawned when ad spoken with Aunt Suzie. It was the Yin-Yang: ah loved her affection, but also loved fighting. They both provided relief. Whether ah was battling or snuggling, ah stopped thinking about Mam for a while.

'I'm waiting.'

'Sorry, Zoë. Some fox-face tried to break Dan's legs. Ah had to step in.'

'Oh, sorry. I've obviously got it all wrong. There's me thinking you're a thug, when all the time you're a hero. Silly me.'

Tentatively ah touched her arm, but she'd turned her back.

'He tried to grab me balls!'

Her shoulders melted a little. 'Do all your stories have to centre around your…' She paused for effect. 'First, the cycling with Scabby Mary, then with the cricket ball, and now this! Anyone would think that you're obsessed with your bits. You've even got that football poster on your wall… and that weird picture of Doogs with codpieces covering their privates!'

'Droogs, not Doogs, from *A Clockwork Orange*. It's a famous scene from a film.'

'Anyway, it's not important. You love football, and I hate people thinking the worst about you.'

'No, yer right. Av spent ages thinking about the match, and ah messed up. Ah let people down.' She cupped her hand around mine and backed in. The tactile touches stirred, but it was no time for cocky innuendo.

'Am sorry, Zoë.'

Her voice became breathier and less husky. 'I just worry.' Tenderly she uncoiled and we rubbed noses. 'People will think all this violence is to do with your Mam.' Her eyelash whispered against my cheek. 'Is it?'

A flower bomb of crisp fragrance fanned. 'Dunno. Ah don't think so,' ah replied truthfully. Me Mam had said to never lie because she'd know. 'What the f-'

'What is it?'

With a cigarette dangling, Wild Bill stood close, pretending that he was checking for a lighter.

'What you looking at?' Ah brushed Zoë aside.

'Just out for a drink. Enjoy your night, kids.' He disappeared into the ginnel. Ah was about to follow, but Zoë held uz back.

'Leave it, he's not worth it.'

'He was in the house when ah left, must've followed.'

She put her arms around me neck. Ah was unsure what would feel better: Zoë's touch, or hounding Wild Bill? The flower bomb, or the sweaty yeti? That was the Yin-Yang. Ah needed both in equal measure.

Isaac

Ham with peas pudding was Geordie Pizza's speciality. It required expertise to provide the right amount of heat and mirrored the Goldilocks scenario: not too hot, not too cold, but just right. Stefano loved the Italian / Geordie fusion, but his son was less than impressed. Sophia's dad thought that traditions should be fervently adhered to. Stefano said that he knew the market and a twelve-inch ham and peas pudding was the shop's best seller.

Shift over, Sophia and I sat on the back step with our knees touching. The radio rejoiced with another League Championship victory for Liverpool, who always clinched it. Being pipped by Arsenal the year before was a one off. At least it'd knocked Strangeways from the news. But the only news that I was interested in was Mam.

Zipping and zapping, I loved the echo of returning Vespas and Lambrettas; they had a distinctive sound. Stefano was a collector and insisted on Italian bikes for the pizza-fleet. Once, when we loaded ovens, he'd recounted a tale. On holy days after a shift at the mine, he had offered the local children a backer around the Island. The men from his Italian village had done that – post Mussolini – when he had visited in the '50s. Stefano had told me that following the war the scooter was the greatest invention, and he had immediately imported one. Once – as legend has it – there had been over forty children waiting to ride on the Lambretta.

Unfortunately, Stefano had to install huge padlocks on the back gates after his vintage mint-green scooter was stolen. Youths around the Island shared Stefano's love of bikes; however, he despaired at their exploits on the Teenage Wasteland where they ripped up turf and scared older residents. Scooter culture on the Island was a far cry from Milan.

Sophia squeezed my hand with what I hoped was affection as I went to lock the gate with the return of the last scooter. Removing his helmet, the delivery boy's cheeks were drawn and his hair dank. Each were given a pizza at the end of their shift. With smiles, they'd plod inside with Sophia whilst I organised the bikes. Even though it was dark, I arranged them in colour order and shielded each seat with a plastic covering before spotlessly scrubbing the tail-trunks. Wearing a light on a headband, I looked like an old miner. Due to my love of bikes, I had asked my Mam whether I could have one, but it was pointless; the rule was non-negotiable. She had thought that motorbikes were the devil's death-trap.

Once the scooters were safely locked up, I checked the yard for inky traces of petrol. There was nothing Stefano liked better than fixing a bike. In fact, clustered around the corner, where the industrial chimney bellowed out the pizzeria's delectable smell, was an enclosed section. It was too disorganised to touch during a shift and caused me stress. Spare parts and metal had rusted.

'Let's have a coffee,' said Sophia. She'd provided pizzas to the riders and Stefano had left us to clear up, so we were alone. I took off the lamp and joined the smell of fresh Italian coffee. Without warning it took me back to the morning of Mam's disappearance, when she had clasped a mug decorated with Bowie's face.

'The floor needs mopping, and the counters have to be wiped.'

'Have five minutes.' She gave a smile which stopped me in my tracks. I was freaky about her. She turned up the music. 'You love this, don't you?' I nodded as The Stone Roses filled the takeaway. The coffee was the colour of her eyes. 'We make a good team, don't we?'

she cooed.

Not wanting to be the victim of misinterpretation, I sought clarity. 'As… err… work colleagues?'

She put down her cup and once again squeezed my hand. 'I like you, Isaac.'

Awkwardly, I placed my free hand on top of hers. We drank each other in, until… *bang*! The sound of spinning metal droned from outside. Puzzlement crossed her brow. 'Did you lock the gate?'

'Three times,' I told her, and the corners of her mouth rose slightly. Despite wanting to spend time with Sophia, I'd never neglect routine. The untouched coffee splashed on the counter, but we left it to investigate. The gates were open, and, judging by the clank, someone was delving through the spare parts. Fear didn't surge through me; it was anxiety at leaving the gates insecure. Sophia held me. Her breath was on my neck. I clenched a pizza shovel. Dull light exposed the yard.

'Hello, can I help?' I gulped, glad my voice didn't break. The clanging stopped, replaced by jangling keys.

'Papà,' Sophia huffed, as her father – booted and suited – stepped into view. My heart dislodged from my throat and returned to its normal position. 'You scared us, what are you doing?'

Glad to kerb the tension, I repeated the routine to lock the gate.

'Your nonno asked me to pick up the takings. I was looking for a Piaggio label. Stupid really, it needs to be done in daylight. Tried to kill two birds…'

'Don't do it again.' She hugged him. 'We've got to give the place a quick clean. Ten minutes?'

Whilst I mopped, Mr. Rossi approached. 'Your Mam was a big David Bowie fan, wasn't she?'

'Huge fan, yes.' I hated the past tense.

'She told me that your dad loves The Beatles. She said

that he knows the words to all their songs. Do you know 'You're Going to Lose that Girl'?'

I rested on the mop as if it were a microphone. 'I know it.'

He held up his palms before collecting the takings. 'You'll lose her, unless...' He winked. Ensuring the place was pristine was difficult, because I'd lost control. What did he mean? You're going to lose that girl... what did he mean by unless? Unless, what? I couldn't remember him talking to Mam. She had never said that they had conversed. When had they met? A lesser cleaner may have missed some scuff marks, but I scrubbed the shop until it was flawless. Whimsically, Sophia clinked two cups together before putting them away. 'We'll share a coffee one day, won't we?'

'I hope so.'

You're going to lose that girl; what was that all about? Was it a message about Mam or Sophia?

Stefano's son – Sophia's dad – had become my prime suspect.

Chapter 5: Photographs

Dad

No news is like being trapped in a fishbowl waiting for electric shocks. When someone disappears, the pain of not knowing is relentless and grief fogs all senses. Usually that cloaked emotion offered protection, but sensory information would sometimes break through from the silliest place. One day when I had collected the washing, the fabric's smell had blasted my world apart. I had held the bedsheets to my face whilst the rain grew heavier. The aroma had made me think of Donna and I fell through the clouds. There was no way I could face our bed, so I had asked Suzie to move in. She took the bedroom, whilst I relocated to the sofa.

Long-suffering looks had become part-and-parcel of my life. At the football club's vending machine, mortification was nailed onto people's expressions. When I moved, coffee in hand, the waves parted. I wished someone would offer human pleasantries: just a simple, 'Morning,' a, 'How are you?' or a, 'Kids alright?' Funny what I missed.

With his back to the sun, holding hands with two lovely girls, was Carter. He was strangely fresh, showing signs of vitamin intake. It was like he'd been scrubbed with a Brillo pad, as pink blotches fought against greyness. Contrasting with his beleaguered work-demeanour, he looked younger in a cagoule, sunglasses, and jeans. He'd volunteered to be our informal Family Liaison Officer, as Suzie had refused anyone else. He had been around most days.

'Hello, Simon,' he said, with the right mix of seriousness and friendliness. From interactions with other police officers, that wasn't part of their training. Lack of sleep had strained my eyes, but they didn't prevent me from offering the girls a full-faced smile. Donna loved kids, and I'd grown to appreciate them when my boys arrived. Each phase brought something new. Carter's girls returned my grin but tugged at their dad, desperate to move on. 'I'm heading to the play-park if you fancy a natter.'

'The lads are in the changing rooms,' I agreed. I'd always hated being on my own, so fifteen minutes with Carter was a relief. From a big family, I had visited my siblings most evenings as the boys were out and about. Before bed we'd convene with the lure of one of Suzie's milky drinks before I'd unwrap my sleeping bag.

'Lovely kids.'

'They're great. Off you go, girls, I'm going to sit with Simon. Careful on the roundabout, remember, it's faster than a flying saucer.' In a flash, the girls inhabited the environment, and their laughter was a poor man's music.

'Funny to see you outside work. Like seeing a teacher on a bus when you're a kid.'

'There's always someone working on Donna's case, y'know.'

'I know,' I replied. 'I dream that something will crop up.' I sipped the lousy coffee, and he lit a cigarette. 'I know how hard you've been working. It's nothing like television where clues miraculously appear through a clever-clogs link.'

He blew out smoke. 'Sometimes they do. I'm hopeful that something will give. For you and the boys, that must be soon. I can't imagine what you're going through. Dennis Nilsen was caught by a visit from Dyno Rod, and I'm the first to criticise inaccuracies in fictional crime, but sometimes real life is like cracked ice.'

'How do you mean?'

'Well, remember the death of that disco dancer?' I swallowed the information, trying to displace thoughts of murder, as I knew Carter was only trying to help. 'We had nothing for weeks. Then we found the bus timetables and the whole case cracked and we were drowned in information. The killer was behind bars within twenty-four hours.'

'I'm just glad that you speak to me like a human. It's like being a leper when people don't interact.' The reflection in his lens showed how much I'd aged.

'They don't want to say the wrong thing, especially a month on.' I tipped out the weak coffee and the vapour dissipated. Screaming with pleasure, the girls were relishing the slide. 'It's the final today, isn't it?' he asked, taking in the gathering crowd.

'Yes, only Isaac's playing. Carl's suspended and Dan's injured. They're in for the team talk with Coach Taylor.'

'Carl's a hothead,' he said bluntly. 'He's a canny kid, though. Judging by my gaffer's nose, he must be good at headers.' I couldn't judge Carter's humour from behind those sunglasses. 'Careful on that seesaw, watch your feet!' he shouted. 'A PC said he's seen Dan's band: Materialise?'

'Fraternise.'

'He said that they were great. You must be proud of how they've kept going. Isaac gave me free toppings in Geordie Pizza the other night.'

To be honest, I had no idea how we were still functioning.

We were going about things our own way.

One breath at a time.

Dan

Three weeks since the dishevelled interaction, and our relationship had grown. A far cry from being The Crow, I had never expected to have sex for the first time in a pub toilet with a girl I didn't know. There were whispers when we had come out for air, and Laura belatedly introduced herself. Since then, we had devoted time to each other. Offering an ear about Mam, we had spent time talking. She loved music and, in her room, we had scattered album sleeves, placing the needle on our favourite tracks. Ashamed about the lust in the cubicle, there had been no repeat. Taking things slowly was great, and lyrics about our first night were coming together: *Drinking passion in a confined place / Pressed against your pretty face / Finally I've joined the human race / There's more to us than that embrace.*

I adored how she held my hand with a two-handed grip, one underneath the other, like holding a cricket bat. From behind, she leaned on my shoulder. We were huddled on the side-lines with Carl and Zoë, whose honeycombed eyes netted the sun. Sophia fussed around her dad and grandad with coffee from an oversized flask. The scooter boys – Isaac's fan-club – kept an eye for dregs. Arriving late, Dad looked frail; he had sore eyes and sunken cheeks. Despite Aunt Suzie's efforts, he wasn't eating. Surprisingly, Carter was in attendance, two little girls dragging him along. From the look of his belly, he had been eating dad's portions. Perhaps that's why he came around.

When the players trotted out, a series of camera flashes captured the teams' stony focus. The local press was in force, and the opposition even had their own cheer leaders. We chanted: *'Canaries, Monkey Island!*

Canaries, Monkey Island!' It drowned out the teenage dance crew.

Experiencing the pain since Mam had vanished had served me well. Clipping toenails until they bled or drinking washing-up liquid until I vomited were my favourite releases. I never told Laura my secret, or the bigger one about suspecting Coach Taylor. Confessing that missing the cup final hurt, and a hair's breadth away, Carl's face showed that he had the same feeling. 'Are you sad not to be playing, Carl?' Laura asked.

Unnecessarily brusque, Zoë replied, 'Of course he is. He's played his heart out all season.'

'Sorry, I was only asking.' Zoë and Carl turned away.

Ever since I'd brought Laura to our house, they'd been hostile. On her first seat at the kitchen table, she had asked whether she could see Mam's belongings. Zoë tutted and led Carl away. Later he had told me that they hadn't liked the way Laura had asked. The pathetic explanation was beyond me.

Unfurling into a classic, the first half pinged end-to-end. Picturing Carl in midfield and me up-front, I felt the team would've had a better chance. Several attacks were prematurely snuffed out, and, stoically conformist, Isaac wouldn't budge from his position. Organisation was his forte, and he was in his element. Most other players had their shirts untucked or socks rolled down, but not Isaac. He was from a bygone age: his shirt's top button was fastened, his shorts were pulled to the waist, and his socks had a three-inch turnover. As a spectator, he looked even classier. All of us were decent players. I had pace, Carl had guile, but Isaac's composure was what set him apart. Gliding between mud-patches, he orchestrated a masterclass of lines and triangles.

Dad had received a coffee from Stefano and was oblivious of the girls' communication. Photographers continued to take snaps. Allowing Carter to stay, Zoë and Sophia braided his girls' hair. Laura continued to hold my hand, her vanilla perfume melting. She and Zoë exchanged poisoned looks. 'She hates me. I've done nothing to her. I think she wants to be the only girl in your house. She's ridiculous,' Laura snapped. I gave Zoë a cursory glance when she viewed Laura with slitted eyes, and her attention returned to the Carter girls.

'It'll be okay; they'll get used to you. Carl's a funny bugger.' I touched her face. 'When they realise this isn't short-term, they'll come 'round.' She squeezed in. 'Come on, we'll stand behind the goal.'

'Okay.'

We moved away from the others. It was the first time that I hadn't stood with my Dad or brothers to watch a game.

Mam wouldn't have allowed it.

Killer

Those cheekbones were stolen from his mother, I thought, as I stepped from the corner flag to let Dan pass. The girl with him was about Sally's age.

My first.

She was easy meat.

Back in the Summer of '82, I had been completely focused. And whenever I thought about her, I'd break. The McCarthy woman was only a month gone and still screamed loudly in my mind. Yet, nothing could compete with the intoxication of Sally. Although my handful of ladies each held a unique place, only the first few days after an operation had reached Sally's heights.

She never faded.

Throughout the '70s, I had raided washing baskets, stealing underwear belonging to my friends' mothers and sisters. Lurking in the shadows, I had stalked girls from school, giving myself points if I made it home unnoticed. Once, I was caught in a girl's shed. After a telling off from the police and my headteacher for being a Peeping Tom, I refined the operation. Astonished at the ease of graduation, I was soon touching prey, but executing these advanced operations had required a mask. Confidence and honed violence rose with a hidden face. The monster lurked beneath with a ravenous thirst. Some ladies had been passive, whilst others fought tooth-and-nail.

Seeing adverts for Italia '90 took me back to España '82 when the operation to tame Sally had taken place. I had seen England destroy the French and, when watching Italy draw their second game, it was time to strike. Terrified of sloppiness, I had spent eighteen months tracking the prey. I had first seen her when picking up merchandise for work. She worked in the garage opposite. Fireworks had exploded inside my head, and I had to make her into my lady. Whenever that trip near Sally was scheduled, I had volunteered and would leave the evening before. The drive provided an hour to plan and dream. Every Thursday she babysat and walked home barefoot, carrying her shoes. Along the shore, on the concrete jetty, amongst fishing boats or smoking in caves, I had been watching.

Sally had wet herself when I had struck. The whack to her head had turned her into a ragdoll, then my hands were around her throat. The ritual in the van had been like a volcanic eruption before I chucked her out. I had stared at her tiny feet, captivated by the chipped polish and smooth heels. Ripping the pin from her kilt had been an unexpected deviation.

Before progressing to cremation and burial, I had dumped the ladies.

Effortlessly, the next day, I had been cheery when I'd picked up the merchandise, and I never became a suspect. Watching the news and reading about Sally had been another unforeseen development. The newspapers had an obsession that the culprit was a drifter or from the travelling community. A picture of a promiscuous liar soon grew, as if Sally had been responsible for what'd happened.

She had no clue how she'd presented herself to me.

A knock from the police had never arrived. It was hard to judge whether it would all end tomorrow or go on forever.

DC Carter

My mother cracked eggs into a jar, while I circled butter into the frying pan. I checked that she wasn't looking before dipping my finger into hot fat. 'I saw that,' she said.

'Impossible,' I replied. 'You were checking there was no shell in the pot.'

'Know you too well, Neil Carter.' For once it was humour and not disappointment in her voice. I went to the fridge, which inhabited half a pig in the form of sausages, bacon, and black pudding.

'Have to get you on the force. With knowledge like that, you'd be the top-cop!' The kettle clicked.

'Go and wake them. I'll finish off here. Before you go, grab the tomatoes.'

'Trying to be healthy?'

'Cheeky.'

'Thanks, mother.' Most of us take our parents for granted. In her pinny and comedy slippers (a present from the girls), I couldn't help but think about the McCarthy boys. They'd never view their mother through adult eyes. A Kylie song started upstairs and simultaneously my pager made that horrible squawk. 'Girls are awake.'

'Never mind that. Why are *they* contacting you? It's your time with the girls. Just ignore it.'

'I can't. It might be about Donna McCarthy.' Judging by the noise upstairs, the girls were entertaining a herd of elephants. I dialled DI Quick, who said that I had to attend the station immediately.

At the front step, my mother's eyes bore, and the girls yelled a cheerful cheerio. The drifting smell of fried bacon reached the car. The streets were busier than usual, with groups wearing football shirts. The radio was all about the match: Sunderland versus Newcastle in the play-offs, both vying for a place in the top division. That week at the station there'd been briefings from specialists and dog-handlers. The showdown was the largest tactical event since the Miners' Strike. Bloody waste of time and money, all those officers to stop lads fighting. Should've just let them get on with it. Marshalling the streets on match day was like taming a bear in heat. They'd chosen a noon kick-off to stop boozing, but I reckoned the fans would start earlier, or just keep going from the night before. That's what I would've done.

Riot vans departed when I parked the Cortina. The station was a hive of activity. Officers were collecting shields and helmets, and, through the back, horses were treading the well-worn path into their boxes. Undoubtedly, there'd be many arrests. 'You're not involved in this,' stated my old Sarge when we bumped into each other. 'Thought you were with the girls.'

'No, I've been pulled in by Barry Manilow. Not sure why, but it might be about Donna McCarthy.' A couple of burly PCs apologised as they brushed us aside.

'If it's nothing serious, get home. You're supposed to be on the same team.'

I rolled my eyes and left the pandemonium. If it'd been a television programme, a tenuous piece of information would've already appeared, which I would clarify through wisdom and street intelligence. Yet, we had nothing.

Subserviently, I knocked on the door. 'Come,' he called. I felt a tremor. He didn't even have the respect to say, 'Come in.' Having no choice but to follow his command, I drew on a Clint Eastwood smile and entered. Stood under one of his special photographs, his hair remained a fire-hazard. Even on a Sunday morning it looked like he'd spent three hours in an old ladies' hair-salon. 'Carter, look at this.' Once again, I felt offended. No pleasantries or apologies for leaving my children. However, I was intrigued. Having spent time with the McCarthy's, I was desperate for a breakthrough. 'Well?' On the desk a newspaper was spread out, gatefold. Pictures of me with the McCarthy family had been nonsensically given inches of print. Prodding with skinny fingers, his self-manicured nails brought up images of witchcraft.

'And?'

'Read it,' he commanded. Feigning interest, I skimmed through and found the journalist's name: Peter David. He had written several articles about the disastrous Dead-Babies case. To say he wasn't my biggest fan would be an understatement.

'I'm not sure why you've brought me in to read this. It's nothing.'

'Nothing?' he breathed fire. 'Negligence, this is negligence, Carter. Cavorting with a dead woman's family. Blurred lines. You're a faux FLO, and there's boundaries. How dare you spend social time with them? I have it on good authority that they're your girls.' He jabbed their image, only pulling back when a nail cracked.

I didn't like him touching them.

A shooting pain drilled up my left arm.

I took some deep breaths.

'Sir.' I decided to be official. 'I was at the park with my children and bumped into Mr. McCarthy.' It took all my effort to hold back the scorn. 'It would've been untoward to ignore him. Yes, I decided to watch the match as my girls were being entertained by older children.'

He looked down his nose. 'Perception. This is about perception. People will think that we're doing nothing.'

'Peter David has it in for me. It's a cheap shot.' I had to escape and get home. My stomach rumbled with thoughts of my mother's fry-up. Quick was destined for the loftiest positions but needed better perspective.

'Look, the Chief Super has said we need to work together, but you're making it difficult, Carter.' He jutted out his chin and I crumpled the paper.

'This is just a pathetic dig. Ignore it, sir. Peter David's a chancer.' Quick sat down, but I could tell that the article had gripped his bowel. 'You know it's been a month.' I offered a new avenue. 'Why don't we use this to our advantage and stage a reconstruction? Get the national press onboard. That'd wind-up Peter David, and *CrimeWatch* on the BBC may be interested. You could talk about some of those other cases you've uncovered from around the country, where women have disappeared.'

'Yes… erm… yes, I was thinking the same thing. In fact, I've already drawn up preliminary plans. Okay, Carter, you can go. No more social interactions with the McCarthy clan or we'll have to insist on an official FLO.'

'Yes, sir.' I sarcastically dipped an imaginary hat. He was so vain, admiring his steepled fingers. He thought it'd been his idea.

Carl

The bloody rag. We were the middle spread of the newspaper. The pictures were out of focus, so readers couldn't see the destruction in our eyes. Dad was drinking coffee with Stefano; Dan was snuggling with that star-screwer Laura; me and Zoë were playing monsters, chasing Carter's kids; and there was a close-up of our policeman hiding behind sunglasses. '*One month on,*' it said, '*and the family appear to be coping well.*' The Crime Correspondent's spite was aimed at Carter: '*Lovely to see the recently demoted DC Carter enjoying the frivolity of a football match with the McCarthy family. Wouldn't he be better employed investigating the disappearance of Donna McCarthy?*'

How unfair.

The bloke had worked his fingers to the bone for us.

Unbelievably, the journalist never mentioned Isaac's performance, just insinuated that we didn't care. Ad got used to sympathetic glances, but on the bus into town, the looks were different. Accusatory. If only they knew how hard it was to get out of bed in the morning, never mind find a smile.

Central Station was mayhem. Lunatics had gathered. The capacity for violence was absolute. Police had made a thoroughfare, and the air was a cacophony of chants. Being pushed, shoved, pulled, and tugged felt great. Ah was an anonymous face in the crowd and had the biggest headrush. Big Eddie grabbed uz. We had been mates since he had stopped uz from mutilating the lad who'd banged me erection with a cricket ball. Funny that we were around casuals. Rumour had it that The Monkey Business (the Island's hooligans) had tied him to a pylon and beat him when he was at school. He had neither confirmed nor denied the taunt.

On leave from the army, ah had asked whether we could go to the match together. Ah knew that going to Sunderland – our closest rivals – was mad. But seeing those pictures had made up me mind. Ah was filled with Mam and unfairness. Fighting was the only chance of escape. At first, he had said it wasn't a good idea. Not wanting to be responsible, he told uz to wait until next season before me first away game without the family. When ah had twisted that ad go alone, his arm practically came down the line. There was no way he was going to let uz walk through Sunderland on me lonesome.

Spit, spirit, and the smell of a violent storm covered the platform. Eddie introduced uz to some remarkable creatures that Dad had told us to stay away from when we'd seen them at away games. Lugless Douglas, who'd had half an ear cut off in a ruck; Wiry Will, who'd taken such a kicking that his jaw had been wired together; and Blind-Boy Bob, a lad in a patch who'd been left partially sighted after fishhooks had scissored his eyelids. The energy throbbed like the town had been injected with adrenalin, and bug-eyed lads tossed bottles and sang with venom. We were like a horde of sports shop's mannequins who'd come to life – robotic and uniformed – in tracksuit tops and trainers. 'Stay close,' Eddie ordered, and ah nodded. Me body was covered in sweaty anticipation. 'There'll be nee fuss unless it comes looking. Bob says that crews are raiding pubs early doors and facing up their lads. We're going straight to the ground, so nowt daft.'

'Is it organised?'

'Sort of. It's not the army, just a bunch of blokes who back each other up.' Our faces practically touched, and a surge jolted when the train appeared. 'People know roughly what they're doing, but it can easily melt into

111

chaos.' Shoved into the carriage, we stuck together like super-glued action men.

'Never had you as a hooligan, Eddie.'

'Am not. Av got friends who are, but av also got army mates, musicians, boffins, OBEs, famous people, tradespeople, students, and coppers who are. Am not in anyone's crew, and most of this lot are a bunch of nobody's.' A lad next to us eyeballed Eddie but turned away when he saw the width of his shoulders. Luckily for him, it was a short journey. 'Ah kna' Bob and the lads, they're me mates, but ah only see thum when we go away. Truth is that ah like watching football. If trouble comes, it comes, but ah don't go looking for it. Away games are like having sex with a prostitute.'

'What do you mean?'

'You need protection. Hence, Bob and the boys, and its recrytisol.'

'Reciprocal.'

'Aye.'

Through the toxic streets of Sunderland, our hatred for them was met by their hatred of us, each side ready to inflict damage. The '80s had been equally disastrous for both clubs and there was an enticing chance of returning to the big time. The match was the karma that people had predicted since Christmas. Hurling mouthfuls of scorched verbal – with strange vowel sounds – they created a cauldron of loathing. Kettled in by the police, our group were a mini-island. Dogs snarled, and horses' hooves scratched concrete. None of this affected Eddie. He marched with a smile. 'Welcome to the jungle,' he yelled to the pondlife in front of us. There was no doubt that ah was alive, because me heart banged and ballooned, thoughts of Mam miles away.

We stood inside the ground before going onto the terrace. Since the Hillsborough tragedy a year earlier, there were raucous calls for all-seater stadiums; these old grounds needed an upgrade, and since Mam's disappearance ah felt the Liverpool families' loss. Everyone had been numb when they had watched the catastrophe unfold. Mam had knelt in front of the telly and sobbed. 'They'd only gone to a football match. That should never happen.' She had followed every second and knew the names of all who'd died. It had changed her.

'Your old peg's missing, isn't she?' Lugless asked. Eddie's cheeks expanded from his chiselled face, and he looked like the fat kid he'd been at school.

'Aye.' Surprise was caught in me throat.

'Yull have to speak up, am canny deaf,' he said, which made Will snigger. It didn't last long as his mouth locked.

'Aye. It's rubbish.' Talking to this lot about me Mam hadn't been what ad had in mind. With their range of facial deformities, they weren't the most compassionate counsel.

'Right, am away for a slash,' said Big Eddie. 'Keep an eye on him, Bob.'

'Av only got one, cheeky,' the lad with the patch kidded.

'If yer get wind of who's done it, have a word. We'll kill him before the police get him. We'll chop him up, cut him up, and stick him in the freezer.' Lugless' hooligan oracle was acknowledged by the others' sincere bows.

'Ad love to.' Somehow ah managed not to spill me guts about Wild Bill.

'Don't know how yer dee it. D'yer take owt?' asked Bob.

'Eh?'

'D'yer take owt? I've got tabs and pills. On the house if yer want thum, under the circumstances.'

'Wouldn't mind.'

Bob gave uz an acid tab which ah hid inside me wallet. 'Say nowt to Eddie, yer know how anti-drugs he is.'

'Av seen nowt,' said Bob.

'Al say nowt,' said Will.

'Av heard nowt,' said Lugless.

In a rehearsed comedy routine, they bumped together as if it were the funniest thing in the world.

Isaac

Stefano had asked to meet. The day before, he had marvelled at my performance in the final, like Inter's *Catenaccio* defence from the 1960s, he'd said. He had spoken with Dad, who'd told him that, for me, summer was a difficult time. Yes, I had my garden, but without football training, maintaining the kit, and writing ideas for set-pieces, I could become manic. Last summer I'd painted seventeen fences on the estate, and the year before I'd fixed every bike for miles around. Dad wanted something away from the neighbours, because friendly interactions were claustrophobic.

'Thought you might like one,' Stefano said, nodding his head towards his trailer.

Curious, I peered inside. 'Really?' My lips cut into a grin. I had dreamed of owning a scooter but hadn't expected to find one disembodied inside a trailer. They were like honeybees pollinating the Island with pizza: they'd hum, find their sting, and fly from house-to-house before buzzing home. I loved hearing them return up the back-alley at the end of a shift. Sticking to a task had never been a problem. I enjoyed seeing something for my efforts and constructing a scooter would be time well-spent. Looking at the wheels, spokes, and handlebars, my mind slipped into the endless possibilities. When a shard of light reflected, I felt the first flash of optimism since…

Mam's image caught in my head. The hours spent welding and buffering could be spent working out what had happened. I'd learned that Mam was always there: when I was resting, she coloured all thoughts; when I was busy, her caresses were lighter than polystyrene. In my head, I saw her smile.

'Are you serious?' I asked. In the ginnel, faint

discussions about football reminded me that I was part of the wider world.

'Of course, my bambina insisted. The only thing that concerned her was that your madre never wanted you to ride.'

Mam had a blanket rule. Knowing us as she did, she would've guessed that I'd observe the speed limit and wear protective clothing. Dan wouldn't ride but would use the bike for a photoshoot. Carl would've been her concern. She would've seen him with no helmet, standing on the seat chasing us around the Teenage Wasteland. When he found out that I was building one, he'd be jealous.

I looked at the perfect row of spotless scooters. 'Doesn't mean I can't construct a scooter as good as those. Once I get started, I'll talk to Aunt Suzie about learning to ride.'

'Your Dad thought it was a good idea; we'll get you a proper licence. All the delivery boys go through training.' I nodded, knowing Dad had decided something against Mam's wishes. 'Mind, this isn't for free.'

'Of course. I've been saving. I wouldn't dream of-'

He put his hand on mine. Liver spots sat either side of a blue vein and his nails were scrubbed clean. He led me around the corner, and, beneath the extractor fan, was the stockpiled metal, old and withered lying inside a cage.

'You won't pay for a thing. Now, tell me if I'm being rude, but I've noticed you like to organise.' How could I take offence? The world would be better if everything was in its place. 'I want you to sort everything in here. That's the price.' Other people would've focused on the beetles crawling through the rust, the entangled mess, or the greasy oil. Me? I saw the finished article: the plot divided into sections, engines here, labels there, and exhausts exhibited in size order. I'd overcome the jumbled disorganisation with gloves, cleaning products, and hard work.

'That'd be great.' We shook hands.

Sophia arrived, looking better than a catwalk model with her hair pulled back and with no make-up. 'Don't mind me, I can manage,' she protested, lugging a box. I sprang up to remove it. 'You're a gentleman,' she said with a suave piece of sarcasm. 'You're sharp. Do you think it's a good idea?'

Before I could respond, Stefano said, 'He loves it, and I'll get that rubbish your Papà keeps bringing in sorted. Did he ever find that Piaggio label?'

'Don't think so.' She shrugged.

Heavily weighed down, the strain of the box took my breath away. Sophia was stronger than she looked. Placed next to the trailer, I scanned what was inside: Owner Manuals (for Lambrettas and Vespas), engineering books on how to strip and assemble, some oil, rags, a toolkit, a pad, and a pencil case. 'I'll pay for these.'

'Not a chance,' Sophia scalded. 'Right, come on nonno, let's leave him to it and we'll have a coffee.'

'Ooh, sounds like a plan, bambina,' the old man responded. He linked his granddaughter, and they went inside as a plump pigeon strutted through the yard.

I wondered whether Sophia's dad had played a part in gifting the scooter. Was he somehow entangled in Mam's murder and keeping me close? They say that killers are planners. Had he organised how to take her and do whatever happened next? Was it like what I was doing with the scooter? Was it him? Was I like him? Fantasies and scenarios were in overdrive. The smell of coffee wafted to the chalked section and caught the pigeon's attention. Revolted by the thoughts of being like Mam's killer and my preoccupation with Sophia's dad, I was filled with remorse. Working on the scooter would allow me to think about Mam and battle the invasive stories.

Ten minutes later, things were far from shipshape, but I'd tempered my thoughts by listing birds from A-Z. Avoiding tripwires and the nagging pigeon, I went inside to borrow a radio for the match. Sophia's infectious laugh echoed from tiled walls. 'Isaac, have a look at these. They're lovely. Not like those mindless pictures in this morning's paper.' Strewn on the counter were an assortment of photographs. 'My aunties opened their restaurant *Sorella* last summer. Papà was so green-eyed, it was hilarious. His big sisters' restaurant is the best.'

'They've always kept him in line,' Stefano chipped in.

'We're going to put together a portfolio with images from their first year.'

Ice covered me. The foreground was filled with white teeth, champagne flutes, and canapés. Like a drunken fabulist my internal narrative spun. No A-Z or list could help me realign. Although I couldn't see her face, those shoes and how she tied her neckerchief were unique. In the background, Mam was in conversation with Sophia's dad.

Carl

Mobs had flocked. We were chased on the way to the station and swarmed into petrol-stained alleys, foraging for ammo, picking up spillage for weapons: bricks, bins, bottles, concrete. 'Get something, this could all go pear-shaped,' shouted Big Eddie. Ah searched for saliva, but me throat was dry. On the ground, ah found a metal pole that in a former life had been a shopping trolly. All easy pickings. In GCSE history, we'd learned that when the Russians retreated, they left only scraps for the enemy. So, we scooped up everything, leaving our nemesis empty-handed.

'Right, lads, everyone stands. There's nowhere to go, anyway. It's a rabbit-warren. Stick together and we'll get out.' A bloke cried from the front. Ammunition was carried in lads' up-turned tracksuit tops. A crew came around the corner and ran towards us.

'Geordie scum!'

'Stand! Stand! Stand!' Like the film *Zulu*, we were coiled springs, and when they were upon us, we unleashed stones for bullets and bottles for artillery. Carnage. A stray plank whistled by me ear as their lads toppled, sounding like scalded cats. Savagely, we got stuck into those left exposed. Groans, moans, and fierce screams were sickening. A half minute assault would give them lifelong nightmares. A boy in a baseball cap left a bloody palm print on his friend's white top. Ah slammed the pole into his ribs and he hacked up bile. 'Come on, daft-lad,' Eddie yelled, as all anger about me Mam slopped out. 'Gotta keep moving.' Usually fights lasted seconds. People got stuck in and it was over, but this was different. There was no exit or time for fear. But ah was afraid. It was a paradox. It was endless. Once the battle was over, we readied for the next. Adrenalin spurred uz on, but the taste of sickly sludge was what ad remember. Dread is the purest form of solidarity, and we wouldn't be battered alone.

The next alley – slightly wider than a car – looked as if a house had been demolished. Broken bricks with vicious ridges littered the backstreet. Berlin Walls – cemented with shards of glass – prevented escape into yards. Ritual cries were amplified. Younger lads began to reminisce about what'd happened, but older blokes kept them in line. War had broken out and ah was shoulder-to-shoulder with Big Eddie.

'Mental, isn't it?'

'It's crazy. Lucky you've had that army training. Am knackered.'

'Ah want to get home and watch *Columbo*. Can do without this.'

Cries went up that more Mackems were coming. Both armies faced each other. Again, we waited. 'THE FULWELL END, IS ALWAYS FULL, THE FULWELL END IS ALWAYS FULL!' they chanted.

'FULL OF...!' we hollered back, but they were upon us before the profanities kicked in. They were close enough to feel their spit in me eye, but they were immobilised by shelled debris. They scattered, leaving the wounded looking for a bolthole. The stomach-turning sound of somebody being hit by flying concrete was like a car being crushed. Clad in a red LaCoste T-shirt, a lad with gooey blood running from his eye squared up. Thinking he was Wild Bill or whoever had taken Mam, I kicked him square in the balls. Staying brutal, the battle rallied, and the grey sky was tinged red. Congealed blood thickened between cobbles. We moved on, hoping we wouldn't be annihilated.

Miracle of miracles, we escaped. 'Thank God,' Big

Eddie said as if he'd just recalled it was Sunday. Our trainers padded onto the main street, joined by our collected spoils. Half of the country's police were arresting lads who were scrapping at the crossroads. Acting invisible, we split into smaller groups to slip by. Warning bells rang when a group of Sunderland lads shouted, 'There's some Geordie scum!' Police horses thwarted their attack, and we traded hand gestures. A hasty exit up the road and it was over.

Once we reached the dog track, Lugless called, 'Think we're okay from here on in.' We blended into the ether. Numerous other groups were walking, some in red, others in black. Scarves of both colours flapped from passing cars. None of them were our concern. Eddie taught, 'Only ever fight with people who come looking. It's like being at war. Most people are civilians. At the match, most fans are there for the football. It's only a few who want to fight. Ad be happy to never fight again, but it turns up.'

At the next village, we slaked a shop's supply of pop. Carefully eyeing the traffic for police, it wasn't much further to the Metro. 'How you doing?' Eddie asked.

'Never had fights like that. Not sure if it's for me.'

'Look, don't feel guilty. The lads you struck came looking for it. They would've done the same to you, and worse. Don't pay thum any mind. If they hadn't chased us, we would've gone straight home.'

Ah understood his philosophy, and ah hadn't thought about Mam in hours. But if the likes of Lugless and Blind-Boy were the answer, then what was the question? Zoë would never see uz again if she knew what ad done. Don't get uz wrong, ah was glad for the experience, but a downer hid behind the buzz. We headed home. Job done. Finished.

Kids who had a murdered parent shouldn't care – but ah did. Ah wasn't afraid to get hurt, not after what ad seen in the dark, but ah didn't want to upset those around uz, or Mam's memory.

Dan

For the family, it had been our first match together since Mam had gone missing, and after Sunday's draw, spirits were high that we'd finish them off at home. But the second leg was a disaster. Sunderland had won 2-0, which meant that our old enemy had a trip to Wembley, and it left us languishing in the useless division. The final decade of the 20th Century looked like it would be littered with more lows. In the end, after the shouts and complaints, we had funeral-marched home in our thousands.

The next day, newsreaders had been whipped into a frenzy by the game's pitch-invasion. Spiel of repercussions and retaliation fizzed from the television. People were told to keep their colours to themselves, and that any football related violence would be severely reprimanded. On the train to Laura's there was no evidence of high tension. As I hugged my guitar, the familiar sights of empty factories, graffitied walls, and of the people daydreaming, flicking newspapers, or having quiet conversations were perfectly normal.

Earlier in the week, Laura's frown had splintered into a smile when I had told her that she should attend the reconstruction. God knows what Zoë and Carl would think. DC Carter had informed us that it would happen. An actress had been employed, but Suzie had startled us when she'd insisted on playing Mam's part. Through his Criminology course, Carl had forecast that the mur... kil... person responsible would be watching. I wasn't so sure. I just wished Mam was home.

Approaching Sunderland, a group of lads who'd been quiet at Newcastle became animated. Starting with 'Red and White Army', they moved onto songs about their

1973 cup win and chants about their favourite players. Obviously cock-a-hoop about their win, they started to act in a way that Carl would describe as "behaving like a dog with two big ones". They jumped up and down, thumped the roof, and wrapped their arms around each other, giving it large. Although I was upset that we hadn't won, I wasn't like Carl. He would've been foaming. For me, it was way down the priority list. Their exuberance was alien to the otherwise subdued manner that evening. Around the train, fleeting smiles graced people's faces. Others raised their eyes heavenward. Some swallowed.

I thought about Mam.

What would the reconstruction bring?

Exhausted by not knowing, I absent-mindedly found my nails entrenched into my hands. I quickly stopped and made sure there was no damage. Although finding new ways to hurt myself was comforting, my hands were out of bounds. Playing the guitar was as much a coping mechanism as hurting myself. As the Sunderland fans jigged, I cleared my throat. My song brought a violin-cord of tension throughout the carriage:

Ah me lads, ye shudder seen us gannin,
We pass'd the folks upon the road just as they wor
stannin.

The old lady sitting opposite squirmed. A man in his twenties shielded his children.

Thor wes lots o' lads an' lasses there, all wi' smiling
faces,
Gannin alang the Scotswood Road, to see the Blaydon
Races.

I sang with a smile. When the four lads approached, I

spread my hands in innocence. 'What yer doing?' the biggest lad, who was wearing a T-shirt flaunting a spliced lemon, barked.

'Joining in with the sing-song.'

'Yer Geordie fool. Your songs aren't wanted.'

'You lot won, mate, fair enough. No need to be upset about a song.'

First there was a fist, then a kick. The floor smelt of shaved rubber and dead grass. I looked at my guitar case. Kicks inflamed my ribs. The old woman yelling, 'No!' burned my ears and children screamed. Being a stickler for punishment, the violence was more brutal than I'd imagined.

When I hurt myself, I had the power.

Pain controlled what was wrong through its delivery.

But this was different.

Uncontrollably, the pounding bassline of their ferocity quickened and darkened. It became sinister. Evil flashes lasered.

Is this how it was for Mam?

How had he taken her?

Was it Coach Taylor?

When did she realise that she was no longer in charge of her life?

Drifting away, I sensed Mam's singing voice as the final pang stung and swelled. Lyrics swirled like a sticky fairground lolly. *I'll skip into your life each night / To soothe the pain and the fright / Sleep tight, sleep tight, sleep tight.* Deeper into the mist, her words repeated and gave a warped pleasure, like writing a sad song.

Coach Taylor's face appeared before I passed out.

Chapter 6: Reconstruction

Carl

Dan was full of fear. His eyes flickered like a light bulb on its final legs. He was pressed against the flimsy seat, his breath shallow. Sweaty abrasions folded as his hand sunk into mine. Slumped sideways, blood oozed from swollen lips that looked like a kid's inflatable, and his face had two halves: the right unblemished, but the left bruised and blistered.

Sean the singer had arranged to meet him at the station, but instead had called an ambulance. They should have been on a double date with that star-screwer Laura and one of her mates. On stage he sang faultlessly, but when he spoke to Dad his voice had faltered. For once, Dad had drove like he meant it, skipping amber lights with nifty gear-changes which made up for that drive back from the midlands. Coach Taylor had met us at the hospital. He said that he had heard the commotion from the next carriage and was flabbergasted to find that Dan was the victim.

Tripping on Dan's guitar, Sean's shirt was scabbed with blood. Ricocheting from walls, he fidgeted like an expectant father. A tranquilliser may have calmed his jitters. Coach Taylor was jumpier and asked if the police had been called. Dad suggested coffee and went to the machine.

'Wha, wha Co Til do ning?' Dan squelched.

'Ah think he's asking what you're doing here, Coach.'

'Was meeting some mates in Sunderland,' he said with far-away eyes. 'Glad I could help, but I'll head off, if that's okay?'

'Of course. Pleased you were there with yer first aid

badge. Did yer see who did it?' Both Coach Taylor and Sean shook their heads.

'I spoke to the passengers, but not anyone involved,' Sean explained.

'Tell your dad to get in touch if he needs anything.' Coach Taylor exchanged a handshake with Sean and ruffled me hair. Before leaving he patted Dan, who flinched. Ah was surprised that the Coach didn't leave through the exit but instead went to the lift.

Left with Dan and the edgy singer, ah was struck by the dreariness. 'I think I should call Laura and Shelly and let them know what's happened,' Sean said.

Ah shook with cold rage. 'What is it with her? She's a right witch.'

Backing off, he held up his hands. 'Hey, cool it, dude.' His voice quivered. 'I'm only doing what Dan would want. We're on the same side.' Dan was barely conscious and snuzzled into me. Sean was likeable. A good lad. Dan had been lucky to find people like himself. At The Comp he'd been too arty but being good at football meant that he had got away with it. At our new school, he was too authentic; he was genuinely into wearing second-hand clothes from the sixties.

'Okay. Sorry mate, yer right. But tell her it's under control,' ah told him.

'Okay, Carl, cool.'

Passing in the corridor, Sean and Dad had a brief interaction. With asbestos fingers, Dad plonked down four plastic cups on an empty chair and blew his fingertips. 'How is he?' he asked.

'Not sure how much he's taking in, they need to see him soon.' Thursday night and movement in A&E was methodically slow. Every time someone was seen before us, ah prickled.

'Where's Coach Taylor?'

'Had to go. Asked if you'd let him know how Dan's getting on.'

Dad nodded and knelt in front of me brother. 'Look at me, Dan.' There was the frailest of smiles. 'Good lad.'

'We'll see him now,' an Irish doctor said, accompanied by a nurse. 'Been involved in a fight, az he?' Her face lacked concern. 'Half the wards are filled t'bursting coz o'this fighting.'

'This is totally out of character, Doctor,' Dad protested. If only he could've said the same for me. Ah liked the power ah got from hurting people. Don't get uz wrong, me bearded neighbour had it coming after his accusation. But could ah say the same for the copper? Probably not. A creeping stillness filled uz. An image from Sunderland of the lad's bloody handprint flashed. Was he a patient who'd blocked up the wards? Ah tried to think like Big Eddie. That lad wanted trouble. Dan didn't. Yet, the people who'd spoken to Sean said that me daft brother had been singing Geordie songs. Did he have a death wish? Did he like the pain as much as ah liked to inflict it?

'Let go, Carl,' Dad directed.

'Sorry.' Eased apart like clingy Velcro, Dan was placed into a wheelchair and Dad wheeled him through double-doors with the medical team in-tow.

Being alone, me mind drifted. We'd never sat in a hospital for Mam. That made uz jealous. All we had was the memory of the broken shoe in a see-through bag. When someone dies yer should have a story to tell: the brilliance of hospital staff, of them dying peacefully in a chair, or being prepared for the worst. Even horrible deaths were improved by loved ones. All we had was the memory of her holding a David Bowie mug with that haunting lightning strike across his face. How ah longed for something different, to know that she'd died painlessly with a smile or happy thought. Nothing. And nothingness gouged cruelly.

'Carl.' Striding towards uz, almost bursting the zip on his trousers, was DC Carter. 'What's going on? I got a call to say a McCarthy boy had been assaulted.' If it'd been the weekend, it would've been me who'd inflicted an attack. 'Dan or Isaac?'

'Dan. The knacker started singing Newcastle songs and some Mackems kicked seven-colours out of him.'

'Jeez.' Eyes heavenward, he put a hand on me shoulder, making his shirt buttons groan. 'I can't believe it. What have they said?'

'He's gone in with Dad. Not life-or-death, but ah reckon he'll have a sore head for a few days.'

'Can I sit with you?'

'Feel free.' Ah didn't like being on me own. Strolling back, Sean's hangdog expression told a thousand words. 'What is it?' Ah bit. Perhaps Dan had relayed me reputation because he stood out of harm's way.

'Look, Carl. I tried to dissuade her, but she's coming down.' If looks could kill, the band would've been looking for a new singer. Fortunately, Carter would be duty-bound to stop me swinging for him or me brother's phoney girlfriend. 'She asked if it'd impact on the reconstruction.'

'She asked what? The f…' Sean stepped back.

'It's set-up, but if you want to call a halt, that's fine,' Carter explained calmly. 'Here's your Dad, now.' The detective took uz to one side. 'I thought you'd taken the law into your own hands and had attacked someone that you thought had hurt your Mam.'

Ah shook me head, but he'd given uz the germ of an idea.

Dan

The sky was grey. An invisible man pressed me into a barbed wire trap. My skull was bolted and each turn throbbed. Excruciating pain from hammered vertebrates caused lightning bolts through each bone. It hurt too much to breathe; my ribs were white hot. Of course, I hadn't expected to come out unscathed. But I had started something that I couldn't finish. Only when I had become a football did I want it to stop. Hiding my hands had been instinctive. I'd tucked them between my legs, allowing the attackers access to my head and torso.

Recuperation was a chore. Being conscious was suffocating, but sleeping was worse. The dull thwack of pain-killer nightmares offered no respite. Inundated by fairy tales of dropping crumbs like Hansel and Gretel, I'd try to find Mam. Trees with Coach Taylor's face wanted to eat me, and dwarves wearing T-shirts displaying spiced lemons sang on-loop. Laura dressed as a princess was stalked by birds of prey. Worst of all was Mam's faint whisper on the breeze. Following the direction led to peaty bogginess underfoot and deep darkness.

Although my bedroom was familiar, the muffled undercurrents were not. Whether they were linked to Mam, my assault, or the reconstruction was impossible to say. Since Dad had agreed to the reconstruction, the BBC had courted and prodded, employing as many people as the police had on Mam's disappearance. The crew's attention to detail was astute: the Bowie mug, the way she wore her neckerchief, and how she'd place her handbag on the backseat were meticulously absorbed.

Suddenly, the door swung open. 'You better have a word with your lass,' Carl remarked. 'Shuz doing me head in.' I wheezed, which sounded like gas leaking from a broken pipe, when I tried to prop up. 'Howay, yer knacker,' he said with softer tones, cupping my arm pits. Thoughts of tickling made a sway of sweat fly from my brow. Being a triplet meant one of us was an outsider. For years, a deadly duo would gang up on a runt, which meant I'd had more physical contact with Carl than he'd had with his harem. But he was only helping. Despite straightening pillows, Carl was the most unlikely Florence Nightingale. Unrhythmic drumbeats entered my head of Carl and Laura arguing at the hospital.

'What's she done?'

Carl shook his head. 'What do you see in her? She's a witch.'

If I could've moved, I would have grabbed him by the scruff of the neck. 'She's my girlfriend, Carl. Leave her alone.'

'Shuz downstairs hobnobbing with the hoi-polloi of the BBC, with her fake laughter as if shuz auditioning. She shouldn't be here. She doesn't get it.'

The inability to think was frustrating, but when Laura bounded in like Tigger on E, I knew things would worsen. 'Dan, it's unbelievable, they've designed a storyboard and there's a crew. The director reckons that there'll be a breakthrough.' Her teeth flashed, and I thought Carl would smash them with my Fender.

'It's not a soap-opera, Laura. This is about Mam's disappearance,' Carl spat.

She shook like an epileptic leaf. 'God, I know,' she said in exasperation. 'I've lived every minute with Dan.' I was convinced that I was about to be killed in the crossfire. Peaceful instruments like the glockenspiel and xylophone could easily become weapons. Carl said nothing more but was so purpled he could've passed out.

Adding further farce, Isaac arrived carrying a jumper. 'Dan, tell Carl that he has to wear it.'

'What's going on?' I preferred the nightmare.

'The reconstruction must be authentic. Carl wore this when we went to Wolverhampton. He says that he won't wear it on telly, but it's in the script.'

'Ah don't care,' Carl screeched. 'Chuck it over; al put it on. Am past caring.'

'Charming,' Laura sulked, pouring petrol onto flames.

'Can you remember whether my Harrington was undone?' Isaac asked, his OCD in overdrive.

Somehow, Mam appeared behind Isaac. Her neckerchief – as always – was theatrically tied to the side to show her grandmother's ring. I passed out with a series of lyrics ringing in my ears: *Old jumper / Lost mother / Deafening sound / From underground / Old grey day / Here to stay / Aching bones / Xylophones / Crumbling gloom / Familiar room...* then I was back in the woods with Mam whispering: *Find me, nothing more...*

Aunt Suzie

Poor Dan buckled. In his state, he must've thought that I was his Mam. The others had seen Mr. Gallagher drop off the uniform (with neckerchief), and they'd seen me change clothes. Isaac had even made Simon buy replacement shoes. When I was younger, I had wanted to be her. Never in my wildest dreams would I have thought it would be like this. But I took a heavy breath behind the front door dressed as my sister, swirling in a whirlpool of guilt. The reconstruction was designed to find her, turn a new leaf, start a new page. But I couldn't help feeling that tomorrow would never come.

Isaac gave me the Bowie mug – containing tea – with a burdened smile. The poor lad had organised everything in a bona fide manner. The fact that I preferred tea to coffee had caused distress. Even though his Mam and I were sisters, we had our differences, just like the boys. With wine she was red, and I was white, whilst I was better in the evening, and she was a morning person: a lark to my owl. 'It'll be okay,' he chirped, reassuringly. 'Our scene was over in a flash.' Bowie's image helped, even though he could've been on a mortuary slab, except for the healthiest crop of red hair. I shook. Was the mug the last thing that had touched her lips?

'Ready when you are,' the director called. Isaac adjusted the neckerchief, mumbling a list. I kissed him to soothe nervousness but understood that he didn't like to be touched. For once, he leant in. Maybe it was what I was wearing, or the circumstances. Whatever the reason, it was not as significant as what he gave me. I was now ready. Not exactly brimming with hope, but steady enough to open the front door and wait for... Action.

On opening, there were flashes. The gaggle of

photographers – jostling for position – snapped indiscriminately. The director allowed this to continue until I was blinded. I fell into fathomless thoughts. Life was a series of snapshots, and some never faded. Snippets from our photo album coloured my mind: Donna and me next to the Christmas tree, I must've been four and she seven; then as teenagers dancing to The Stones at the local disco, fashioned in mini-skirts and Jackie O sunglasses; her wedding day and us stood back-to-back like we were heading for a duel, jollity captured in our smiles; holding the boys, me, Simon, and Donna cupping their tiny frames; queuing outside Wembley for Live Aid, self-righteously doing our bit for Africa, but secretly dreaming of being close to Bowie. The memories were like precious antiques behind glass. They were brittle and priceless and would grow in value as the years passed without her.

Squinting back into view, Bowie's pallid skin reflected my own. Despite rising nausea, I was only making a small gesture. Gathered around the press were a horde of neighbours. Descended into a hush by the camera crew, their pitying looks created a backdrop of respect and excitement. I knew exactly how Donna stood. Arms folded, resting the mug on her forearm with a smile wider than the Tyne. Painstakingly, I'd rehearsed non-stop. Sight returned, I was ready.

'Action.'

'Hey, Carl, that's a crane…. Ooh, sorry.' I'd fluffed the lines, penned so fastidiously by Isaac. Automatically, I cursed and muttered, 'Sorry, Donna.'

'No problem,' the director called. 'Even happens to Meryl Streep. At least you've perfected the accent.' His playfulness nourished my resolve. 'Okay, Don… I mean, Suzie.' A sharp communal intake of breath murmured when he almost called me by her name, but it gave me something. I was doing it for Donna. 'We're re... ready for a second act... shot?' The thick interest on the street had got to him, but as his confidence shrunk, mine grew. 'Silence on set... ... ... Action: Take Two.'

'Hey, Carl, that's a canny jumper; are you really wearing it?' *Pause, allow the editor to do his job.* 'I would've ironed your new top.' *Count to three in my head.* 'Have a safe journey. Love you.' *Remove arm and wave – raise Bowie.* Nailed it.

'Cut. Excellent, Suzie, really well done.'

'Should we do it again?' I asked, pleading that he'd say no.

'We'll quickly look through the rushes, but I think we've everything we need. Thank you.'

'No. Thank you.' Inhaling a large breath, I made way to the kitchen and embraced Isaac.

'Sounded good from here. It passes so fast,' he said, wriggling free. I could see that he wished it had been real. All of us wanted to say goodbye, properly.

At the table, my parents were hunched together. They'd hardly spoken since she'd gone. Dad's knuckles rattled the wood, creating an echo that sounded misplaced. Not a beat of music had graced the house in weeks. It was as if Donna's soul had sucked away harmony and verse. With an unhealthy gasp, he shuffled over. 'Let me look at you, girl.' A film covered his eyes. 'You look magnificent.' I remembered years earlier – when he was younger and tougher – how he had half-heartedly told me off for taking Donna's Biba dress without permission. He'd had no clue what the fuss was about and even pronounced it "Dibba"!

Visibly broken, his wrinkles looked like a toddler had reconstructed a smashed ceramic. He stroked and squeezed my shoulders, feeling the silky neckerchief before circling the ring. Donna and I had both received the special gifts from our parents' mothers. Donna joked that it'd be my only betrothal. Northern Goldsmiths had mounted them tastefully on necklaces and they were worn with pride. Until that moment, I'd never thought about the missing ring; it was part of her. Dad's long look let me know that his mind had departed.

The director wasn't the only one who'd mixed up Donna and me.

DC Carter

The scene spotlighting Donna's final interaction with her family rocked me on my heels. Suzie's smile had a palpable sense of sadness which betrayed her acting prowess. On the street, empathy was in abundance, even Wild Bill held a cap in hand. Buffeted by the wind, the neighbours disembarked with a whisper of white noise. I questioned ever mentioning the reconstruction. Known to reap rewards, they weren't always successful, and, if it didn't work, the McCarthys would have to abandon any lingering hope. Over excruciating weeks, the family had made every attempt to behave normally. What could be worse than not knowing? Every night I imagined Donna being exposed to unspeakable deeds, so God knows what Simon thought.

Leaving Dan with his grandparents, Suzie left the house. The make-up artist had created Donna's doppelgänger. 'You're doing great.' Almost speechless, I gulped to clear my throat. 'Are you ready for the next scene?'

'I think so.'

With Isaac in the front, Carl jumped into the back of the Cosworth with the girls who'd braided my kids' hair at the football.

'Do you want a lift, love?' I asked Dan's girlfriend, who'd made Carl go berserk at the hospital.

'No, it's okay. I'll walk,' she said. Her translucent eyes were blue water. Simon set off to the hallowed spot, and the girl dragged her feet.

'Feels weird,' Suzie sighed. In position, the leftover crew assembled to video her departure.

'Why's that?'

'Driving her car, wearing her clothes, walking in her

shoes – well, a version of her shoes. Everything seems so normal. She had no idea what was about to happen.'

'That's why we must do this. There's a chance it could trigger something.'

'Do you think it'll work?' she asked, her hand resting on Donna's Fiesta.

'I hope so. I really hope so, Suzie.' Having spent all week persuading the family with statistics about successful reconstructions, I felt fake. 'I'll see you down there.' I radioed that I was on my way but would park up on the terraces. Driving the Cortina, I saw Dan's girlfriend striding back with a purposeful stare. She must've forgotten something.

Scores of people were pressed along Brass Band Road. My old Sarge's uniforms had prevented a logjam by shepherding them to one side, allowing precariously positioned cameras to pick up Suzie en-route. On screen, the Island would look as deserted as it had been on Good Friday. Utterances were that we had missed clues due to lost time at the beginning, whilst the press had called us incompetent. Despite this, everyone was desperate for success, even if the groundswell of solidarity for the police had long gone. There'd been too many cases like New Cross, Orgreave, and Hillsborough.

Carl's eyes were on stalks. 'How you doing, young 'un?' I asked. 'Thought you were going to the old pit.'

'Ah asked Dad to drop us here.' Zoë, standing next to him, gave me a quick wave. She was paper thin, and when the aroma of pizza-dough caught the air, I wanted to buy her a Hawaiian. Carl's head pivoted like watching a game of swing-ball.

'What is it?' I asked him. At that moment, Donna's car passed, creating a solid silence. There was no need, as a voice-over would be applied to the journey. 'Look at me, Carl. Why aren't you with the others?'

'Same as you, ah reckon.'

'How do you mean?' I'd thought I'd trust my gut and see if the film would winkle out the killer. But the jostling crowd left me disappointed. All I saw were old miners, regulars from the pub, folk I'd nicked, and a splattering of faces from the Dead-Babies case.

'Me Criminology course says that killers often turn up to these things. But it's like a football match.' Zoë's bony hands clasped his arms. 'He'll be hiding in the shadows,' he said as his football coach and teammates looked on.

'Don't believe everything you read,' I lied. 'There's no way he'll be here.' Yet, our thoughts were aligned; part of our investigation had covered the same ground. We'd switched on the warehouse cameras, but had only picked up dog walkers, kids playing football, and courting teenagers practicing their fingering skills. In fiction, the cliché during group gatherings is that the cop and the killer's eyes meet and they "just know". Following a chase, the cop apprehends the killer, and, after years of concealment, the murderer unburdens themselves by explaining the entire plot in a page and a half.

'Howay, I'll drive you there,' I said, whilst jealously viewing the queue outside Geordie Pizza.

*

On the fresh tarmac, the family were reassuring Suzie, whilst my SIO pursued a discussion with the director. Powdered and coiffed, DI Quick was being tended by the miraculous make-up artist, his hair a puffy summer cloud. Smyth loitered like a spare part at a wedding, surreptitiously hiding the evidence bag containing Mrs. McCarthy's shoe. Exacerbating my hunger, the crew grew familiar with Geordie Pizza's boxed delights.

'Cheers, Carter!' Carl called as we went our separate ways.

'Over here,' Quick commanded. The choking hairspray was enough to wipe out an army of ants, and he still hadn't been on that "*Manners towards your Minions*" course. 'Did you bring Carl McCarthy here as part of your pseudo-FLO duties?' Dusty make-up quivered from his face.

'Certainly, sir. Made sure he's with his family.'

He glared at Carl before creasing a fake smile to a crew member grappling with a sachet of garlic sauce. 'Apparently, everything's gone well. Next, it's your scene.' He transmitted a bucketful of envy about my acting role. 'We've filmed everything: the shoe, and Smyth's line saying what he found under the car,' Quick said. I put on my sunglasses like Clint Eastwood. 'All we must do is catch your facial expression and Suzie getting out of the car. Finally, I... well,' he patted his hair, 'the SIO and I will talk through the case on camera.'

Thankfully, my cynicism was hidden behind dark lenses.

Killer

New Order's song for Italia '90, with John Barnes rapping ripped through the rafters. Singing along, I almost missed a knock on the shutters. How could I have been unprepared? Talk of the reconstruction had sent me into overdrive. Deciding where to stand and how to behave was all I had considered. Pigman Carter, who'd allowed a baby killer to walk the streets, had conducted the earlier interview, but two policewomen arrived with minty smiles: the plain clothed one that smelt of stale horses, and the uniformed one who'd caused my younger staff to buy extra tissues and that looked like she was on a catwalk. Acting mock-offended at catching me unawares, I complained about how they could've called ahead.

Even in dappled light, the lock-up was spotless. And, when an advert about the Garden Festival began, I switched off the radio. The duo scanned the place and checked the arrangement of tools and equipment. My sanctuary was impenetrable, but I'd allowed them in as Aladdin's Cave was triple-locked. After formalities, they explained that they were checking van tyres. Stating unequivocally that I'd do anything to support the McCarthy case, I asked tentative questions. They checked the tread and took an impression, but they could tell the indentation was not a match. They used their script about taking precautions to eliminate people from their enquiries.

As if I'd be so stupid.

I always changed the tyres.

After photographing the van, they apologised for the inconvenience. 'Are you attending the reconstruction?'

I thought carefully but knew that everyone would attend. 'Yes, it's terrible. I hope it'll jog someone's memory. That poor family.'

'Better be quick.' I was watching their perfect behinds when the uniform turned. 'You've got a few freezers.'

'Lots of merchandise,' I replied.

She flaunted a photoshoot smile. 'I'll pop in for food soon.'

'Please do. See you then.' Police ate at all my establishments.

I propped against the van, thankful they hadn't looked inside. A bag containing the McCarthy woman's belongings still hung from a hook and would bring nothing but harm. Inside my pocket the ring moved with each heartbeat, and I circled it with my fingers. Happy they'd left, I escaped through the back door – bag in hand – into the ginnel. My feet made echoing acoustics on the cobbles. Glad to find the back gates open, I thought of an excuse as to why I was there, but my visit went unnoticed. I dumped the clipboard, keys, and pager amongst the scrap.

Back onto the streets, I was amazed by the solemn sight of grieving people, and quickly mingled with my group. Pigman Carter was talking with Carl and a tissue-thin girl as the car passed. With avid interest, I inhaled the choking sight of the McCarthy woman's resurrection. Whenever I saw a replica of one of my ladies, my throat contracted.

Back at the lock-up, I stared at the mementos stored inside Aladdin's Cave; my shrine. After unwrapping the tinfoil, I picked up the bejewelled pin that had belonged to my first; Sally. I thought about how long I had left. Were the incompetent police closing in, or was the visit a consequence of operating near home?

I needed to blow off steam.

Zoë

Wires, left by the camera crew, meant that wind was winding through a gap in the front door. After some gentle negotiation it closed, and we said goodbye to the outside world. I was glad to have Carl home; he'd been like a cat on a hot tin roof all day. In the hallway, we heard nothing due to the conversation. Only in the kitchen with Carl's grandparents could we hear the distinctive hum of music. 'If Dan's got the radio on, tell him to switch it off,' Carl grunted. 'Can you go, Zoë?'

'Of course, dear.' I curtsied, playing a subservient role, which raised a smile from Isaac and Sophia. An unwritten rule since Carl's Mam vanished was that the house was devoid of music, which was a stark difference from the wall of sound when each McCarthy had blasted out sounds. Moving between tracks had been dizzying. Signed pictures were arranged symmetrically in the stairwell. They showed pop stars with weird haircuts, and Bowie's peculiar eyes were dead centre. The Beatles in varying states of drug misuse – hairier the more drugs they'd took – were well represented. Stopped in my tracks, I had to find my bearings. The rhythmic riff from Bowie's 'Moonage Daydream' strutted around the landing. But it wasn't from the loft rooms, it came through Carl's parents' bedroom door. Seeing Suzie dressed as Carl's Mam had made me cold, but now it was like an ice bucket had toppled over me. It was a stupid thought, but had Donna's ghost materialised? I tiptoed on air and sensed rummaging. Next, I smelled Donna's perfume, one of the Chanels. Slightly ajar, I peered through the gap, spotting silhouettes and shadows. I thought about calling for Carl, but that was insane. I stroked the door and was met by an inconceivable sight.

Rolling on the bed, Laura was soul-snatching. I hadn't noticed her since she'd chatted like a demented dolphin to the film crew. Wearing Donna's vintage pale-blue Biba dress, she was miming Bowie's song, lost in her own world. Donna's shoe collection had detonated onto the floor, and Laura tossed heels into the array. She was now on her feet with her hair like Donna's. She sprayed more perfume and walked through it, then emptied the jewellery box. I was baffled. She deposited items into her shoulder bag. I found a voice louder than shrill. 'WHAT THE HELL? WHAT THE F...?' In a trance, druggier than a hairy Beatle, she flipped focus.

A storm of people ascended the stairs and were stopped by an invisible force-field as they toppled and absorbed the sight. Expecting to see a shamefaced Laura, or a damsel in distress routine, we were met with frostbite. 'What's the fuss?' she bleated in a little girl's voice. Instinctively we held Carl, expecting a hurricane.

'I told you, she's a nutter!' His words were almost inaudible as he fought to keep the lid on. All of us were living on the edge of rage. Simon marched downstairs, stopping Carl's grandparents and taking them to their usual spot.

'Get rid of her, just get rid of her.' Isaac slumped and shutdown with Sophia consoling him. I clung to Carl like cement on concrete; Suzie's look was blunt stupefaction.

'I'm leaving,' Laura said.

'Not in that – take it off!' Suzie commanded.

'What's the problem? You're dressed like her.' Laura yanked off the dress in one sweep, causing an audible creak in the stitching.

'Not because I want to, you silly girl.'

'And empty your bag,' I added. Jewellery dropped with letters, photos, and the boys' childhood drawings. Carl bit his knuckles. Barefoot, we shoved Laura downstairs, avoiding the treasured possessions. 'She's wearing two T-shirts!' I added. At the bottom, Carl turned his back and Suzie made Laura strip down to her bra. She'd hidden Bowie's *Serious Moonlight* Tour T-shirt beneath her own. Tickets from gigs fluttered from the sleeves. 'I think she's got kleptomania,' I said.

'Ah think she needs locking up!' Carl replied.

'I need my shoes. I can't get home without them.'

I fetched them and flicked off the music. Only after we'd thrown her out did the emotional wreckage join the house's deeper hurt. Dan hobbled from the loft. 'What's going on?' I grasped Carl's arm.

Isaac

Cleaning should be done alone. At work, I'd arrive early and stay late to maintain standards. So, I flapped like a landed fish when Sophia made a beeline to help clear Laura's devastation. I was as surprised as anyone when I accepted. Inexplicably, the brick wall that usually appeared wasn't there. Everything had to be returned to the exact place and Sophia waited for directions. Watching her fingers fold Mam's things meant that Laura hadn't been the last person to handle them.

She initiated holding hands as we walked to work. Branches waved and the wind whooshed. Making a mental note, I told myself to ask her which hand cream she used. Tender and smooth, I'd smell it before washing my hands. 'How's the scooter coming on?' she asked.

'Haven't really started. Still sorting the metal.'

'That's a big job.' She swung our arms a little quicker. 'Mind you, the yard looks great.'

'It's taken longer than I thought. There was so much in there and the trailer. I'm on first name terms with Scrapyard Stevie. Mind you, I think half the stuff came from him in the first place!' She squeezed my hand and laughed. On Brass Band Road, the cameras used in the reconstruction were being dismantled.

Panic pulsed when we skidded on dirty tiles. Unsurprisingly, the pizzeria didn't have its usual soapy hygiene. The film director had asked Geordie Pizza to feed the crew and, as a one off, Stefano had agreed. Judging by the disorder, it'd been a success.

'Hey, you two,' Stefano said urgently. 'Great to see you. We haven't stopped – I think most of the Island have had pizza today. Ooh, so sorry.' Stefano bowed, suddenly slowing down. 'I hope it went well.' Sophia and I put on our aprons.

'As well as expected,' I answered. The benches were overflowing with ingredients, so I helped create a slicker working area and provided Casio with a well-deserved break. He looked like a victim of an exploding flour bomb. Whilst I was sorting the chopped Italian sausage from the saveloy, Sophia kissed me on the cheek. I turned to jelly.

Although confused by the kiss, her smiles when presenting boxed pizza helped the evening pass. Even Wild Bill's presence didn't disturb me. When Sophia's dad collected the day's takings, whistling 'You're Gonna Lose That Girl', the stresses of the week – Dan's beating, Carl's anger, the reconstruction, writing the script, and bloody Laura's antics – didn't matter; they'd been wiped out by Sophia's caress.

Out of her earshot, Casio said, 'She loves me, she loves me not,' with each slice, making the tattooed love heart between his thumb and finger look like it was beating. Songs on the radio reminded me of Mam – 'Nothing Compares 2 U' and a song called 'Killer' (which never mentioned that word) – but I was buoyant. Whenever Sophia and I made eye contact, my shoulders relaxed. It was good of Coach Taylor to check in and buy a twelve-inch Buffalo.

The scooter-boys were finishing their shifts, but Sophia and I weren't on the back-step. En-masse, a flurry of partygoers had appeared, and we frantically loaded ovens. As a creature-of-habit, this threw me. The pattern was that we'd peak between seven and nine-thirty, then it would be steady phone calls before a few drunks would grab a pizza on their way home. Fridays were quieter, as traditionally that meant fish and chips.

Puzzlingly, four lads from the chippy came in. Why weren't they at their shop? 'Hey, Stefano, do you think

147

it's right that you're making a profit from that dead lady?' asked a deep voice. The oven's timer moved in slow motion, and Casio flicked off the music and headed out back. The partygoers huddled in the corner like frightened rabbits. The exit was blocked by the chippy-crew.

'Wha' ya mean? The BBC asked.'

'Doesn't mean you should be open all day,' Freddie, the fish shop owner, twisted. 'Thought we agreed to work the same hours.' He was small but looked like a pit bull at the counter.

'We opened later than you on Good Friday, as it's your most important day.' Stefano made the sign of the cross. I was unsure whether it was for the holy day, or for Mam. 'So, you owed us one.'

'Bloody greasy Italians, never to be trusted. I should've had you when you came up with that slogan. *Cheaper than Chips*. Taking liberties, that was.' Freddie picked up a menu and ripped it in half.

'Hey, now, wait a minute, wind your neck in,' Sophia protested.

'You shut your mouth, you,' said a chippy lad who was about six foot six; his voice gritted with gravel.

I considered making a list but instead came to the counter. 'You all know it's my Mam who's missing.' I disorientated the big lad.

'Didn't think you were working,' he explained, but Freddie and Stefano were eyeballing – neither flinched. The partygoers shrunk further when Casio returned with the scooter-boys.

'I wanna po-lite-ly say, on your bike,' Casio informed them, like repeating an order. He and the boys roguishly leapt over the counter and confronted the chippy's crackpots, who fancied themselves. The violence was deeply dirty and uglied the pizzeria. Both sides brutally spiralled, toppled, and dived. Swarming and screaming, the partygoers squeezed into the corner as grown men exchanged blows. The smell of burning pizza should've caused alarm, but I was transfixed and couldn't avert my eyes. Only Sophia's touch, as Stefano called the police, pricked my senses.

Carl had told me that violent interactions were over before they began, and this was no exception. The chippy crew soon spilled onto the street, the door was locked, and a heated debate began. Only some final pangs of bravado, as the chippy crew pounded the windows, caused squeals amongst the partygoers. Stefano offered them a refund and free pizzas.

Speckled blood stained the floor. Despite itching to clear up, Sophia made coffee for the fighters and provided first aid to those who'd taken blows. Returning riders wanted every detail. When the police interviewed Casio and the scooter-boys, Stefano and I cleaned whilst Sophia created steam with the coffee machine. 'Oh my God!' he shrieked. Not one to blaspheme, I asked what'd caused the upset. He pointed. Sophia and I made haste.

Cowering in the corner, glistening blue and gold under fluorescent lights, was Mam's ring.

Dad

Whether we should've been laughing, crying, or seriously talking was hard to decide. I was on autopilot, harbouring excitement in case the reconstruction failed to bear fruit. Wholeheartedly, we needed light to be thrown on Donna's disappearance, but what was equally harrowing was the thought that it'd be another failure, another dead-end, another reason to lose hope. Another reason to be dead.

We missed her with a fierce ache. Positioned in the front room, Carl lay in front of the TV with his head in Zoë's lap; she brushed his temples. Dan had made his way downstairs for the first time in a week and curled into Suzie, occasionally grasping my hand. Suzie was muttering to DC Carter, who was perched on the arm of the sofa. Donna would've gone crazy, saying, 'Arms are for arms, not for bottoms.' Sophia and Isaac sat on armchairs. He was like an upright meerkat, whilst she nestled a cushion.

The television programme went through its paces, and we learned of other families who'd been destroyed by murder and rape. A screenful of mugshots showed a den of liars wanted for heinous crimes. Previously, I had watched the programme with a voyeuristic gaze, this time I seethed in the trauma caused by evil minds. My heartbeat peaked when our house surreally appeared. Suzie – dressed as Donna – was on the step. Nick Ross provided a sincere, honey-toned voice over. 'Hey Carl, that's a canny jumper; are you really wearing it?' Suzie said. Inside, my feelings disassembled. Thoughts of how we had driven away clawed. It'd been so innocuous. When Donna had called to Carl, I'd only been half-listening. I remembered how Isaac had explained the contents of the mixed tape, and Dan had sniggered at his Mam's words: 'I would've ironed your new top.'

'It's okay, Mam, it's me lucky jumper,' Carl replied. 'I always wear it when we play away.' I hadn't realised how brave he had been, he was the only one who'd repeated words from that fateful day.

'Have a safe journey. Love you,' Suzie called. That was the last time I'd heard Donna's voice, the last time I'd seen her face, the last time I'd taken her for granted. I watched myself drive away, knowing I'd rewind the scene a million times, wishing for a rewrite.

Why hadn't the match tickets been lost?

Why hadn't the car broken down?

Why hadn't she come with us?

Nick Ross explained the circumstances of Donna's appointment as Suzie drove through empty streets. By the time she reached the warehouse and it cut to DC Carter crouching next to Donna's shoe, my sight was misty. Intractable thoughts had gone further than CrimeWatch was allowed to speculate, and I saw her bludgeoned in a van. That featureless industrial estate should never be associated with someone so full of light, so full of energy, so full of life.

Next up, Nick Ross interviewed DI Quick. The boastful detective had been on local radio pontificating about "the breakthrough" and the "importance" of the BBC reconstruction. But he'd never spoken to me since issuing the warrant. He repeated DC Carter's words: since Isaac had discovered the ring, a search of the pizzeria's yard had unearthed Donna's clipboard, keys, and broken pager. The incident room had sprung into action with over forty officers.

The answer lay on the Island.

The main problem was that almost everyone had eaten in Geordie Pizza that day. Interviews were taking place.

Intrusively, a week after the items were found, the national press had a renewed interest in the case.

'Are you one-hundred percent sure they weren't there earlier?' I asked.

'Absolutely,' Isaac replied. 'I've arranged everything the way I want.'

'It was a total mess,' Sophia added. 'Now it's perfect. He would've noticed his Mam's things.' She squeezed Isaac's hand. If it'd been anyone else, I would have questioned their authenticity. But Isaac was so scrupulous that he provided a faultless account.

'Just glad that your grandad recognised the ring.'

'He remembered seeing it when she'd dropped off Isaac for his shifts. She'd once explained where it had come from. He thought it would be great to do that for his daughters.'

'How did it end up in Geordie Pizza?' I asked.

Sophia bristled, as if someone had walked over her grave. 'It's horrible.' Suzie comforted Sophia when the tears arrived.

'Cases can disentangle on things like these,' DC Carter remarked. 'It varies the pattern of an investigation because we now have something new to work on. In books and films, this would mean that someone is playing with us. It's rarer than hen's teeth for a criminal to do that; they keep as far away from us as possible,' Carter continued. 'I think they've made a massive whopper. I'm not making promises, but we've more of a chance. We've interviewed the partygoers, the nutters from the chip shop, and everyone who's come forward who was in the pizzeria that day, including your neighbours and the BBC. We won't stop until we catch him.'

Chapter 7: Suspects

Carl

A girl in a wheelchair about my age opened the porch door but locked the one behind. 'What yer looking at?' she snapped, folding her arms.

'Am looking for Bob.'

'You mean the pirate that lives upstairs?' Ah gawped and almost dropped me bag. 'Use your brain, pretty boy,' she continued. 'You're better looking than most of his pals and I saw you on telly. Once you've been with a girl on wheels you never look back,' she flirted, and ah beamed; for once ah was speechless. 'Pirate Bob,' she hollered. 'Sex-on-a-stick is here.' Ah now knew she was messing, so winked. 'Wait here; he'll come down. Sorry about your Mam.' She closed the front door. There were children playing football on the street and a couple climbed into a taxi. The door reopened.

'Alreet, Carl? Come in.' All three of us lingered in the porch-way. 'Only one door's open at a time. Security. Ah see you've met Ironside.'

'Shut your face, one-eyed Jack.' She headed to the front room and began a conversation. Ah followed Bob upstairs where he explained that his sister had been involved in a hit-and-run when she was six, but the driver roamed free.

In his room, evidence of the bright, chilly early summer evening was hard to find. Blackout blinds and a black carpet were stifling. A dangling light glowed, exposing interesting carpet splatter. The room a microcosm of me life: boxed in the darkness waiting for light, only to find nothing but stains that needed wiping away. Beneath a poster of The Happy Mondays were a couple of metal suitcases. We engaged in general chat and ah explained why ah was there, watching his every move.

Blind-Boy Bob's eye-patch was an acid smiley face. Bright yellow, it absorbed the bulb's fragments. Strangely, he had a bushy unibrow that needed clipping and looked like a hairy caterpillar. Slicked back hair revealed scars and mole-like ears. A black Fila rollneck helped him become a chemically modified Bond villain and he tugged the sweaty neckline. Football hooligans were known for their steely balls, so Bob's twitching limbs showed an odd edginess. A Roman nose – which ah couldn't believe hadn't been broken – reddened nostrils, and sunken cheeks gave clues of an alternative lifestyle. Sharp white teeth that reflected his skin were either false or had experienced extensive work. Another surprise were his short hairy hands with accompanying Yin-Yang tattoos. Ah would've expected them to be shovel-like with less profound artwork. No point stereotyping, as life was full of surprises and mine had caused unease. The cyclops eye burned with a mottled mix of intrigue and scepticism.

By turning up uninvited, he'd had no alternative but to let uz in. Even drug dealers showed reverence to those with a missing mother. Despite the hospitality, the warmth of his welcome quickly dispelled. 'Are yer sure that's what you want? Ah mean, ah understand, but think it through. Did yer enjoy that acid tab ah gave yer at the Sunderland match?' he asked in monotone. On many occasions – especially when dealing with Dan's nutter girlfriend – the euphoria of a trip had been tempting. Yet, the minute square remained safely in me wallet. Keeping a flimsy grip on reality was important.

'Aye,' ah lied, 'great stuff, it shunted me head al owa the place.' He rocked with a shoulder shaking laugh and his teeth scissored. The ice was broken, and his shadow wobbled faintly against black wallpaper. But we were far from an agreement.

'Look. Don't yer reckon you'd be better off with some more acid, wobbly-eggs, even a white-line, or that party drug that's turning me pals into dance-crazies? Once upon a time, yer knew where yer were with us lowlife, now we're all drugged up and loving each other. Ah blame people like me!' he joked.

The sound of that lad being hit by a slab of concrete at the battle in Sunderland often joined the other horrific images in me head. Being shoulder-to-shoulder with the upper echelons of me team's thugs had been hellish. Sombrely, thoughts of a rematch instantly scarpered. Although Big Eddie had kept his physique through disciplined training with the army, the others were withering on the vine. Bob must've been twenty, but if you'd said he was thirty ah wouldn't have argued. All hooligans were adrenaline junkies; ah just hadn't realised how much it aged yer.

Ah suppose all highs must have their lows.

'Howay, help uz with the case.' He spat out the words whilst dragging it up. 'This is what yer want, not the other stuff. Seriously, since me and the lads have been raving, ah feel much better. Ah mean, we all like a skirmish, but not so much now.' He'd become totalitarian, but ah wouldn't be browbeaten. 'Welcome to me treasure chest.' On the bed, he opened the lid; Isaac would've been proud of the organisation. Tidy bags of powder, weed, tabs, and pills had their own homely section, but the distinctive, throat-grabbing smell of skunk pushed uz onto me bag. From next door a toilet flushed. Bob systematically snapped the door securely with three padlocks. 'Av got everything to lose yer mind.'

Ah knew that one misstep and ad be chucked out, so

after clearing me throat ah praised him. 'Bloody hell, Bob, you've got enough to take us to the moon and back. But ah don't need it.'

He flipped the patch, but ah evaded eye-contact. 'Ah know but am not happy.' Little beads of sweat formed under his nose. 'If Big Eddie finds out what y'doing, yer didn't get it from me – d'yer hear? Am in two minds. There's nee way ad upset me big mate. Yer have no idea what he's capable of. Said you were off limits.'

'Ah get it,' ah parried. 'Eddie keeps an eye out for us all.' Ah cringed, hoping he hadn't picked up on me Freudian slip. 'Al keep me mouth shut. Of course, ah really appreciate it. Am not in two minds. In fact, am one hundred percent. If yer do it, it won't be for me, it'll be for me Mam.' Feeling like a charlatan for using her that way, ah somehow managed – quite literally – to look him in his good eye. Despite the flippancy with his sister, ah knew if he found out who'd driven that car, they wouldn't be breathing much longer.

Yin-Yang.

'Al help. CrimeWatch is me favourite programme, and it was dead sad seeing her last night.'

'Ah can't thank yer enough.'

'But am blameless, just facilitating yer needs. Yer didn't get it from me. If Eddie says owt, yer on y'own.'

'Aye, it wasn't from you.'

The eye-patch was back in place and the smiley face made everything surreal. We leaned in until our heads touched. 'If ah was you, ad do the same thing, but think it through. Yer don't want to end up getting into loads of trouble by not planning. Reet? Ah can just see how it could gan wrong.'

'Aye, ah know. Al be careful.'

With control we slid the second case onto the bed. Like unveiling an ancient relic, we handled the lid with respect. Inside were knives, machetes, knuckle-dusters, and chains. Bob lifted the prized possession, and ah regulated me breathing. Pulsing with anticipation, ah took hold. A very singular odour, stronger than fireworks, drowned out the smell of skunk. Weirdly, the intoxication was enticing. A smell ad never forget. Allowing me fingers to dance around it, me base thoughts stewed. Ad sidle up with icy detachment, stick the gun into his face until he spilled his darkest secrets like a cowering dog. Ah couldn't wait.

Ah was ready to wipe away the stain.

Dan

I met Laura at the Swing Bridge. A subtle layer of make-up accentuated her sharp features. She wore a short blue skirt, trainers, a fitted denim jacket, and a retro bag hugged her shoulder. Swept-back, her wet hair smelled distinctive, but I couldn't put my finger on what it was. 'You look good,' I said, wondering whether she had a bag for every occasion.

'Been swimming.'

'Not in there, I hope,' I joked, pointing at the river.

She laughed and adjusted the strap. ''Course not. In town.' It was chlorine that'd clung. 'I'm glad that you're back on your feet. It was scary at the hospital. Can't believe it's been over a week.' With a furrowed brow, I took in the surroundings, wondering how to start the conversation. Opposite, the ship with a night-club on board hadn't opened yet but looked unseaworthy. More grey than white, grime had spread towards deck. 'You alright?' she asked.

I thought about the incomprehensible things my family had said about her, but I had to hear it from the horse's mouth. Everyone assumed we'd split up, but nothing had been confirmed. 'Yeah. Fine,' I lied. My hands choked the black rails.

'I thought the reconstruction looked good. So different when you're on set. I couldn't believe it.' She'd spoken to the side of my head. 'This is bizarre, Dan. Pete the drummer said that you wanted to see me, but if Carl finds out he'll go mad.' Not touching was torturous. 'You'll never guess what's happened?' I shook my head as she changed the subject. 'I got an offer to go to summer school in Leeds.' She rested her heel on the railing. 'I thought you'd be pleased,' she stropped.

'I am. It's just…'

'Just what, Dan?' Her darting eyes studied. 'Come on, Dan. Why am I here?' she challenged, and I sensed a flirty tone, her mood alternating with each sentence. Disdainfully, I wanted to kiss her. I hated myself. She brought the sweetest pain.

'Honestly, Laura, I want to say loads of things, but I don't know where to start.' We snuggled and her hair cleansed my chin.

'Is this about how your family have treated me?'

'No.' I bit my lip in shock. 'It's about what you did.'

'What do you mean?' Her nostrils flared as she huffed. 'They completely over-reacted. They've hated me from the start.'

'Can we get a drink?' Not wanting events to overtake us, I tried to bide for time, but her unexpected response had scattered my thoughts. Were there too many obstacles between us?

In silence, we passed queues of laughing weekend boys and skimpily clad girls. Ceremonially, a mass exodus had arrived in town and pub culture colonised the streets. Lined like colourful zombies, they were ready to be encapsulated by trendy drinks and poor chat-up lines. We found a beer garden away from the humour and loud music. Above us, pigeons treated the gigantic bridge like a manmade nest. The metal chairs were uncomfortable, but the heater provided warmth. I ran the gauntlet of being asked for I.D. and passed the test. Laura's latest tipple was gin and tonic.

I grasped the nettle. 'What was that freakish stuff with Mam's clothes? You can't blame my family. It was odd, Laura.' My voice tried to find the correct tone between warmth and command.

Distractedly, she rattled the shaker eight beats to the bar. 'Coz I'm sick of them. I wanted to be like her… I tried to understand… to get it – I dunno.'

I squinted. 'What do you mean?'

'Since we've been going out, I've only wanted to help – know more about your Mam. But it's like a closed shop in your house. Zoë and Carl have treated me badly, as if I'm responsible.'

I held up my hand. 'We're trying to be as normal as possible. You have no idea how it feels – not knowing where she is. We're a mess.'

Resting her cheek on her palm, she scowled. 'I can't believe this, Dan. You agree with me. You know I did it for the right reasons.' We were on a different page. What she'd said was incredulous. I didn't agree with her one iota and couldn't understand why she thought differently. Was she really that mad? Nevertheless, I scratched my chair closer to her.

'I don't agree, but when I was convalescing, I missed you. It was better when you were around, before you… well, before the reconstruction.' I cleared my throat. 'I love you.' My cheeks flared.

She hugged her bag. 'You can't say that. With your family, I'm an outcast. What we had was special. They don't understand.' Thinking of those explosive minutes in the cubicle had kept me going, but we had something more.

Although it was a brisk evening, the crowd were filling the decking. Some women who'd had too many sunbeds and not enough meals huddled for heat. I worried about their safety and wondered how Mam was chosen. Although the conversation with Laura had gone cold, the womens' cackles were warm, even if their conversation was thinner than their dress straps. Sometimes Mam and Aunt Suzie had shared wine with their friends in our kitchen. In harmony, the women's hoots sounded similar. I missed that.

'This is useless, I'm going.' Laura's drink wobbled but didn't spill when she shot from her seat. The women's sympathetic looks were joined by nudges; they must've recognised me from CrimeWatch. I caught Laura at the door, where we became a spectacle.

'Is that all you have to say?'

'I don't believe you, Dan. It's over. If you can't see why I did it, then what's the point?' She strode off and I banged down my bottle and sped from the bar. Following her along the Quayside, there'd been no explanation as to why she'd dressed in Mam's clothes or the attempted theft. 'How should we behave now, Dan?' Cold wind spiralled from the river.

'I dunno. This hasn't worked out.'

Itching my head as she left, lyrics about her dim blue eyes materialised: *You – you're blue and you're cold / But in the night / I've been bought and sold / A dim-ming light.*

DC Carter

Propped against the wall, my copper's eyes watched the unfolding chaos. A dozen officers scratched around like blind vermin. Projecting a sense of panic, DI Quick was in the lead role as a hair-sprayed king rat. Less than twenty-four hours since CrimeWatch, the team were incapacitated by useless information. Led by that upstart Peter David from the local rag, the press had printed headlines like 'Fiasco' and 'Feckless', and that morning's photograph showed detectives walking through the mist with the strapline 'Not the Foggiest'. The top-brass were on the war path with rumours that heads would roll.

Forensic-free evidence was housed in plastic bags: Mrs. McCarthy's shoe, ring, keys, broken pager, and clipboard. I'd seen the puerile atmosphere before, and it was bound to descend into finger-pointing accusations. Little piggies had to save their bacon. With hair like a hurricane, Quick slammed down his hands and howled, 'Stop! Come on, we look like a bunch of amateurs. We're better than that. Everyone, take a seat. They'll be here in five. We need a coherent message.'

Reluctantly they plonked down, but I remained against the wall. Anticipating a shambolic show gave no satisfaction. That would mean that we were no closer to finding the abductor. Around the table, people awaited the sound of the four horsemen of the apocalypse. The DCI, DSI, Chief Superintendent, and our local MP had called the meeting. We knew that their pensions would not be affected, but many in the room were checking the friction on the greasy pole.

'Aren't you joining us, Carter?' Quick asked.

'I think better on my feet.'

'We need to show a united front.'

I sat. My old Sarge had said that I ought to work with Quick, but his weaselly stare was scurrying, deciding whom to scapegoat. These new coppers wouldn't think twice about drowning a colleague in formaldehyde, but we had to be united. Spellbound by déjà vu, I knew what Quick was going through. Yes, he was jumped-up, and his two-faced toxicity had caused distress. But when I was in the pit of despair, contemplating throwing myself into the kohl gut, I had promised never to allow anyone else to feel that way. If I could prevent one person experiencing what I had survived, I would. Unfortunately, I hadn't anticipated saving my nemesis.

A bleak anagnorisis lived inside his eyes. Even licking our superiors' backsides with an iguana's tongue wouldn't be enough. He knew he could be cast overboard quicker than a diseased fish. On the Dead-Babies case, I had felt like a fraud when roads led nowhere. Many of the team partook in my downfall. But being depressed had taught me perspective. Our petty squabbles and blame-games meant nothing – absolute zero – against what the family were going through. Instead of in-fighting, we had to pull together. Did they all have nightmares about a decaying Donna McCarthy?

'So, Carter. You've failed twice before, and this could be a hat-trick. The inability to locate the missing football hooligan and the failure to find the baby-killer have gone down in folklore. What can we expect when our superiors arrive?' Flummoxed by his passive-aggression, I looked to the ceiling, realising that God did indeed move in mysterious ways. There I was preparing to save the wavy-haired worm, and it was me whom he'd incriminate. The acid rose but I remained professional.

'They'll want a root-to-branch breakdown, sir. They'll want to know everything that we've done, and where we're going next.'

'Come on,' he boomed, moving the evidence around as if he were a magician. 'We must be missing something.'

'I think a body's what you're thinking of.' I hadn't meant to be openly sardonic. Razor slits – rawer than hornet stings – glared and eye-contact avoidance infected the group. Then he unstiffened.

'Maybe another search for the body is not a bad idea.' He was more troubled than I'd imagined, happy to accept any advice. 'Widen the net.'

'What about the interviews? Something must've come up,' I pleaded. 'Even if your gut said someone was lying.' A cliché in books and films is that something connects like magic during these conversations. Usually, the youngest member of the team reluctantly reveals something and the dominoes fall. There was nothing.

'The answer's on the Island. We've always known that,' Quick preached.

'We interviewed the partygoers, but they just went on about the fight,' DS Pearson reported.

'I don't know how many times we've interviewed the estate agents about who knew of Mrs. McCarthy's appointment. He must've been tracking her; it couldn't have been opportunist. Hence, why the Island has so much to answer for,' I added.

'The staff from the fish shop were stroppy. But they were glad not to get nicked for disturbing the peace,' added another colleague.

'The pizzeria staff produced a detailed list of who'd been in that day. We've almost interviewed them all, but there's nothing of interest,' recounted a detective who'd been snapped in the newspaper that morning.

'I've interviewed Wild Bill, Slasher-Sloan, and the other usual suspects on the Island. Nothing,' concluded Quick. 'There have been thousands of missing person cases coming through from around the country; we can't keep up.' Shifting through the nonsense was a skill he'd have to develop. To be fair, that was the DCI's speciality.

'Everyone on the Island with a van is being alibied, as well as Mrs. McCarthy's clients for the last six months. The problem is that she dealt with commercial property, so all her clients have vans,' the youngest DC shrugged.

Silence descended as a sound like galloping hooves reverberated and grew louder. Quick swallowed and a watermelon replaced his Adam's apple. Recognising the pain, I decided, despite everything, that we would stand shoulder-to-shoulder. My twin – Clint Eastwood – would've called him something smart. But Clint had never worked a nightshift on the Island. I knew it would probably backfire, but I was an old cliché and that's what I did. After all, we were on the same team.

'We stand by DI Quick!' I blasted. 'Tell them we're making an interactive list to see if people appear more than once. We tell them how the DI is going through all interviews with us to establish anomalies. Say how we're rechecking forensics and re-examining the ginnel in a fingertip search.'

Quick didn't smile. Instead shock or guilt occupied his face. I hoped a comforting wink would build a bridge.

The door handle moved.

Killer

Bobby Robson was on the radio. The England manager repeatedly snarled: 'Garbage.' Accusations of traitorous behaviour for accepting a job with a Dutch team that'd commence after the World Cup had hurt him. Everyone knew that the FA weren't going to renew his contract and offered no help when the press exposed his personal life. 'Garbage!'

Focusing on the garbage blaring through the lock-up was testing. Bobby's problems were nothing compared with mine. This time, keeping a public face had been difficult. Coffee mug rings orbited my eyes. Operations meant that I was no stranger to not sleeping, but it'd been a hectic week since losing the ring. News had spread like garlic butter that the killer had been in Geordie Pizza.

There was a jackrabbit off, and there were journalists everywhere. Yes, I'd discarded her clipboard, but I hadn't meant to lose the ring. I cherished my keepsakes. I may as well have lost a lung; it's how I breathed. Reverting to the bracelet from the previous lady hadn't offered the same feeling.

Aladdin's Cave provided research. I read newspaper cuttings, observed crime-scene photos, and scanned books from those who'd gone before. I was a connoisseur and schooled in the mistakes they'd made. Due to permanent insomnia, I'd been reading ornithology books in preparation for a homecoming with Mrs. McCarthy. It'd be risky. Since word of the reconstruction, I'd been in a state of flux. I believed that I'd become a media spectacle heralding the power of CrimeWatch. Was I paranoid to think I was the subject of a surveillance operation? Were the police collecting evidence? Listening to the garage breathe, I expected the door to collapse at any moment.

Losing the ring had a huge effect, and anyone returning to an operational site when being monitored must have a screw lose, but it had to be done. Yes, sampling her family's suffering was pleasurable, but I needed more. A plan had formed: I'd leave the van with a spade, camera, and tripod to dig by her grave. Convinced that they'd sweep in a pincer movement, my alibi would be photography. Barn owls hunt best at dawn, and I'd tell the police that the trench was to capture the best shot. A quip about a bird's eye view would avert capture.

I had to get the photo.

But that wouldn't be the real picture.

For each lady, I had photo'd where we'd become one.

In the plan I saw myself under the shadowy trees at daybreak, smelling the fertiliser from a nearby field. I would tick off images in the book and snap close-ups of talons and beaks. The unwitting eye would never know that the shot was of a lady. I'd reappear every morning to dig the new grave.

Since the discovery of DNA, my operations had become more technical. Changing the MO from dumping ladies to burning them had been progressive. Yet fires caused disturbance. McCarthy was my first burial. I had to spill my "garbage" over them, so the changes were necessary.

I switched off Bobby's rant, crouched in the corner, and cut the headline from the paper: 'Not the Foggiest'. Blu-Tacking it in the scrapbook, I didn't believe a word. It was more "garbage". They were on my tail. I could feel it. Desperately, I hoped there'd be a new grave for a new lady.

The garage breathed.

Tomorrow the plan would become real.

Isaac

'Isaac, Isaac!' she hollered. She must've exhausted a lungful of air to rise above the music. I turned and saw people corkscrewing from bars, and travellers alighting trains. I had time to spare but hadn't banked on Laura's superficial talk. A quick glance at my watch told me that I had seventeen minutes. It would take precisely eight-and-a-half to reach my destination (half the time is always a good yardstick). I'd calculated that I'd need a nerve-induced toilet break. So, a bar with no bouncers, underage drinkers, and a toilet near the door was selected. Conservatively, this would take another three-and-a-quarter minutes, thus allowing over five minutes for emergencies. I hadn't thought there'd be one.

With a retro bag and pursed expression, her presence stopped me. For Dan's sake, I waved and hid my weariness. Naïve and drugged by sex is how Carl had described Dan's infatuation. Self-centred and unlikeable, she'd been a spectator without the sense to understand the rules. Saying she was out of step was more than generous. Laura asked the wrong questions and made everything about her. Zoë and Sophia had selfless compassion whilst she was the polar opposite.

Aware of her emotional volatility, I prepared an excuse to leave, already counting the seconds. Nothing would deter me from a date with Sophia. I couldn't understand Dan's fascination; Sophia was worth a hundred Laura's. All she had brought was pain.

'Did you know Dan still loves me, but I had to dump him because of you lot?' She was inside my personal space.

'What? Have you seen him?' We danced around but she was determined to go nose-to-nose; I was nonplussed by her temerity.

'Dan said he still wants me and understands why I dressed in your Mam's clothes.'

A dubious look took valuable seconds. 'No, he doesn't. We all know that you did it for some weird self-satisfaction.' There wasn't time to pussyfoot around, and all courtesy disappeared. 'You sullied our memory of her in those clothes, and you tried to steal her things. He might be in some loved-up state, but I'm sorry, you're not welcome. You make things worse. I think me daft brother must like the pain.' She breathed on my face, so I pushed her away.

'Remove your hands from me!' she screamed. Stern faces turned towards us. Getting into a futile fight with her was unnecessarily time consuming. Reconnecting with my timeline, I strode off. Suddenly, she blocked my track. I would have to scrap the toilet break and go after ordering.

'Do you know what?' Unguessable was Laura's middle name after what she'd done with Mam's things, so I shook my head. Pecking like a vulture, her words stabbed. 'You're right. I dressed like your Mam because I wanted to know what it's like to be dead. I wanted to be loved. I wanted to be missed. What's so strange? If you ask me, it's you lot who are weird. I screwed Dan so I could smell the death.'

Carl would've thrown her through a shop window. But, with head held high, I didn't break stride. There wasn't time for nonsense. Her blatant deceit had only fooled Dan. Yet, a confession was a confession. Keeping what she'd said to myself was a simple choice; I wouldn't hurt Dan any further.

After she'd scuttled off to waste someone else's time with malice, I briskly stomped in the opposite direction. I shook off her words. The last thing I craved was to discuss Laura with Sophia. Our relationship was about to begin and getting to know her during this time could only mean that we were right for each other. Even though it was an understatement to say she was out of my league, nothing could now thwart us from that coffee.

Sophia

'Hi, Sophia.' Their slurping tongues were hidden behind fake smiles. If I'd seen them coming, I would've slipped down the alley. With an icy aura and penetrating stares, they slithered around me. Striking first was the queen-cobra Clara who secreted secrets with venom. She stroked my face with a chilling touch. Leading the entourage of poster girls, she'd smoothly glide amongst prospective parents on school open evenings with cold-blooded efficiency and transparent charm. She was from landed gentry and all the snakes' families were monied.

When I was in my GCSE year, we'd joined the same revision groups. They'd tempted me with weekends at Clara's parents' Northumbrian farmhouse that had horses and endless freedom. Validation from the snakes had felt significant – well, for a short-while. Losing real friends was the price I'd paid; the snakes had asked endless questions about them. It even caused a family rift. Papà had loved the new contacts, but nonno loathed the snakes' stench of entitlement.

During those weekends, a sea of older boys in kitsch sports cars would arrive for pool parties. Up to that point my experience with boys had been like my experience with nuclear weapons. So, the snakes had set me up with Henry, a member of the entourage who wore the uniform of corduroy trousers, side parting, and a square-jawed smile. He had been pleasant, complimenting me on my skin and hair, but I don't think he listened to anything I had to say. It wasn't until afterwards that I thought I had been coerced. Not by smiley Henry, but by the vacuous snakes. Transfixed by their provocative laughs, I thought that I was ready. A sales pitch had guaranteed satisfaction, and they had demonstrated with roll-on deodorant bottles.

The Hoorays had danced around the pool with school-ties on their heads, causing a fit of giggles. Later, we had all gone to separate rooms. In a second-skin Speedo, Henry had embarrassingly hobbled to the bed with an obvious erection. His smile had vanished, and, after the shortest foreplay, he had gritted teeth and a frozen expression. He had made no attempt to satisfy and proceeded with jerky, inconsiderate movements. Overpowering sharp and dull pain had made me wince and whimper. My stomach had churned. He had mistaken this for enjoyment and said, 'Take it, fillet.' Fortunately, the whole thing lasted no longer than a wrong number phone call. But when he collapsed on top of me, refusing to meet my eye, I felt used. Before slouching off in his pal's MG – probably boasting about my deflowering – he had thrown down his phone number.

*

'Thought you'd be working, Sophia.' Clara slunk around me. I wished I'd stood in the foyer, and that they hadn't seen me. 'If we'd known you had a night off, we would've jovially asked you to join us. Wouldn't we, girls?' Clara's voice curdled with plausible etiquette. I should've known that there'd be a chance of bumping into them.

'Of course,' added a snake with a mesmerising look.

When they had found the bloody sheets, their jokiness had made me feel reckless and lonely. None of them had shown any care. Initiating me into their hothouse of pretence sexual experience had been their goal. I had felt useless and dirty. All I had wanted was to be in the arms of my family, so I asked to learn the catering trade. Thankfully, this had terminated my membership in their weekend club.

'You must be meeting someone. This is the key

rendezvous point. So, who's the lucky boy? You've got something. Henry still asks after his fine Italian fillet.'

'Yes, said you were the best he's ever had.' Being outnumbered, I remembered what they'd taught and adopted a phoney smile.

'I wish I could say the same for him!' I answered with a kaleidoscopic stare.

'Ooh, you witch, Sophia. Is it the boy who was on CrimeWatch last night with the dead mother?' Clara asked with emptiness. How had I ever been impressed by her flamboyant vanity?

'Well, she's missing. I hope, well we all do, that she's still alive.'

'So, it is him!' sniped a snake and they coiled. 'We heard on the grapevine that he has OCD. Is that right?' Even under the dreadful circumstances, getting to know Isaac had been like being bathed in milk; I felt warm and safe when we were together. Asking me out for coffee in the cinema's art-deco coffee rooms was a brilliant choice. He was due any second, and these creatures wouldn't destroy our date. I knew how to get rid of them.

'OCD has its benefits – he knows how to satisfy,' I fibbed, adopting the floozy-tone that'd paid them such dividends. The finishing touch was to evocatively waggle my fingers.

'I bet he'll use the rhythm method,' Clara clowned.

'Yes. I can't wait for my OCD boy's rhythm method.'

'Promise to let us know. We're aware of Henry's moves.' She winked so slowly; it looked as if her eyelids had run out of batteries.

'I sure will.' They left thinking they'd collected more secrets, but I'd played them. Next door, the jeweller's golden clock showed that Isaac was late. How could that be? Isaac's timekeeping was legendary. He'd caught more worms than the early bird.

173

Carl

Isaac festered with craziness. Clattering into uz at the bus stop, ah seized me bag but grabbed him, too. 'Calm down, bonny lad,' ah instructed. Breathlessly, he produced no words. Ah throttled him so he couldn't hot foot away. Panic-stricken, he trembled with a phlegmy cough. Isaac was never overdramatic, so ah knew that he was genuinely freaked. Ah just hoped he wouldn't hyperventilate. Once he stopped shaking, we sat down. 'Take some deep breaths, like this.' Scrunching his forehead, he followed me lead, and a few minutes later the soles of his shoes had settled.

The bus driver recognised us and refused to accept a fare. Upstairs, ah silently looked at the bridges whilst Isaac lungs calmed. Me brother's red mist – that ah knew only too well – turned to dark clouds. 'Why was she making fun of me?' he asked.

'Who? What's happened?'

'It keeps going through my head. She was in our house to watch the reconstruction, and she's the only person I've spoken to about Mam.'

'Has something happened with Soph?'

He shifted his weight on the uncomfortable seat. Ah got up from where ad trapped him and sat in front, hooking round so we were face-to-face. It was hard to fathom what'd happened and ah was all ears, clutching me bag.

'We were supposed to be on a date. Sophia was talking to a bunch of girls.' Ah pulled a *so, what?* face. 'I ducked behind a pillar, because I didn't want their hugs, or to talk about Mam. They were the type: confident and false. So, I stayed out of sight.' Isaac snivelled.

'What's the craic? Come on, Soph's a diamond. It

can't be that bad.'

'They talked about her screwing some lad, and my heart sunk.'

'Come on, Isaac, she's seventeen, not the Virgin Mary. You've got to accept that lasses would've been with other lads.'

'I know, I'm not stupid, but it wasn't that,' he responded, and ah willed him on. 'She even talked about Mam. Okay, she was polite, but I didn't like it. Carl, you should have seen her. It was like she was the triplet. It was her, but she was different. She moved differently, spoke differently, and was as two-faced as them.'

'What did she do?'

'She waggled her fingers, as if they were... well, I'm not sure what her fingers represented, but certainly nothing that we've done together.' He made a twanging motion, like grabbing a bowling ball. 'She made up stuff that we hadn't done together. Why would she do that? I should be tougher, but I can't take anymore knocks.'

Isaac was sharper than an axe, but ah couldn't help thinking that he'd got it wrong. Ah wasn't about to say that, though. 'As a spectator, you don't know what was going through her head. Once you've calmed, why don't you talk to her? Av regretted loads of stuff. Ah agree it's weird, and she sounds bang out of order, but she's a canny lass.'

'She went on like a floozy, shallower than a thimble. She told them that I've got OCD.'

'She didn't!'

'Aye. And she said that once we had sex, she'd tell them about it.'

'Never in the world.'

'I swear down. They laughed saying I'd use the rhythm method, whatever that is. Suppose it has something to do with how abnormal I am.' For a short

175

second, ah felt like calling her a snake but stopped. He needed help.

'She comes across dead unaffected. Al talk to Zoë, she'll know what to do.'

'I want nothing to do with Sophia and her family. I don't trust her or them. It's broken, Carl. You know trust is the most important thing.'

We fell into silence. A ripple of laughter from girls in the front seats and arctic air from an opened window filled the stillness. Mulling things over, we took in the sights as tower blocks changed to terraced streets. It was a stroke of luck that ad been at the bus stop, otherwise me brother could've ended up in a state.

'Carl?' He leaned in. 'I've tried to stop myself, but I've something to tell you.'

Ah tasted metal. Unwaveringly staunch, Isaac would resist four years of torture and never utter a word, so this was a first. 'What is it?'

He moistened his lips. 'I suspect someone who's involved with what happened to Mam.'

My heart quick-stepped. 'What the f... who?'

'Sophia's dad – her Papà.'

'Come on, ah know you've had a shock but that's a serious accusation.'

Unruffled, he explained steadily. 'I wouldn't say it if I didn't mean it. He rummaged around amongst the scrap one night when he thought there was no one around. But here's the thing.' Me back was an ice rink, knowing he was on the level. 'He knows stuff about Mam, like loving Bowie, and said so before the reconstruction. He mentioned conversations they'd had together about Dad.'

'Jesus H. Christ.'

'I saw photographs of them that nobody knows about. He never said a word.' Me eyes bore into the dirty floor and ah felt like smashing the bus window. Instead, ah swallowed and bade farewell to secrecy.

'Am listening mate. Av got a plan to find out for sure.'

In a trance-like state, he asked, 'What do you mean?' Ah opened me bag and a faint smell radiated. Ever so slowly, ah moved me football kit and revealed the gun. His neck cricked, our eyes met, and ah knew he was in.

Dan

My world wasn't the only one that was falling apart, but what greeted me in the kitchen was disturbing. To which depths would my brothers descend? Like Robert De Niro and a crony in a gangster movie, they glared at a gun. A gun! *What the...?* My eyes burned a hole of bafflement. I struggled for words. Exasperated. 'Where's Dad and Aunt Suzie?'

'At his brother's.'

'What's that?'

'An umbrella,' Carl quipped. 'It's a gun – what d'yer think it is, yer muppet.'

'Me, a muppet! Why have you got a gun?'

'To exorcise some demons.'

Slouched at the table, I opened my palms. 'What are you talking about? Exorcise what? You need to exercise your brain.' I turned to Isaac. 'Are you involved with this? Please tell me that you've told him it's crazy.'

Looking self-absorbed, he whispered, 'If we're going to do this, we need a plan.' Both the gun and the mood were tainted in danger.

'What, and you've got a blueprint for success? What's the plan and who's it for?' My voice hit falsetto heights whilst wondering how, when you thought you were in the bowels of hell, things got worse.

'Not here. Let's head out,' Carl crooned. A wild streak of lunacy ripped through his face. For weeks we'd lived a coexistence, like soldiers who were almost out of range, hanging onto a final sizzle of interference. But our disjointedness paled into insignificance compared with the contents of Carl's head. He traipsed off ahead and we followed. Something must have soured Isaac's brain; he marched, trance-like, across the bridge onto the Hill. The yards between us when we entered the dark jowls of the copse felt like miles.

Mam loved to bring us here when we were younger. How the formation of trees changed during the seasons had caught her imagination. Her aura was always near, but here it felt intense. There was never a second when I didn't picture her or hear her voice but being in the long grass was like the smell of her perfume or a Bowie riff in how it created time travel. I remembered Mam treating our wounded knees with copious amounts of TCP on the copse's pathway. She'd cringe as if it hurt her more than us. Also unforgettable were how she'd howl at Billy Connolly, cry about Hillsborough, lose herself in Bowie's music, or look at us as if we were Greek Gods, calling us three peas in a pod. How disappointed would she be with us strutting around like characters in a rubbish western? *Walking around without the sun / reaching out for the blast of a gun / Ending up on the loneliest run / Beating to the sound of some other's drum.* Country and Western lyrics created an escape from Carl's mission.

Deep in the dark trees we made a triangle. Despite everything there was always a fizz of excitement in the copse. In our early teens we had found some dirty mags in the undergrowth and looked in wonder at the hairy bushes. To escape GCSE revision, Carl had sniffed white powder from a picnic bench and didn't come down for days.

'Where shall we three meet again?' asked Isaac.

'When the hurly-burly's done, when the battle's lost and won,' replied Carl.

'Stop messing about!' I screamed. 'You've got a gun – it's mad, man.' An anti-Shakespearean rant wouldn't do; I wanted to bang their heads together. 'What's going on?'

'You've seen the papers. Carter's trying, but the police haven't got the foggiest. We need to take this into our own hands. Me and Isaac know who did it, well... we think we do.'

'You think you do. Well, that's just great. You're prepared to tarnish Mam's memory with a poxy brainwave. Carl, I know you're hot-headed, but Isaac, I'm surprised at you. This is ridiculous.'

'Look, Dan, everyone knows yer spaced out because yer think yer gonna marry the first nutter yer slept with. To be honest, two pumps and a squirt in a pub toilet hardly makes yer Romeo.' Carl wrong-footed me with the personal attack. I deflated, which gave him encouragement. 'There's no point in us moping around like a cloak of goths at a druid's birthday party. What would yer do if we caught the murderer? You'd try to talk him to death, wouldn't yer? Well ah want to stab him through the heart, make him a eunuch, or blast his head off.'

'This has nothing to do with Laura. Come on, we can't go around the Island with a gun – it's crazy! You can't shoot someone! We're not American. Carter will catch Mam's abductor.' In the dimness, I expected to hear Isaac's voice of reason, but his knotted tongue told me that he'd drunk Carl's fatalism.

'Isaac's planned it, and we should all be involved. Are yer in or out?'

'Isaac's planned it! Have you both had a brain transplant? Not a chance, no way! Imagine if we get caught. The first time that I want to read about this is in the *News of the World*. I haven't even heard your ridiculous plan, yet.'

Carl leapt on my words in the same way that he taught us how to chat up girls. 'Yet? So, yer want to hear it. Yer interested.'

'I'm interested in keeping my brothers out of jail!' I cried, wishing I could flog myself with a branch.

'We're going to intimidate some blokes until we find the truth.'

'Bloody hell.'

My words were deafened by a gunshot.

Isaac

The blast was a starting gun. We flew off in different directions. 'Meet in the old schoolyard,' I called, hoping they'd heard. Expecting a SWAT team to materialise, goosebumps bigger than grapes covered my body. Feeling out of control was never good, but Sophia's words had already shattered my mindfulness. Never one to bleat, keeping the masked axeman of a secret about Sophia's dad had been strenuous. It was liberating to share with Carl, and he had suspicions of his own. We both wanted revenge and agreed on a hitlist of two.

Dan fumed, pacing Brass Band's schoolyard like a caged tiger. Carl was the last to arrive and Dan went for the throat. 'Why did you fire the gun? Everyone for miles must've heard.'

'Ah had to make sure it worked,' he replied with an unfortunate smirk, which made Dan throw him to the ground.

'Come on, you two,' I intervened. 'Dan, at least hear our plan.'

'Howay, Dan,' Carl begged, his hands raised in surrender. 'Hear us out.'

With arms folded straitjacket-tight, Dan listened to our suspicions and the planned confrontations. Shelving his better judgement, he agreed to participate, if only to make sure Carl didn't go too far. Stakeout one would happen the next day.

*

The following afternoon, the England team boarded the plane for Italy. Tearing newspapers in support of Bobby Robson was hardly the greatest preparation for a World Cup. Whilst watching, I needed to organise to calm the bucketful of thoughts. I was attaching Post-it notes into my homework files with specific colours when Dan came in. 'If we do this, we can't see The Stone Roses.'

'This is more important,' I replied.

'We've paid petrol money and everything. They say Spike Island will go down in history.' The gig was that weekend, and Pete the drummer's dad had hired a minibus to transport the band and a few hangers-on, like myself.

'Dan, nothing matters more than finding out about what happened to Mam.' No one could argue with that. Possessing unique empathy, Dan had a huge heart. He couldn't understand why I supported Carl's therapeutic justice. When I explained what I'd heard Sophia say, he was shocked. 'Are you sure that you didn't mishear?'

'No way, she was like a different person. It wasn't just what she'd said, it was the way she said it.'

'She thinks you're great – she's been a star, not like Laura,' he defended.

Deciding not to mention that I'd seen his poisonous girlfriend, I took the yellow Post-its and stuck them down, making sure that they were spirit-level perfect. 'I think she's just like Laura. Both leeching off our distress.'

I felt his temper rise, struggling to comprehend. 'But you haven't got an ounce of spite in you. Why did you tell Carl that you suspected Sophia's dad?'

'Nothing spiteful about it. It's been in my head for weeks, it came out,' I explained.

'If you don't feel the same way anymore, we'll tell Carl.' Dan was flicking through my CDs. Later, I'd make sure everything was in order. It'd been drummed into us over the years that we stick together, and Dan was trying to form a majority. But I had the deciding vote. Since summoning the courage to mention Sophia's dad, I wouldn't change my mind, and he knew it.

'I think we should confront them.' I said with steel.

'But your plan means that they won't be able to tell that it's us.' He was browsing at lyrics from a sleeve.

'I've made up my mind; we're doing it. I agree that we need to rein Carl in, so it's best we're both there.'

Sniggering sarcastically, he placed a CD in the wrong slot. 'Rein him in? We may as well suspect Coach Taylor. He came around the house and couldn't keep his eyes off Mam's picture. He drives a van. I saw him in Pete the drummer's pub, and he was on the train when I got beaten up. Maybe he's following us around. He loved taking Mam out when they were fundraising for the changing rooms. He loved celebrating with Mam when we scored. Do you know where he was when Mam went missing? Do you know that the police interviewed him? Does that mean he's Suspect Three?' Dan challenged.

'Course not. Do you want me to mention your suspicion to Carl?'

'No! You're both seeing stuff that's not there. How you think about Coach Taylor is what I think about Sophia's dad. We're going to end up in a world of trouble. If they were suspects, the police would have evidence.'

'We know things that they don't. It could work.'

'You do know that we're going on the rampage with an impulsive person who'll be carrying a shooter? That'll be like trying to shove the reins on a wild mustang fifty metres from a cliff edge. We'll be powerless to stop him. If we miscalculate this, we'll be dragged through a hundred miles of sludge.'

Quickly, I stuck down the green Post-its. I had to keep control. When Dan went to his room, I put the CD in the correct place, but it almost slipped through my fingers.

Carl

Isaac was a schemer and set it up carefully. A genius at recalling routine, he knew how the pizzeria customers made their way home. His shadowy outline was veiled by the trees and ah wondered how he felt as we settled into position. Biding time, ah hoped it would soon commence. Dog walkers, joggers, and courting couples passed with no idea that we were hiding in the night. Then, it began. Down the Wagon Way ah heard the suspect's voice, but he was not alone. Although Isaac had planned everything down to the T, there was no plan B. We'd agreed not to deviate, so this could muller the whole thing.

He felt her up and her head disappeared inside that ragged beard. The repugnant man lifted her skirt. Ah didn't want to watch so ducked down. It was like some elaborate prank. 'Come on, wild man.' Am sure her words were supposed to sound sensual.

'Just give it a minute, love.' They were pressed against a tree next to me hideout. 'Howay, man, come on.' Pitiful frustration filled his voice.

'Are you okay? I'm not hanging around with my knickers down all night. Why don't we go back to yours?' The house was probably as vile as him, ah thought.

'No, let's do it here.' Anger and desperation were rising. Listening to his grunts and profanities made me legs buckle.

'Don't worry, this happens to lots of blokes, especially after they've had a drink,' she soothed, backing off.

'Not to me, it doesn't. Come on, Jenny. Let's try again.'

'Sorry, Bill, you've had your chance. I'm off home. Maybe we'll catch up next weekend.' Departing through the tunnel of trees, she waved.

Stood cursing between Isaac and me, the suspect was in pole position. If he confessed, we wouldn't have to attack Sophia's dad. Further down amongst the trees, ah saw Dan's silhouette. He adjusted position and the suspect must've caught the movement as he paced a few steps back.

'Who's there?' the suspect called, but Dan melted. Trapped in the silver moonlight, our bearded neighbour's face was set in deep-routed lines. There was no time to alter course.

Ah knew Dan would be ready to fill his pants. When we were four years old, he had done just that. He had tried to hold on but had made a mess. Unfortunately for him, we were in town and the shops had closed. Mam managed to find a public toilet and had cleaned him up. We had been swimming, so we had our trunks. He had to wear those with socks and shoes. It's the first time that ad felt embarrassed. Dad had walked ahead with Isaac and me. Mam had held Dan's hand. The little bathers with divers on the front were as wet as his eyes. Ad hoped that nobody thought it was me with us looking the same.

Despite his complaints about missing The Stone Roses, ah knew that we'd pull Dan into our plan. Whether it was brotherhood, or whether he didn't want uz to make a great big tool of meself didn't matter. The three musketeers were together, and ah loved the sense of oneness.

Ready for the ambush, ah pulled on me balaclava. The suspect was perfectly positioned for a pincer movement. 'Ooh, yoo!' ah called in a Scouse accent, and we faced up. Ah was on him. Isaac spilled from the trees and Speedy Gonzalez clumsily lugged up behind. Expecting him to fight or take flight, he did nothing when faced with three balaclava'd faces. Me fist struck his face, and he went down like before. Ah jammed his shoulders with me knees, pinning him to the floor. Smelling like Dan had in town, further vapours of alcohol, kebabs, and the menopausal Jenny filled me nose. The bloke was gurgling vomit, spraying puke into matted hair.

'Right, mate, you need to tell us all about how you killed Mrs. McCarthy.' Ah spoke through me nose like a poor John Lennon tribute act. 'Or wool do yer.'

'Yeah, spill the beans,' Isaac added, more akin to Ringo. Ah wished he'd kept quiet! *Spill the beans*, bloody ridiculous. He sounded as tough as candy floss.

It mustn't have gone unnoticed by Wild Bill, as he suddenly struggled. A toothy grin sprung from the clumpy mess that looked like a barber's floor. 'Sod off. I know who you are. I'll get yer.' We frogmarched him into the gully, splashing through dark water and throwing him in a ditch, but he immediately sprung up.

Then he saw the gun.

Click.

I'd removed the safety catch.

'Move another inch and al blow yer head off.' Me voice was me own. 'Ah think yer killed me Mam and tried to set up me Dad.'

'That's not bloody real, what do you take me for?' He let out a sour laugh.

Ah knew ah shouldn't.

But ah squeezed.

A nearby tree absorbed the bullet; it cracked and splintered. Isaac and Dan scattered like pigs from a pen. Wild Bill fell to his knees and prayed. 'Don't shoot, please, don't shoot. I never touched your mother. I liked her. She wasn't a witch like my wife. I can't even drive, I can't even drive, I can't even drive.' Anchorless, ah shoved the gun into his mouth and cracked a tooth. His head jerked and the gun burnt his beard.

Inside me head, Mam's voice created pressure behind

the eyes. *Stop it, son, just stop it.*

Me brothers were back, shaking more than Bill. 'Last chance.' Me voice muffled by the balaclava. Ah withdrew the gun and pressed it between his eyes. 'Is it because you can't get it up? Is that why you killed her?'

'Not me, you've got the wrong bloke.'

'Come on, Carl, it's not him. Mam was taken in a van.' Isaac's timorous voice warbled.

'I believe him,' added Dan. 'The police are sure she was taken.'

'Could've been with one of his mates,' ah wheezed in a final desperate act. 'Did yer plan this for someone else?'

'I haven't got any friends. The only thing I plan is where my next drink's coming from.'

Click. The safety catch was back on.

Grabbing me broken neighbour's testicles and twisting one-hundred-and-eighty degrees, ah told him: 'If yer go to the police, they'll do nowt. After what you did last time, they won't take the risk of a second screw-up. If yer go for me or one of me brothers, al tell some football hooligans that yer abused your kids. Ah know yer didn't, but they don't. If they get hold of yer, you're gonna wish ad shot yer. They'll chop yer up, cut yer up, and stick yer in a freezer. Do we understand each other?'

Wild Bill rasped like a dying walrus. Unsure what me brothers would say after ad gone rogue, ah chased after them. Ah felt sorry for Sophia's dad, because he was next.

Faint blue lights splattered through the trees.

Chapter 8: Snakes

Isaac

I'd heard Carl call some girls "snakes". Sexism like that annoyed me, but did it apply to Sophia? Had she belittled me? Was she a snake? One of Mam's Bowie songs sung about a cat with a screwed-up face, and, no matter what, I couldn't remove that look from my face. What Sophia had said to those fake girls in town had contaminated what'd gone before, infecting all integrity, and had derailed any chance of a relationship. I felt like an astronaut cut from the mothership, drifting aimlessly through space. 'Isaac, could we have a ten-inch Hawaiian, a twelve-inch Ham and P-P, and a twelve-inch Meat Feast, please?' She wiggled three fingers before pressing the till, which catapulted me back to how she'd entertained those phonies. Evading eye-contact, I swirled dough. Every shift had been torture. Our flame had burned to a smoke-filled sadness. My brothers were convinced that I had got it wrong, but I knew what I'd observed. I wasn't on my high horse like they'd suggested.

It had been a week since we'd sank to the lowest depths, and Dan had been right. Allowing Carl to stomp about like Dirty Harry had been psychotic. We would've only stuffed more victims into the world. Although we didn't want to be identified by Wild Bill, my plan had been ludicrous. Pretending to be Scousers in balaclavas – what had I been thinking? Mam used to watch Brookside, but that didn't make me Bobby Grant. After Carl had beaten our neighbour, we had called him every name under the moon. Getting home had been a quest. Avoiding the police's blue lights, we had skipped through the invisible child's world, climbing over the cemetery wall, rejecting houses with dogs, slipping through back gardens, and finding gaps in fences until we had arrived home. What we had not expected was Aunt Suzie to be sharing an aperitif with Carter. Guilt had poured from Dan's translucent skin. Luckily, we had Carl whose skill on the football pitch was to turn defence into attack. Despite the enormous mind-split when he had fired the gun, he had shaken the policeman's hand. For amusement, he had made insinuating comments about Carter's intentions towards Aunt Suzie. We had laughed, but it had taken the attention away from us. Especially when our neighbour had bashed walls and growled like a caged bear. We just about managed to stop DC Carter from knocking at his door.

All week I had tended my lawn, constructed the scooter, and realigned files, but to no avail. Finding an equilibrium had been impossible. Partaking in something so out of control had an effect. When I closed my eyes, I saw: my mutilated mother, Sophia having sex, or the smoking shooter. I'd had no choice but to alter my deciding vote. Admitting to my monumental mistake had been important. Confronting Sophia's dad was no longer an option; my nerves couldn't take it. I had hidden the gun, which caused Carl extreme stress. He had badgered and badgered but knew the Spanish Inquisition wouldn't make me budge. Dan had no idea where it was stashed, to which he was eternally grateful.

After relaying the pizzas to the customer, she snuffled into the yard. Even though I couldn't hide the malice when I passed over the box, I didn't want to hurt her. We were strangers. 'What are you doin'?' asked Casio. As usual, we looked like we had different jobs: his uniform was stained like he'd completed a hundred shifts whilst mine was cleaner than an angel's dress.

'What do you mean?'

'Breaking the poor girl's 'art.' He scraped the pizza shovel as I cleaned surfaces. Italian tricolours and buntings of St George triangulated from the ceiling as anticipation for the World Cup reached fever pitch. 'It's obvious that you're bloody besotted with 'er. Then you stood 'er up on your big night out.'

'It wasn't like that,' I blocked, rubbing at a resistant stain.

'Well, tell me. We can't go on like this every shift. You two not talking is terrible.' His eyes popped from his head. 'We're the frontline, 'ere. The atmosphere's been great, watching you lovebirds grow close. Reminded me of getting together with the wifey. I know it sounds soppy, but it's true.' He dabbed his cheeks with a napkin. 'But she came 'ere in floods last Friday. She said you didn't show. She couldn't believe it. She thought something dreadful 'ad 'appened.'

Remorse was counteracted with bitterness. Casio's words sounded like the old Sophia. 'Just bad timing; we're *finito*.' I'd told the truth. If I had arrived earlier, I wouldn't have witnessed Sophia showing her true colours. But Casio took it another way.

'Is this to do with your madre?' he asked, dipping his brow.

'No. Nothing,' I said with tetchiness.

The door tinged and Sophia returned. Unable to face her, we changed position. I went out back. On the radio there was an interview with a local singer, Charlotte-Anne. Her velvety tones were momentarily distracting; she was introducing a singing contest at the Garden Festival in Gateshead. Through the sound, I heard Sophia's dad and grandad's voices. My name was mentioned, so I crouched under the office window. In hushed tones, her dad said, 'With Isaac's Mam gone, we'll have to get someone else. Another one.'

'And you're convinced that neither Sophia nor Isaac suspect a thing?' I stuck to the floor.

'Why would they? Look, I'm desperate to do it.'

'I know. I suppose another one won't hurt, and this one will be special. But be patient,' her grandad said. My brain detonated.

'Donna was great, though.'

'The best.'

I paced to the scooter where my billowing breaths clouded the mirror. I couldn't make a list. Minutes later, Sophia's dad approached. 'On a break?' I couldn't think. 'Bike's looking good.' Booted and suited, he wiped an imaginary thumbprint from the exhaust with a pocket square. Wafting it out, he strutted stone-faced to the gates. 'You're a silly boy, though.' The scooter almost toppled when I gripped the seat. 'Other guys keep ringing,' said the glorified waiter – or was he Mam's killer? 'I told you that you'd have to play your cards right, or you'd lose that girl.'

And you'd lose your kneecaps, if my brother had his way, I thought. Hating being at sixes-and-sevens, I questioned my deciding vote. But allowing Carl access to the gun was not an option. My heart couldn't take it.

How could I keep what I'd heard to myself?

Was Stefano also involved?

I was more convinced than ever that the Rossi family weren't on the level. There was no plan except from burying what I'd heard… along with the gun.

Zoë

'A snake!' Dan gasped. 'Is that what he calls her?' I was a feminist and found my boyfriend's silly words revolting. More articulation was required, and I felt shameful about branding another girl, but Laura *was* a special sort of witch!

Demonstrating expertise, Dan was tuning his guitar. 'We were worried about you,' I said. 'She's voyeuristic. I know you couldn't see it – and I don't blame you, she's incredibly pretty, those eyes – but... well, she wasn't right for you.' I didn't want to hack him off but was shocked by her evil mind.

Dan twisted. 'I know what she did with Mam's clothes was crazy, but we had some good times.'

'Sorry, Dan.' I tried to pacify whilst remaining honest. 'I'm glad you've split up.' His body language was streaked with sorrow.

Earlier, when he had arrived, both he and my dad had given each other a huge double-take. From dad's point of view, he had seen an image of Carl, but it was obviously not him. The fact that Dan had carried a guitar must've been off-putting, not to mention his monkish disposition compared with Carl's liveliness. Dad knew Carl was a triplet but had only seen his brothers on CrimeWatch. For Dan, seeing a six-foot-five black man would have been as rare as seeing a featherless bird. My dad was used to it. He had trained in Newcastle and had worked in the hospital for twenty years, so he had grown accustomed to a second glance. Most people weren't racist – he swore volubly – just startled by their doctor's good-looks. Maybe he wasn't too different from Carl, after all. My friends thought Carl was a hooligan or womaniser, but those catcalls had hushed since the news of his Mam.

Due to being in the middle of my GCSEs, my dad only allowed me out when he'd ticked-off a study chart, but Carl was just as important; I wanted to be with him.

'Have you had any ideas?' Dan plucked the guitar strings with a focused demeanour.

'A few,' I replied, but was embarrassed. 'Thought a U2 song for him, a Bowie one for your Mam, or anything, really. Is there a tune that Fraternise do that would suit my voice?' Deep in thought, he was strumming when Mum arrived with a pot of tea. Despite the unnecessary formality, it was a welcome distraction. If I was flustered in my own house, what'd it be like on stage? 'Thank you, Mum. Could you pop them on the table?'

'Of course, darling.' She smiled; her rusty-coloured ponytail looked beautiful against a bottle-green summer dress.

'How are you feeling?' she asked Dan, adopting her doctor-tone, which – like the tea – was out of place, even for the Hill. To be fair nobody really knew how to communicate with the McCarthys; there was no manual.

'I'm okay. Just glad my hands are all right after what happened on the train.'

'Terrible business.' She took his hands and checked them over. 'Anyhow, Charlotte-Anne's been on the radio; they think there'll be hundreds of applicants, so you better begin. I'll be listening from the kitchen,' she cooed and gave Dan a playful wink as she dropped his hands.

'Mum!'

I poured, but it was so hot that we only managed to sip the tea. Dan looked serious. 'Right. We'll do a few and hear your range. A couple of old songs should be cool. Then maybe something modern. What do you reckon?'

'Sounds great. I'll follow your lead.'

When he wielded the guitar, it was like sprinkled

fairy-dust. 'Wild is the Wind', a Nina Simone song covered by Bowie, reached a plateau and I came in. Soon, the poignancy was too much, and we stopped for a few tears, but I savoured what we'd achieved.

I was entering the competition for Carl. It was my way of saying thank you. He'd leave little love notes under my pillow with lines from songs. In recompense, I had phoned Dan, who said that we should stay tight-lipped and see Carl's face when I dedicated a song to him on stage. At times, he was a tearaway and filled with contrasting emotions. He was impossible to pigeonhole and only saw what he was doing or what immediately followed. After watching the reconstruction, he had said that life was pointless without love, hate, and passion. Fighting tooth-and-nail so our relationship wouldn't be trapped in the tunnel of trauma surrounding his family, he had earned my respect.

'How about 'Sweetest Thing' by U2? I know I shouldn't say this, but he played it non-stop when you first went out.' Gently, he patted the guitar and I beamed.

'Go on, we'll give it a go.'

Somehow, I managed to sing "*losing you*", and Dan gave a thumbs-up. 'That's a possibility, Zoë. You were brilliant.'

'You weren't too bad yourself.'

'Better with a guitar than with the girls,' he said, dejectedly.

'Just haven't met the right one. We'll fix you up after the exams.'

I went to quench my throat with tea, but I was trembling after putting everything into the song and the whole scorching lot gushed over me. In a panic, I wrenched off the clinging dress.

Shock.

Sharp breaths.

Dan yelled, 'Mrs. James come quick, Zoë's spilled hot tea on herself!' With my back to him, I fearfully stared over the copse. Huffing and puffing, I intuitively covered my bra cups hoping nobody was walking amongst the shadowy trees. Dan flapped behind. 'Does it hurt, how much does it hurt?' he asked with a strangeness to his voice. Seconds later, fussier than Isaac, my parents arrived with their medical know-how.

DC Carter

'Snakes, filth, or any words that dehumanise,' I said as we sauntered into the gully off the Wagon Way. DI Quick's lustrous locks looked out of place and his bloodshot eyes revealed that sleep was a thing of the past. 'That's how a murderer views his victims.'

'It's hard to get inside the mind of a killer. Sometimes I wish I could glean how they go about things so I could catch them quicker. If I could have one super-power, that's what it'd be,' he replied whilst holding back a bramble so I could squeeze through. When we were grilled by the top-brass, we had stood shoulder-to-shoulder and he had been taken aback, but it had been fabulous for morale; the team couldn't have tried any harder. For him it had been a first, but to me it was a core element of being on the force. Everyone had come together despite the schedule and scrutiny. Speculation that he'd be moved from the case was a huge untruth – that only happened in fiction. But, judging by his slumped disposition, it was taking its toll. Since the Dead-Babies case I had a season ticket with a chiropractor who pounded knots. Heightened stress was another cliché, and I hoped Quick wouldn't suffer the same fate.

'For me, it's about the victims. Imagine if they were forgotten? It'd be degrading.' Yet, the investigation was in tatters. In a quandary, we couldn't believe that the reconstruction and missing items had brought nothing. Every avenue was blocked off. I continued, 'There's so much human suffering, everyone connected is affected. Best to remember the names of the victims, not the murderer. In real life, no one remembers the cops.' I'd grown to like him now that he no longer lorded over me.

Granted, we'd never be bosom buddies, but it felt better to breathe easily at work. 'The bitterest pill is not solving a murder. Every family deserve to know the truth,' I said, stopping him from slipping into the creek. 'You should buy some shoes with grips.' Even though he'd changed on the inside, he was still a sharp dresser, but patent-leather loafers were hardly the thing for a walk in the woods. I'd have to recommend my cobbler.

'Thanks, Cli …Carter,' he said, removing his hand with an embarrassed look. He'd almost called me Clichéd-Cop and I was pleased his gaffe had caused discomfort. To be honest, it'd been a nightmare not referring to him as Manilow, so I was in no place to judge. 'I only call you cliché because of how the old team used to go on about cops in books,' he lied, but I played along.

'I know. If this were a book, then there'd be no outside world and all the characters would be stuck inside a forcefield and they'd only talk about the case.'

'I wish it was like that,' he said seriously. 'The killer would already be known to us – hidden in plain sight. It's always the most unlikely person. Perhaps it'd be you or the DCI! Now that would be a cliché. Don't know how many books I've read where the cop is the killer, or the killer is a relation of the cop.' The lack of humour was alarming. The case had consumed him.

'I know, but we still read them, and I love watching *Inspector Morse* on telly. If this was a book we'd stumble over clues: a footprint of a shoe when only a hundred had been made; a ripped jacket with fibres from a particular part of Africa; or, some unusual plant that we'd seen in an interviewee's house.'

Acknowledging each other with caution, the snap of falling branches grabbed our attention. The air was fusty and, in reduced light, the plastic-suited forensics were like extras from *Doctor Who*. With the silkiness of mammoths on ice, we approached. A week earlier, on separate evenings, gunshots had been heard in the copse and gully. Every police officer knew that violence takes place off the beaten track. With hitting a brick wall in the murder case, we were looking at other crimes, praying for a tenuous link. After initial small talk, the forensics explained that they had retrieved fragments of a bullet. Unfortunately, there was nothing else. Spongy earth, the passing of time, and a shadowed area had infected the canvas. 'Don't know what's become of the Island. Missing women and guns going off. When we first started there'd be a couple of Friday night punch-ups,' Frazer the forensic stated as his colleague packed. He was chiselled, old school, and hard as nails with a strong sense of justice. My mam would've described him as a fist in a velvet glove. 'What's happening with the McCarthy case?'

'Just keep hitting dead-ends,' I replied. Frazer grumbled at the misfortunate pun.

'I can't believe that we didn't get a thing from the ring or the items in the yard, did we?' Frazer's colleague responded with a head shake. 'The answer has to be on the Island,' Frazer added with conviction.

'We've always said that,' Quick interjected. 'How did the ring get there? There's no escape from it. Somebody in the pizzeria that day must've done it. We've interviewed everyone, though. Bloody everyone.' The DI's animation was reaching meltdown levels. If he wasn't careful, he'd brew an ulcer.

'We'll just keep going. We'll get a break.'

I hoped my cliché would stop Frazer from detecting Quick's stress, but the forensic grimaced. 'Don't mind scum killing each other, but when it comes to lovely women like Mrs. McCarthy, then that's another thing.

Could've been my missus.'

'I'm doing my bloody best,' Quick shrieked and almost knocked down Frazer's colleague as he stormed past, but I knew what the DI was thinking.

'What's with him?' asked Frazer.

'Taking it personally. Reckons we should've nailed it by now.'

Frazer itched his ear. 'You know better than anyone that every search is different.' Whilst he gathered his things, my insides chilled. Would Donna McCarthy become another Dead-Babies case? Heading out of the trees, Frazer unzipped his plastic suit, letting out that manly smell that was vanishing from society. Back at the car, Quick gave Frazer a nod, salvaging a professional air. Just then, we turned to the sound of reverberating footsteps. Carl McCarthy sped by like a bullet from a gun.

'Carl, Carl, Carl!' I shouted, but he leapt onto a stationary bus with a picture of the England striker Gary Lineker on the side.

'Still think those McCarthy boys could have something to do with it. One of them found the ring,' Quick shrugged.

'Come off it,' Frazer grizzled. 'It's their ma. If that's the best that you've got, maybe you should pack it in.' Almost writhing the car into the gully, Quick yanked the door and darted inside.

Whether my clichéd ticker could take it – not to mention Quick's foetal ulcer – was unclear. Cases could break the best of us. Not only was I tracking a murderer, but I was also staking-out my DI. He wouldn't end up a victim like I had on the Dead-Babies case.

I wouldn't allow it.

Killer

People assume that those who do what I do view females as snakes. Nothing could be farther from the truth. Photos of me perched on their vanishing points were majestic. They were true ladies.

That's more than I can say for my sisters' tarty friends whom, many moons ago when they had been teenagers, had drunk cheap cider. At weekends, they had allowed their boyfriends to grope them in our house. Being younger, I had hidden under the table in my astronaut pyjamas, looking up their skirts. They had writhed teasingly as the boys tried to jab fingers into their knickers. Inexplicably, a rocket of my own had stormed. Everything stiffened and they had laughed, both the boys and girls. 'Pocket rocket!' they had tormented.

Then, that night arrived.

The patter of rain had woken me, and I found my eldest sister's friend hovering in my room with unblinking owl's eyes. I was her prey. She had tugged down my pyjama bottoms and hooted. 'The size of your cock will get you nowhere.' Rubbing it red raw, fear refused to let it grow, which ruffled her feathers. 'Come on my little astronaut, it's time for blast-off.' I had been too young to ejaculate, and she became increasingly aggressive, threatening to come back with sandpaper. I was saved when outside there had been a smattering of voices and the distinctive sound of dad's motorbike. The owl flew back to my sister's room.

Unable to sleep, I had sung nursery rhymes until, like a virus, she returned with a hungry rage. I had been halfway through 'The Grand Old Duke of York'.

'Are you calling me names, saying I've been with ten thousand men?'

'No!'

She had shoved my pyjama bottoms into my mouth and brutally molested me with a tube of sandpaper.

*

The photos inside Aladdin's Cave failed to provide relief. Since the ring was in an evidence bag, I'd lost something vital. Off-kilter and consumed by grief, I sank lower. Dropping it had taken vim and vigour, and the replacement bracelet failed to reenergise. Even though I had a box of stolen underwear, snatching souvenirs had been unplanned. I had wanted to be one-hundred percent pure and not a derivative of another operator. But, when I had peered at Sally's scuffed knees, the kilt's pin had been too inviting. It was as if all Christmases had rolled into one. Since then, they had all offered something.

It had been eight years since Sally became my lady. But lately all I wanted was to stroke her pin. Like an addict who'd fallen off the wagon, unwrapping the tin foil revved my engines. Eyes closed as I buffed, I could see her diamond eyes – sharp and precious – reflecting the morning sun. I even felt the splash-back from her thighs, which caused heavy breathing.

That would've shown the owl.

Carl

Since when had Zoë become a snake? If anyone else had said so, I would've laid them out. But when ah passed the detectives, bussed into town, and mounted a Metro, that question swirled. If ad known where Isaac had hidden the gun, ah would've been toting it around. It was a quirk of fate that ad seen them. Ad sneaked into her back garden to throw stones at the window like Romeo and Juliet. Her Dad would only let her out once she'd completed "enough revision", so ah thought it'd be fun. Then ah saw her, looking flustered in her underwear with me lecherous brother perving! The sheer audacity.

He must've wanted it.

She must've wanted it.

They both must've wanted it!

But, why?

Images of them doing unspeakable things bubbled. The little git. Zoë and I had performed countless bedroom gymnastics. We'd been in more positions than a carpenter's slide-rule with her legs akimbo. So, what did she see in Mr. Premature with his toilet-sex? He'd hardly compare. We'd sometimes go for time immemorial, whilst Laura had spent more time playing inside his head than inside his boxer shorts. What was Zoë doing? If they were messing with uz, it'd worked; ah was mashed to pulp. If Dan really did love pain, then ad inflict it until he was on hospital food. But how could ah? Mam's voice wouldn't allow it. *Ahhhhrrrr* – it was too much!

The carriage was sparsely populated. Ah took out Zoë's photograph, smiling sweetly. On the back she'd written "forever" inside a love heart. To the revulsion of a balding man, ah spat on her image. Spurred on by psychotic thoughts, ah scrunched her up. This wasn't enough. Ah kicked the ball before shredding it and scattering the remains. Tiny pieces fluttered like ash from an urn, whilst a poster proclaiming "Keep Britain Tidy" looked on in horror. Wind blew through windows, picking up the death of our relationship and spreading it through the carriage. An old woman shook her head, but I had no remorse for the state of public transport.

As ah put away me wallet, ah remembered the hidden acid tab from the Sunderland game. Stories of flashbacks from friends who'd dabbled stormed me mind. Calculating that a bad trip would be better than reality, ah slid the minute Union Jack under me tongue.

Thank you, Blind-Boy Bob.

Nothing happened.

Sat away from the other passengers with me head in me hands, the train travelled from station to station whilst ah couldn't link one thought to the next, but ah hoped the journey wouldn't be me final trip of the night. Would the acid dissolve the deliberations?

Bang – a depressing thought.

Bang – another.

Bang – something worse, still.

Alighting the Metro, ah followed the sea's salty smell. Eventually, ah reached the fairground where the waltzer twisted into oblivion, cars transformed into huge polo mints, and passengers' hands ground through chalk. My self-control vanished. After ad spun away from the deformity, ah was confronted by a gigantic centipede that roared pure venom. The bug tossed and tortured its victims, swirling them in a ferocious game. The more ah told mesel' it wasn't real, the more vivid the visualisations became. A midge bit and ah scratched me arm, but, in despair, me hand shredded flesh like tissue paper. With a flapping limb ah tried to escape from the worst place to be when under the influence of mind-altering drugs. A man on stilts, surrounded by children, approached carrying balloons. Our eyes met and the giant's flickered with fiery-red beams. Fangs dripped with vomit as the pied piper led the children away. Ah couldn't stop him. Me Mam's image zipped into me head like someone had flicked a switch. Then Scabby Mary wearing holy plimsoles was crying and asking for help. Every child with the thirteen-foot man had Mary's face. Why was she entwined with Mam?

Ah escaped along the promenade where a plague of overgrown rats passed with miners' lamps for eyes. Fingers in me ears deterred the colourful winding drone from pubs. Ah arrived at the bay after hours of dawdling. In daylight, the concrete breakwater created a safe cove in which children could swim; at night it looked like giant pincers reaching out to sea. Above, grand Victorian houses stood like centurions facing the embittered sea. It was difficult to balance, because the sand had transformed into treacle. Me feet disappeared into the cold stickiness. Repeatedly, ah lifted me legs in exaggerated movements which sapped all energy. Heavy lids made uz topple. In the water, a techno-coloured dolphin leaped and splashed. Its yellow tail surfed the waves, and it laughed through chattering teeth. Soon the treacle crystallised into sugar and the sweetness plunged into me sweaty skin. Ah drifted from the illusion into an impenetrable sleep, which searched every cranny of me mind, inventing new shades.

Ah missed me Mam so much – she was everywhere, walking with Scabby Mary.

Sophia

Just south of self-loathing, I felt how I'd done when I was in Clara's company. My real friends said that I'd become a snake. Lacking Isaac's habits, I still had a Saturday morning routine. I listened to music and had a long soak. My parents also recuperated through a lazy start. Often the family would meet for lunch at one of our restaurants. When Papà called to say that I had a visitor, my thoughts scattered. Dreaming it was Isaac arriving with flowers to reassemble our wrecked relationship, my cheeks reddened. With a pout, I brushed my hair and changed from a towel to a silk dressing gown. Trying to look sexy, I tripped on the stairs. It wasn't Isaac but Carl's elfin girlfriend; the morning sun ignited her layered freckles. Although we both lived on the Hill – Zoë near the copse and us in the orchard – we attended different schools, so our paths had only crossed through the McCarthy boys.

When we went upstairs her lightness became heavy. She sunk onto the bed and explained that the night before she'd spilled a hot drink down herself. 'You don't mind Soul II Soul, do you?' I asked. The funky sound filled the room. 'What can I do for you?'

She revealed why Isaac had stopped talking, and I coiled like the proverbial snake, feeling utterly helpless.

Soon after, my parents watched us leave. Zoë and I trampled by the Hill's huge dwellings and within minutes the houses shrunk as if they'd been on a diet. Entering the graveyard – an evening love haven for couples – I ordered my thoughts. Duped once more by my fair-weather friends, I reflected on what'd happened when Isaac hadn't arrived. Zoë listened with *ooh*s and *ahh*s in the right places. I appreciated her kindness. Completely on my side, she was wise to the mega-manipulation to which some girls were prone. She told me that she would've reacted the same way. I cringed at how I had flicked my fingers, which I never would've wanted Isaac to see. He was so strait-laced there was no surprise that he found me ridiculous.

'I'm really scared, Zoë.' My spine ached when we turned into the boys' cul-de-sac.

'Come on. You can't let this drift. You're great for each other.' She held my hand as my helplessness intensified.

'You haven't seen how he's been. It's heart-breaking. He's looked at me like a stranger.' Memories of exhaustive shifts made me shiver.

'Don't you think he's thawing?'

'Not at all. He's frostier.' Her warm hand was calming, and I recalled how I had wanted to rid myself of the snakes before Isaac arrived. Yes, I remembered the fingers – but was that the juiciest part? Oh my God! They'd mentioned my liaison with Henry. Had Isaac heard? Had I said anything about his Mam? No way. I took some satisfaction in my thoughtfulness but understood that adopting a persona had jeopardised trust.

We were at the front door. Jerking and juddering, I swallowed three times. Zoë drew circles on my back. Thankfully, Dan answered with an embrace. I tried to present a confident aura but only managed a weak grin. 'He's out back, sorting the garden,' Dan informed us. 'It'll be okay. We've told him he's got it wrong.'

'I hope so. I miss him.'

'Howay,' he said. Dan's arm felt safe around my shoulder. We walked through the house. 'I bet it's been painful,' he remarked with genuine concern.

Outside, Isaac was shovelling turf. Rigid about routines, the back lawn was lined like a football shirt, and he'd laid new paving stones. Knowing his strong ideals of right and wrong, his hooded stare failed to appease. Simultaneously, I wanted to both run and stay. Singing birds heralded the beautiful morning, but over the fence stood the drunken man who'd order gluttonous mountains of pizza. Pretending to de-clog the lawnmower's blades, his interest was unhealthy, undressing me with his eyes.

'I've been talking to Dan and Zoë.' They flanked me like prison guards.

'That's nice,' he gritted back, resting on the spade as the neighbour's metal clanged.

'Isaac, listen to her. You've got it wrong,' Dan rebuked.

Isaac blew out a burst of air. 'Okay, then.' His feet made a tune on a loose paving stone. 'I'm listening.'

'Isaac.' I'd never felt so embarrassed. 'I'm not saying what you saw was wrong. In fact, I'm devastated by the whole thing. But those girls... well, the only way to get rid of them was to act like them. We used to hang around together, so I know what they're like.'

'Carl would call them snakes,' Zoë interjected. 'Where is he, anyhow?'

'It was an act. I was pretending to be a total fake, like them. That's what you saw. But only because I wanted them to leave. I wanted to be with you.' I wiped away a slither of sweat.

'See,' Dan said. 'We all – well, maybe not you – act differently sometimes. C'mon Isaac, she wouldn't be here if it wasn't true.' Risking it all, I stepped forward and he allowed me into his personal space. Feeling his minty breath was glorious, and he didn't flinch when the spade fell.

'What about the rhythm method and those waggly fingers?' he asked. Words caught in my throat, and I was beaten back by tears. Surprisingly, he squeezed my hand, and Zoë and Dan hugged us. 'Should I come to your house for coffee? I'd like to get to know your family better.' It was the sweetest sound.

But once again, we were thwarted.

Carl barrelled in.

He almost ripped the gate from its hinges.

Dan

Akin to a poisonous spider, Carl's demeanour lent towards extreme violence. I'd heard the thunderstorm and acid tongue a hundred times. 'What yer doing here with him? Yer snake!' We jostled, caught in a web of confusion. I thought that he was lambasting Sophia and Isaac.

'What you on about?' Isaac barked, picking up the spade, blocking his advance like a lion-tamer. Perilously close to the spade's head, shabby sand spilled from Carl's body. That's when I realised that he was hollering at Zoë and me.

'That tart and him, the perv. She must want jerky sex with the guitar hero!' Revved like he'd been with the gun, he eyeballed me, but it was Zoë that I felt sorry for. Her fingers marked my arm. As usual, I liked the pain.

'Carl, calm down,' Sophia hoarsely whined. 'What's the matter?'

'Aye, Carl,' Isaac added. 'You look like a homeless person. What do you think Zoë's done? You can't speak to her like that.' A jabbing spade was required to prevent Carl's advance.

'Suppose your little foursome are laughing at uz.' When Bill had discarded the lawnmower, I don't know, but our hairy neighbour was loving every minute. Carl fired a pneumatic drill of earth-shattering swearwords and looked like those lads who'd battered me. I turned my backside towards him like a petrified primate. Yes, I liked to suffer, but I needed to keep control. My brother had lost it and I wanted him nowhere near me.

'Those two. Mr. Premature and the snake. I saw yer. I saw him. In yer house. In yer underwear. Him perving behind. Yer dirty…!' Zoë's mother-me-eyes were ringed with terror. Like me, she must've been transported back to the incident with the spilled tea. Unfortunately, she laughed nervously. Carl went ballistic. Words whistled through gritted teeth. 'Are yer joking? Don't laugh at me.' He clawed at the spade, kicking out. Isaac had no choice but to pang him in the throat.

'He's a liability,' Wild Bill barked. 'He'll end up killing someone.' Zoë quivered and her nails drew blood, which felt strangely good.

'Carl, stop it, stop it, STOP IT!' Zoë bawled. Sophia now held a rake, and with Isaac, they'd pinned Carl against the shed. Staggered to his haunches, he held his windpipe and was gulping for air. 'I spilled a hot drink down myself. I had to take off my dress. That's what you saw. Nothing weird. Nothing pervy. Nothing strange. That's just your filthy mind.'

'It's true, Carl. I wouldn't look at your girlfriend. You're my brother.'

'It's another misunderstanding,' Sophia added, exchanging a reserved smile with Isaac.

'What a fistful of lies. What were you doing at her house in the first place? I bet you can't answer that, yer perv. Yer just a snake!'

'They were practising for that competition – you know, the Charlotte-Anne thing. It was a surprise for you, you idiot!' Isaac explained.

'What yer on about?' Carl staggered to his knees and the rage appeared to lessen.

'It's true.' I dared to speak. 'We were doing 'Sweetest Thing'.'

'Sounds like they were at it,' Wild Bill cruelly interjected.

'Do one, Giant Haystacks. Think about a gun blowing yer brains out.' Carl's words were layered with threat and promise. I sensed the fact that Carl was different was dawning on Zoë.

'Dan was helping. They'd planned it as a surprise,' Sophia said. 'There's no way that she'd hurt you. Just like I wouldn't hurt Isaac.' Carl looked tragic with his legs pulled up to his chest. Fecklessly, he'd demonised his girlfriend. Suddenly, it became clear how bad Laura had been. She'd deliberately set out to use me, yet I had liked that pain; Carl didn't look as though he liked the appeal.

'How was I to know?' Carl whinged. 'Ah thought you were up to no good. Am sorry.'

Zoë's clutch weakened. I wasn't sure whether she'd approach Carl or walk away. She took a few steps, and they exchanged a long look. I could see him pleading. Virtually inaudible, her voice – thinner than her – hit him between the eyes. 'I'd never do anything to harm you. My dad has wanted us to cool it during the exams, but I told him to stuff it. How dare you call me names?' With steps daintier than her freckles, she moved to the gate. 'At this moment, I don't know what to think about you.' She disappeared.

'I'll go after her,' Sophia said and pecked Isaac on the cheek.

'What about that coffee?'

'One day, I promise,' she fretted.

Curled into a ball / Waiting for the fall / Feeling so small / Laying out your stall / Losing something tall. The lyrics appeared as I took in my shattered brother's tableaux.

'You messed that up. Couldn't happen to a better lad. You're right, though – women are snakes. Bet she's a right one.'

'Shut it, wild man, just coz yer impotent.' I'm convinced that I heard the sharp snip when Carl snapped.

'Come on, I'm ready for you this time.' Carl and the hairy wife-beater were having more bouts than Ali and

Frazer. Leaping over the fence, he clotheslined Bill and there was a sharper snip. Convinced it was our neighbour's solar plexus, Isaac and I dragged Carl inside. So much for Bill's prediction; he writhed in agony on the half-mowed lawn.

We had Carl pinned on the sofa when Dad came in with a newspaper under his arm. 'Is everything okay, lads?' he asked with a yawn.

'Yeah, of course, Dad.' How he couldn't see the volcano erupting in Carl, I don't know.

What would Mam have made of it all?

Chapter 9: Simon

Dad

Suzie hadn't wanted the house to descend into a place for men only, so I was grateful when she'd moved in. Imagining a house strewn with takeaway cartons and empty beer bottles had never materialised. Isaac wouldn't have allowed it. Besides, it was a front, and she wanted to be there for the boys.

The bedroom was the worst place to be without Donna. That's where she lingered – where we had our privacy, where we shared our dreams, where we were intimate. I couldn't have felt any lonelier than in that room, so sleeping on the sofa was crucial. I'd often sneak a peek; Suzie hadn't moved so much as a curtain-ring, but I'd never set foot in there again.

Four days earlier, England had played their first World Cup game. I had hoped we'd watch it together, but the boys were out. The match against the Irish was one of the worst ever, but I had missed their company. Persistently neglecting them, I had no idea what was happening in their lives. I had allowed them to drift. Recapturing normality was impossible. In the fullness of time, I'm sure they'd understand.

I'd been numb all week and had no resistance to the negativity. I traipsed to the suspension bridge where Donna and I had stolen several happy hours, staring into the kohl gut. If I was to join her, it'd be here. Although it was a sun-drenched evening, the water could have been no darker if the antichrist lurked beneath. Dirt and decay from years of neglect festered, waiting to siphon my soul.

How many victims does a killer make? Certainly Donna was gone, but the aftermath, like deadly fumes, had taken me down. Of course, I thought about my boys, our three peas in a pod, but Suzie was there. She'd know what to do.

Outmanoeuvred by pain, I readied to fling myself in.

Out of the blue, I heard an urgent tone. 'I wouldn't go in there, if I were you.' Surprisingly, there was no jolt through my body. There was nothing. 'Seriously, Simon. You'll be limiting your options. People don't come out of there,' DC Carter advised, sidling towards me, his body-size deriding the fact that he moved like a ballroom-dancer.

'I wasn't going to throw myself in,' I lied. The fantasy shattered, and I felt like a fool. With his hand on my back, we looked downstream to where the old waterway infested the dismantled pit, backing onto the warehouses where Donna last stood.

'I believe you, mate. I've been there, and I haven't been dragged through the miles of pain that you have. Hats off.'

My thoughts were coated with dread. 'There's no way out.'

'I know you think that, Simon. But you've got the lads.'

'They'd be better off without me. I've been worse than a chocolate fireguard. They rarely come home.' Articulating how I felt was impossible, but Carter gave an understanding nod.

'Do you know that they call me the Clichéd-Cop?' I looked at him quizzically. 'Well, in every detective story you read or watch, the lead cop is driven, sometimes through self-derision, or a reason from their past; other times through brilliance or being anti-establishment.' I listened. 'Anyhow, it doesn't matter – they're always a loner and married to the job. They have a fabulous gut.' He grabbed his ample beer-belly, which – even despite my encroaching shutdown – made me laugh. 'No, they have nous, follow their nose, know the wheat from the chaff.' He was right; it seemed to be the make-up of all literary detectives. 'Their personal lives are a mess because they care too much about the job. Often, they have a destructive element like drink, and they overwork like a Mediterranean donkey.' Somehow, he'd roused my interest, and I moved my eyes away from the darkness. I exhaled at the sight of a dilapidated air-raid shelter where Donna and I had once met during our courting days.

'It's unfair.'

'I disagree; I am a cliché. Most police action is teamwork, and nobody behaves like they do in books or on telly. There's nowt more boring than the real thing, so they must make it more exciting. But I'd tried to do too much on my own. Right here,' he tapped the suspension bridge, 'is where a football hooligan went missing.' I remembered the story of a particularly nasty lad from the terraces who'd tried to kill his parents and was wanted for a stabbing. 'I used to come here and wallow.' His expression matched mine. 'Then there was the Dead-Babies case.'

'You don't have to talk about it, Carter.' Two babies had gone missing from the Island's terraces. Reminiscent of the Mary Bell case from years ago, the babies were found on the Vicarage doorstep. There were no leads. Like with Donna, everyone agreed that the answer lay on the Island.

'Every night I came here when I should've gone home. I started drinking here. I was useless. I should've sought help. I should've saved my marriage. I shouldn't have got so close to the case.'

His pearls of wisdom dropped into my brain. 'I need help, don't I?'

'Look.' His brow wrinkled, whilst his voice grew

more decisive. 'It's already there. If it hadn't been for my girls, I would've joined the babies. I wanted it to be me instead of them. In the end, I had to think of my kids; they're alive.'

'I'd swap places with Donna in a heartbeat.'

Carter didn't bat an eyelid. 'That option's not available. My girls are my protective factors – the boys are yours.'

My throbbing pulse pumped in alarm. 'I don't know how to help them.'

'Let's give it some thought.' Carter cocked his hip. 'I don't want to sound like a cliché, but I'm going to get legless. Would you care to join me?' My parched throat itched, and I knew that it'd be better quenched with Carter than by the gut's dark water.

DC Carter

When I saw him at the bridge, there was a ramrod up my spine. I knew how inviting that murky darkness could appear. Part of me thought that it was luck, the other thought it was small-town divine intervention. Either way, it gave me a shot at redemption. The crushing limbo I'd experienced when I had walked the same path as Simon was difficult to recall. But we had both contemplated a permanent solution to a big problem in the same place. Since those awful days when I had thought only of death, I'd somehow got better. The enormous breakthrough had not been apparent straight away. Due to becoming wrapped-up in everyday activities, I had suddenly realised that it had been days since I had perched on the bridge's rails. That had started the recuperation. As soon as I saw him, I knew what he was thinking: *can I escape the pain?* Simultaneously, I thought about my label, the Clichéd-Cop, and getting too close to a case, dreaming of saving others – not myself, never myself.

What choice did I have? Someone had to keep an eye on him.

'Bloody hell, Carter,' he remarked. 'You drink like a fish.' I had to admit that I was no stranger to a Friday night pint.

'I reckon that I could get a game for England if supping was a position.'

'The way they played the other night, I reckon some of the aged miners would do a better job.' Passing in a blur, I raised a hand to some of the old-timers as Fleetwood Mac told me from the juke box that it was another lonely day. On the television, the Germans were pummelling a team of Arabs in a World Cup match.

Undoubtedly, they'd be the team to beat. Simon gave my arm an affectionate squeeze. 'Here's another, Carter. I can't keep up, mind. Think that's your sixth, and I'm on my fourth.' He blasted out an almighty burp, which caused an old fella to yell, 'Go on, my son!' Simon was long-gone, but fortunately it looked like him ending it was like Scotland's chances of winning the World Cup.

My plan had worked.

'What'll your superiors think of us drinking together?'

'Pure coincidence, isn't it? You were here – so was I. We both drink in The Monkey Bar. Okay, Quick might get his knickers-in-a-twist, but – like when I watched the lads' football – I could hardly ignore you, could I?' I offered him a cigarette. Obviously, killing himself slowly was not on the agenda. He refused the cancer-stick with a disgust that only drunks can master.

'I feel sorry for you, Carter,' he said thoughtfully. Once you've pulled a suicidal man from a bridge, whose wife is presumed murdered, the last thing you'd expect is to hear that they have concerns about you. Despite this, I managed to hide the surprise and lit a cigarette.

'How do you mean, Simon?'

'Well, I find this emptiness impossible. The whole world gives me a wide berth. But for you – no-one knows.' He circled his glass.

'I'm not in your league. My ex-wife's with my girls. I cared about some cases, but I failed. I needed to man-up and deal with it – it was a cliché. What you're going through is unimaginable.' I had wobbly knees. Able to lucidly communicate without falling on my face was welcome, but I wished I'd been sober. He put his arm around me.

'You're a good man, Carter.'

'Cheers!' I exclaimed.

'Tell me about the Dead-Babies case? How did you

get to where you are now?' He didn't see a grown man sleeping at his mother's, he saw a success story.

'One day at a time. Keep doing the small things. I nearly lost everything. But the operative word is *nearly*.' The world swung, but I gurgled the truth. 'It squeezes at your goodness, doesn't it? But keep looking for the light. It's the kids, man. The kids keep you sane.' He raised a glass, and we drank some more.

*

Muzzy and in need of rehydration, we left later than advisable when the landlord went from table to table emptying ashtrays. 'England match tomorrow, Carter,' the landlord crooned whilst sucking a cigarette. 'Did you hear that Gary Lineker followed through on the pitch the other night?'

Outside in the pooled moonlight, we laughed at the landlord's line as we emptied our bladders. Using the one-hand on the wall trick caused a vibration, and, consequently, wet shoes. That's when we sang. *'Heat Harrow-line, hood blinds never taste so good!'* he boomed, which faintly resonated with the Neil Diamond classic: 'Sweet Caroline'. Of course, I followed up with: *'Oh ah gloved that dozy child / she got in the way in her nappy!'* I was hoarse and was surprised at how difficult it was to regurgitate lyrics after ten pints, but thought that I sounded like my namesake, Neil. Blurry screams filled the night; whether they were better than profanities was open to interpretation. *Bed Bed swine / Go to my Fred / Make me forget that / I can't knit or sew.* As we neared Simon's house, we shushed and whispered, *'Hurl – you'll be a spunnin' soon / Sneeze inside your hand,'* until we fell about laughing. It'd been an eventful evening for me, but crazier for Simon. Okay, he'd pay for the alcoholic grin in the morning, but he'd moved away from the bridge.

That's all that mattered.

Auntie Suzie

At first, I thought that he'd brought a woman home. In my semi-conscious state, I listened intently and realised that he was downstairs with a friend. Men become little boys when they get together. Okay, sometimes they can be incredibly serious when it comes to money, status, women, territory, religion, or war. But all they require is a sniff of alcohol and a voice telling them it's "free time" and they return to the schoolyard. Amongst laughter, there was a series of spluttering one-liners and the male species' favourite gag – ripping farts. How they can comment and reminisce about historic sounds and smells is impossible for females to comprehend. With a pillow over my head, I had drifted off.

In the morning, I'd almost forgotten about the night's disturbance until I passed the lounge door. The mustered stench was so strong that I expected to see yellow smoke billowing through the crack. Worse was the snoring. Even if a colony of chain smoking sea lions had sunk into beanbags, drugged up on sleeping pills, the noise couldn't have been louder. I tightened my dressing gown and tutted.

Banging cupboards, I checked for painkillers; I was sure there'd be a stampede for them. As the kettle boiled, I took in the symmetry of Isaac's lawn, but instantly the solitude was in tatters. 'Hello, Suzie.' To say I was surprised to hear the furry voice of DC Carter was an understatement. Stood in a shapeless Fred Perry T-shirt with saggy leopard-skin boxer shorts, he was a sight for sore eyes. I tightened the belt once more and distanced myself from his alcohol breath. 'Any chance of a thick black coffee?' My blush was hotter than the kettle. 'We had a skinful.'

Whilst stirring, I asked, 'How bad did it get?' The slit on his crazy boxers was difficult to ignore; I expected everything to spill out.

'How do you mean?'

'Well.' I handed him the cup. 'Tell me that he didn't sing Neil Diamond.'

Sluggishly, he stroked his stomach. 'Aye. We did. Why?'

'Oh my God!'

'What's the matter?'

I hugged myself. 'He hates Neil Diamond. He hasn't got any of his records. When he's drunk, he bafflingly knocks them out. When he's had too many the words come out all wrong.'

DC Carter looked guilty. 'We polished off a fair few. Let's be honest, we wouldn't win that singing contest at the Garden Festival. But when we trawled the terraces, we covered Neil's anthology.'

'Think that's his Saturday done for. It takes him days to blow away the cobwebs of a hangover. Usually, he'd play Beatles' albums back-to-back, but now there's no music in the house, I'm not sure what he'll do.'

DC Carter stifled a burp and closed the kitchen door. 'Look, I know he's catatonic, but I don't want him to hear.' Even though he whispered, segments of stale booze lurked like a big cat's urine. To prevent an unwanted retch, I opened the backdoor and motioned for him to join me in the garden.

'What is it?'

'I found him at the suspension bridge. Looked like he was on the edge of a nervous breakdown, staring into the abyss.'

Involuntarily, I placed a hand over my mouth. 'Oh my, do you think, do you really think, he wouldn't, he couldn't, he can't!'

'Come on, Suzie.' He put his arm around my shoulder. Despite the stale sweat, it offered comfort. 'I need to tell you. I think he's reached an inevitable conclusion about Donna and was testing out solutions. He can't escape, it's impossible.'

'That's no solution. He couldn't do that to those kids,' I said, managing to stifle tears whilst looking up at the bedroom windows.

'I'm no expert, but I reckon he just doesn't know what to do. He feels disconnected from them.' I headed onto the grass and held out my palm and he stayed at the backdoor. The last thing we needed was for the neighbours to see our link-policeman in his underpants.

'It's all my fault. I've wanted to help, but I've been totally ineffective.'

'Don't be daft. Everything is down to who took your sister.'

I shook my head. 'I convinced him to go to work. I've encouraged him to eat with his siblings instead of coming home. I've told him to go out for a walk or a pint. I've allowed him to ostracise himself and only see the lads for ten minutes before bed. I've believed his lies when he's told me he's okay. How could I be so stupid, when I'm frozen inside? Of course, he'll be feeling the same, well… worse.'

'Don't blame yourself.' Carter pointed a finger and spoke with the tone of a grizzled headmaster. 'He's got a double-tongue so not to upset you; he'll say one thing when he means the opposite. He's thinking of you.' I viewed Carter differently. I had no idea that he had a grasp on human psychology. Whilst fussing around hoovering, I had been in denial. Losing Donna had taken our souls. Emerging through the bathroom window was the unmistakable sound of vomiting.

'What should I do?' For the first time, Carter showed

224

an awareness that he was barelegged and tugged at his T-shirt.

'We need to find a way forward.'

'What?'

'England are playing tonight. Why don't you get Simon to ask the boys to watch the match with us?'

'Great idea, Carter,' I said, hoping that coming together would fill the void.

Carl

The Metro Centre looked shabby. Shiny red bricks had been battered into a dreary brown and the tag of Europe's largest out-of-town shopping complex was almost forgotten. Inside, ah could've been anywhere. All the usual high street stores had moved in and the original hope of a shopping adventure of a lifetime had turned into monotonous familiarity.

We'd often wander the indoor metropolis for hours and when ah stepped onto the escalator with the boxed perfume, there was a rush of nostalgia. Shoppers milled around in short sleeves and an elderly couple complained about the draft whilst standing under air-conditioning. Shoplifters blended into the crowd beneath baseball caps, young couples munched burgers, and ah found a wooden bench near ten-foot green letters spelling "Marks & Spencer's". Waves of excitement kept hitting uz and freshly mopped floors made uz sneeze. Ad missed Zoë exactly as much as ad thought. But making-up was the best.

Being watched by a group of schoolies wasn't in the script. They looked identical: tracksuit tops, dark roots, and hard-faced expressions. The glossy woman who'd sold uz the perfume looked like she'd been dipped in bleach, but this lot actually had. For once, ah felt self-conscious. Then ah switched off me paranoia with a spliced grin. Stories developed in the same way and ah knew that ad screwed theirs. Ad spent many afternoons people watching. Ah remembered being chased when one of me mates had made up a story about a shell-suited man who looked like Jimmy Saville. The man had heard and tried to hit us with an umbrella. Priceless.

When ah saw Zoë, ah wanted to run over and sweep

her in me arms. She was checking her image in a shop window, twirling spirals of hair. Her legs looked amazing in tiny denim shorts. Ad seen the movie when the hero gets the girl, but we weren't on a Hollywood set. Obviously, the bleached girls weren't old enough to have seen the movie and they lingered like a wet weekend. 'Got a ciggy?' one of them asked. The last thing ah needed was to be stalked by a thirteen-year-old.

'No. Am waiting for me girlfriend.'

'Girlfriend? Yer were smiling at me!' the girl shrieked, as if she'd inhaled helium. Raising non-existent eyebrows, her lacquered fringe was on the verge of snapping.

'Eh. What yer on about? Shuz over there. Leave uz alone.' Ad pointed, which caught Zoë's attention. Her eyes were muddied stone. She must've also missed the movie. Her stare remained fixed when she approached, and ah wanted to hide inside a bin.

'Yer boyfriend's horrible,' snarled the Domestos girl, brushing Zoë aside.

'I know,' she grumped.

'Bloody hell.' In the fortnight since ad last seen her, ad imagined a romantic rendezvous. That frittered when she wriggled from me advance. Her perfect breasts rubbed against uz and hooked into me skull. Carelessly, ah thought about our first sexual encounter. Me hand had ascended her thigh, and ad never felt so aroused. The sheerness of her skin had slunk against mine and her nipples hardened. Then she had relaxed and uncrossed her legs, showing black, silky knickers before she bent over, her tongue wet…

'How dare you look at me like that,' she raged with a flat voice. She was looking down from two steps above on the escalator. 'Or do you just see me as a piece of meat – a tart?'

Quelling me horniness was difficult, because the imagery had taken root. 'Course not,' ah blurted in haste. 'What ah said was stupid – am a fool. When ah saw you in your underwear, everything scrambled. Dan was behind you, and…' More frightened than ad been in any fight – even the one in Sunderland – ah felt the status change between us.

'That's the problem, Carl. You never checked it out. You just became vexed. You just became volatile, like a mini-volcano. Shooting off on some hare-brained scheme, becoming that messier version of yourself.' Ah reached out, but she shrugged uz off, which was spotted by a nearby security guard. With a comforting smile, she extinguished his interest. As he turned, she leant in. 'It's your pièce de résistance, isn't it? Blowing things to the max and everyone having to pity you because you can't control your temper.'

'Am sorry, Zoë. Am really sorry.' The make-up plans scrambled, and our telepathy evaporated. 'Ah got it wrong – ah admit it. Zoë, the things ah said…'

'You called me awful names, but worse than that – I was scared, Carl. You frightened me.' Leaning over the rails, we watched shoppers come and go. Not being allowed to touch her was agonising.

'Ad never hurt you, Zoë. Never.'

'Your brother had to stab you with a spade! You'd lost control.' When she walked away, me nails cut through the plastic bag where her present remained untouched. Something in the way she moved told uz not to follow.

For the first time, ah felt like the person who'd attacked Mam.

Had he lost control?

Had he got things wrong and gone off on a tangent?

Was ah any better than him?

Before Zoë, ah had a different girl each week. Ah had

called them names like snakes. Me temper could reach murderous heights. Ad never hurt a lass, but was ah rotten to the core? 'Am sorry, Zoë. Am sorry, Mam,' ah said out loud, which the bleached girls, who were tracking, found most amusing.

At the bus station, ah walked through a downpour. Ah thought better of watching the match with Dad. Me mood would bring him down.

Ah was a fool.

Dan

Rehearsals were great. Sean had penned some great words and our rhythm section shone. Okay, it wasn't exactly 'My Generation' by The Who, but it had a great vibe. Bravado and adrenalin made us feel drop-dead cool. We settled on the half-moon sofas but chickened out of performing the song at Charlotte-Anne's music competition. Without doubt, it'd be unplugged once the lyrics kicked in. 'Minis Skirts and Wet Dreams' was a corker: *Your mini-skirt blew me away / Turned night-time into day / Flash of underwear made me scream / You're a walking blasting scorching wet-dream!* An inevitable build to a huge crescendo on a filthy bassline heard my guitar scream in time with Sean. Once we calmed, we decided to use a safer option, a track Sean and I had co-written called Blasé. Thankfully, Fraternise had endorsed my plea to support Zoë. We had a pact that we'd only play live with Fraternise, but as it was for Mam, they had agreed unanimously.

Continuing to rehearse behind Carl's back with Zoë felt fraudulent. Despite their split, she still wanted to perform. It was the end of her exams, and she was so low without him. I hadn't really considered how difficult it was to support us. To say the McCarthy boys weren't easy was an understatement.

Earlier it had been sunny, but we'd missed a deluge due to the pounding session. Met by a bleak sky, I'd planned a quick drink with the crowd before heading to the train. Mild palpitations, reminiscent of the bassline to 'Mini Skirts', took me back to the night that I was beaten. It happened every time I thought of being alone in a carriage. Cherishing pain was part of being close to Mam, but it needed to be harnessed. What'd happened was so out of control that it hadn't helped.

'Great song, Sean,' I said, patting him on the back; his shirt was drenched in sweat.

'You liked it?' We were very competitive, but it spurred us on. I couldn't wait to bring in a song to compete.

'Brilliant. Sounds great live. I reckon we should have it as an encore.'

'Pint?' he asked at the bar. I nodded. 'Be brave to do one of our own. People love to sing along at the end of a gig.'

'I don't know, mate. I think it's strong enough.' There was a huge cheer when Gazza appeared on television. I wondered how he'd perform against Holland – it was the next level.

'Are you watching the match here?' Already, just after opening, the pub was bustling with my bandmates' friends.

'No. I said that I'd meet Dad. We always watch the match together. Anyway, there are a few Geordies playing – wouldn't want to watch it with you Mackems,' I joked.

'God, you sound like your Carl. Bloody hell, I was well worried that night at the hospital. Not only was I nervous about you, but when I'd told him Laura was coming down, I thought he was going to kill me. He had all the charm of a shark in a swimming pool.'

I laughed. 'That'd be a good name for an album.' My mind drifted as to whether I could arrange the words into a song, but Sean's expression changed. 'I never meant what I said about Mackems, mate.' He grimaced as a finger ambled down my spine.

'Don't get hooked in,' Sean whispered before joining the others. I was taken aback to find Laura with a finger like ET, smiling sunnily. I sunk – like falling onto a crash mat – into her misty eyes. I knew that my family could never forgive her, but I missed what she brought.

'Hi, Laura.'

'Why don't you buy me a drink? I'm nipping to the loo.' She leaned in. 'Where it all happened.' The breath on my cheek took me back and her butt-skimming mini-skirt was a wet dream in the making. I ordered her tipple and felt toothless.

Why couldn't I just say no?

When it came to Laura, I was a passive puppet. I knew it but chose to do nothing.

I liked the pain.

Half-heartedly, I wondered what Carl would think. Yet, he hadn't considered us when he was firing bullets, or getting it wrong about Zoë. Stood holding the drinks, my defences dropped. I wanted to talk to Laura. On return, she squeezed my buttocks, causing spillage. 'Lush to see you, Dan.' She took her drink. 'Come on, we'll see where the night takes us.' When we sat, she crossed her legs and there was a glimpse of knickers. It was like a video for Fraternise's new single. Artificially, she air-kissed her friends and Sean pulled me to one side.

'Look mate, tell me to stuff it if you want. But you're fawning all over her. Remember, she's poison.'

'I know, mate. But I like it.'

'I thought you were meeting your Dad. Why don't you go?'

Travelling on a train by myself or chatting with Laura? There was no competition. 'Nah, I've changed my mind. I'm staying.'

He rolled his eyes.

Isaac

If he'd attempted to caricature a stereotypical Italian, Casio couldn't have been more precise. '*Dove sei? Dovresti essere qui ormai. Hanno bisogno di un po' di tempo insieme!*' he screeched; the phone was strapped under his chin as he fought to gesticulate.

'What'd he say?' I asked Sophia whilst boxing pizza. The customers were also transfixed by Casio's histrionics.

Blushing a little, she replied, 'Just asking where his wife is. Says we need… erm, some time together.'

'Wouldn't like to be whoever's on the other end,' a customer said.

A scooter boy arrived with a multitude of shrugs. '*Non dimenticare il telefono. Dove song le pie pizza?*' he sneered through the visor, banging his helmet. Fluent Italian was not required to know that he didn't want to hang around. A great night for tips was on the cards due to innumerable orders. Italy had won two games, and Stefano had agreed that the Italians and English could have time off when their nation played.

'She says *scusa*. The babysitter 'asn't arrived. I am sorry, too. You deserve some time alone.'

It was my turn to grow red. 'It's okay.' I found it difficult to mask my nerves. Sophia had suggested that we walk to her house, and afterwards she'd drop me at the pub to meet Dad. After what, I was unsure. Far from a frosty atmosphere, my stomach had somersaulted when she'd suggested time alone, insinuating more than coffee.

'Are you sure it's okay?' she said with a flirtatious look, which created paralysis.

'*Mama Mia!*' Casio shrieked, becoming the complete cartoon Italian, shunting the scooter boy as they loaded pizza. With a tightening timeframe, their antics freed my nerves. If we stayed, my ineptitude wouldn't be exposed. After all, Sophia had far more experience.

Cleanliness was important, but Sophia made it impossible for me not to interfere with myself. When I *thought* about her, it ended quickly. In fact, it would take longer to mop up and inspect the sheets for stray splashes. Afterwards, I always felt guilty. She was so precious that it seemed wrong to think of her that way. Reconnecting had been great, and we were closer than before. White-hot branding of her name lived next to Mam's on my heart; it sizzled. I imagined telling Mam about her. Overlooking the conversation between her dad and granddad had been essential. There was no way they had been discussing Mam's abduction and locating another victim. That would have been madness. Only at 3:33 in the morning did I have a morsel of doubt.

Once the scooter boy left, Casio dripped with guilt. 'I know you 'ad plans. I will bloody *kill* that babysitter.' I loved how some of his words sounded Geordie, like *bloody*. 'I wanted you to av some *kissy-kissy* time.'

'Casio!' Sophia seethed, much to the amusement of the customers who jeered like a crowd when a goalkeeper takes a goal kick. Rhythmic waves walloped inside my head. Privacy was important, and enough of my life had been played out in public. Wanting to swaddle Sophia in cottonwool was a dream.

'Casio, it's fine,' I said, whilst removing pizza. 'I'll work until she gets here.'

'I am so 'appy that you've sorted things out.'

The phone rang, but mercifully it wasn't another order. We were already overrun. 'Okay, I'll let him know,' Sophia said with a smile. 'Your wife will be two minutes; the babysitter's arrived.'

'I 'ope she doesn't expect to be bloody paid! Usually

take her a pizza 'ome – she can forget it. Better not av her boyfriend around, snogging on my sofa.' Casio let off steam. 'Go on – you can go. 'Ope you two enjoy *your* sofa snogs!' The chant resumed for the full forty-seven seconds it took to wash my hands.

On exit, a customer patted me on the back, as if I were a substitute entering the field. In the window, Ciao – Italia '90's mascot, made from Lego pieces of the Italian tricolour with a football for a head – looked through me. Sophia was recycling pizza boxes, and there was a lurch of excitement when we caught each other's eye. Bejesus, even the smell from the wet street couldn't take away how gorgeous she looked. 'I've called Papà to pick us up. It'll give us more time.'

'I don't think so. There won't be time. I'll meet Dad.'

'Time for what?' she asked, flirtatiously.

'Sorry, I didn't want to be presumptuous.'

She laughed. 'You weren't. Please come back. We need some time without Casio or the boys. I'll wash my hands.' It was good to hear after she'd binned those boxes.

'Hey, Isaac,' Casio's wife called as she went inside. Beside the splurging drain, she and Casio exchanged vigorous retorts. Inside, my confidence waned, and I was overheating. Routinely, I made a "cold" list: a swimming polar bear, a growing icicle, a leaping snow fox – I didn't reach ten. I was distracted by a horn. Sophia's dad was sat in a van with *Cheaper Than Chips* on the side, his arm protruding through the window. Everything erupted: the metal waste, conversations with Mam, the photograph, the plan with Stefano. With Mam's killer still at large, all those thoughts came burning back.

Could Sophia's dad really be involved?

'Come on, Isaac!' she yelled, as she came out. I hung my head, my face on fire. 'Papà will drop us off.' She walked towards me.

'I never knew your dad drove a van. I've only ever seen him in his car.'

'Of course.' She touched my arm the way I liked. 'You know the business has a few, one's usually in the lock-up down the ginnel. He sometimes picks up supplies, but rarely drives it because I hate the smell after it's housed fish. Can't get the stink out, it hangs around for days.'

'I'm going to the pub. We'll do this some other time.'

Disappointment replaced flirtatiousness. 'Please, Isaac. I need to know that I'm forgiven.'

'You are. I got it wrong. I think I've got everything wrong.' I wished we'd mobbed Sophia's dad instead of Wild Bill.

With head bowed she joined him in the van.

'You're gonna lose that girl!' he sung. 'I might pop into the pub later to catch the second half.'

Could he really have anything to do with it?

I waved when the van sped off. Shades of grey weren't good. I needed certainty, not doubt. I struggled for breath.

Oppressive blue tobacco smoke clouded the pub. Sat drinking in a booth were Dad, Carter, and Aunt Suzie. She had an ironed-on smile. 'Where's my brothers?' I asked.

'Don't think they're going to show,' she snipped.

Dad stared into space. He looked a hundred-years-old.

Killer

Cigarette smoke and songs didn't disturb me as I squeezed into the bar at half-time. England were doing well enough to provide a reprieve for Bobby Robson. I eyed the McCarthys and imagined a séance amongst the rowdiness. Once again, the sister's likeness caused disturbance. I felt ravenous, but I couldn't understand why that Pigman Carter was with them. Sampling their grief, I could see that dreams of his mother were haunting Isaac, but he was collateral damage. Mr. McCarthy looked more broken; another side-effect of my operation. In the past, all I had to inform me of how my operations had affected families were articles and videos from TV. Seeing it first-hand was an itch worth scratching.

It was nearly a month after losing the ring, and I'd dug a new grave. Only recently I'd realised that the police weren't on my case. Why I'd worried during those sleepless nights, I don't know. They were incompetent: *not the foggiest.*

I skimmed through a newspaper article about crop circles at the bar. Except for the World Cup, all people deliberated in the shop or restaurant was whether these imprints were naturally formed or created by UFOs. Why people would creep around at night to flatten corn was beyond me. There were more fulfilling ways to spend an evening. If anyone admitted to artistically manufacturing crop circles, then the word would be out. Once that happened, there'd be no way to put the toothpaste back in the tube. Operators like me knew that better than most. Leaving no clues was vital. Deep down, I hoped there was a secret society lurking at nightfall.

As the players came out for the second half, I supped my pint. With Sally's pin in my pocket, a new operation was required. It had been eight years to the day since we'd become one, and celebrating with my most recent lady's family felt strangely fitting. Usually, I'd leave it longer, but losing the ring had left a hole – like the grave – that had to be filled.

Chapter 10: Rave

Sophia

If I hadn't seen Carl act like a mindless hooligan, I would've thought he was soft-hearted. When Dan strummed the opening bars and Zoë coyly whispered, 'This is for my friend, Carl,' he visibly shuddered. She sang U2's 'Sweetest Thing' with earnest, and Isaac informed me it was *their* song. She was fabulous and looked so attractive. Only those who knew her well would've heard the nerves. There was a smile to her voice, and when she crooned, '*losing you,*' the boys teetered. Every facet of their lives had been affected by loss. Minutes later the crowd cheered, and we hugged in our trio.

'I'm meeting her off-stage,' Carl informed us.

'Good luck,' I said. Isaac squeezed his brother's shoulder.

Watching him go, I took in the fabulous surroundings. Dreading that it'd be litter strewn, I was pleased to find an immaculate area. Without doubt they'd cultivated a spectacle in Gateshead. An industrial wasteland had been given a massive facelift. Being with someone who appreciated gardens would've been weird for most girls, but I loved Isaac's quirks. Fed up with being strangers, we had grown closer. But it'd been a week since our last foiled effort, and I'd dismissed the glitch. If that meant discussing the merits of begonias and bluebells, I was happy to do so.

A monorail gave a bird's eye view of the festival. However, the flowers and gentle atmosphere were the exhibition's greatest assets. Wooden coal staithes – made famous in a Michael Caine film – were central to the experience, with a huge model Gulliver floating in the river. The stage was in front of the Big Wheel, near my family's pasta stall.

'Papà's here today,' I told him as we mooched from the stage. But his fingers didn't fold around mine when I took his hand. I thought he'd be as keen as mustard in this organised environment and wondered whether our relationship was a non-starter. Was it already in a state of disrepair? Maybe beginning something when someone's mourning is impossible.

'There's thousands here today.' We found a seat where children shrieked on inflatables. 'What did you… well, your family, do on the day my Mam went missing?' Not wanting him to flounder and to enjoy the day, my instinct was to dismiss it. But there was a grim edge to his voice.

'Why do you ask?'

'I remember Stefano saying that the pizzeria opened later.'

'That's right. All the family's takeaways and restaurants were closed for lunch, but the flagship place on The Quayside opened for family only. My dad's sisters love to fuss. Good Friday is an important day for Italians.' I smiled. He looked glum. I'd put a foot in my mouth. I'd tried to be funny. *Important*. What day was more important to the McCarthys?

'I bet Stefano loved it. Is that the restaurant where a scooter's suspended from the ceiling?'

'Yes, nonno was in his element – strutting around pouring wine, telling stories and singing songs.' Eventually, Isaac's fingers soothingly curled around mine.

'And your dad? I bet he enjoyed it.'

'No. Unfortunately, he wasn't there. Well, he came in for an ou d'oeuvre and a quick ciao, but he had to leave.'

His grip tightened.

'What time was this? Where did he go?' I couldn't understand why he'd asked but thought it was his OCD talking.

'We met at one. He stayed for about a quarter of an hour. He had to see someone about meat and fish supplies. It was the only convenient time. He was so apologetic. Nothing's more important than family.' That was something we had in common. 'Do you want to talk about what you did that day?' He turned green. 'Isaac, are you okay?'

'Just a bit sickly; I didn't have breakfast.' I let go of his hand and found a bottle of water in my bag. He quenched his thirst. 'That's better.' He attempted to smile, but his eyes were preoccupied.

'Let's grab something to eat. Casio's wife is on the stall. She does an amazing aglio olio.'

'Okay.' From nowhere, he hugged and squeezed me. My breath changed. He never initiated contact. 'Whatever happens, I think the world of you. In my head, I talk to Mam about you.'

I had no idea what to say and hung on for dear life.

Carl

Knowing you've been the architect of yer own doom is of no consolation. Ah weaved between people on the grass horseshoe and was recognised by some. It'd become part-and-parcel of our lives, and ah ignored them. But ah wanted to proudly say that the performance had been dedicated to me. What ah didn't want to say was that ad messed up. Having me hair stroked in Zoë's lap was the best, and ah wanted it back.

'Carl, Carl!' a voice called. It was Coach Taylor, dressed in combat shorts and a sleeveless T-shirt advertising Owl and the Pussycat Stotties. He dashed towards uz. Ah hadn't seen him since the reconstruction. Dan had seen him everywhere, and Isaac said that he was in the pub for the Holland game. He shook me hand. 'How are yer? Daft question. Sorry. Hope you're good.' His exuberance waned. It wasn't the first time ad had stilted conversations, people blethering as they dug a hole.

'Calm down, Coach. Am alreet,' ah lied. Different topics arose when ah did so. 'Did yer see Zoë and Dan on stage?'

'Was that dedicated to you? Yer little bugger.'

'Aye. Am off to see her.'

He raised his fists like when we scored a goal and ah remembered how he'd swing Mam around. 'England did well to qualify. Started slowly, but it could end well.'

'Be tough against Belgium.'

He agreed with a neck jerk. 'You look tired, kidda. Sure yer okay?'

'Al live.'

We made our goodbyes.

Top of me list was Zoë, but bouncers weren't known

for their courtesy. In tight penguin suits and with necks pumpkin wide, ah knew their smiles would disappear if our world view differed. Their perspective would be: '*ye shall not pass.*' As a guitar twanged and drums clattered, ah presented a confident persona. 'Alreet lads? Been some decent music, eh.'

'Canny, aye. Can ah help?' asked the emperor penguin with the gruffness of a hundred-a-day smoker.

'Yeah – me lass was the last singer.'

'Hoarse scrawny coloured bird?' Getting needle, sexism, and racism into four words was an impressive skill.

'Aye,' ah hid the rising fire, 'she was class.'

With a Robert De Niro nod, the lesser-penguin – six-foot-four – agreed. 'Reckon shur might win it. Great legs an 'arl,' he goaded. Ah didn't respond; ah didn't have Dan's death wish.

'Can ah go through?'

From nowhere, he produced a clipboard. 'Name?'

'Am not on the list. Just want to see her. Me brother played guitar, as well.'

Blinded by golden fillings, they couldn't have been happier. 'Not on the list, yer not coming in. This is for celebs and performers.' Behind him were Mike Neville and Kathy Secker from the telly.

'Come on, lads, it's dead important.'

'What's dead important is that nee undesirable crosses that line.' He moved his arm like a Jedi master.

'It's okay, he's with me.' A voice rose behind the TV presenters. Fickle and baffled, the penguins stepped aside when Big Eddie – who'd spoken – arrived faster than quicksilver.

'Seems like a canny lad, Eddie,' growled the emperor penguin.

'One of the best. He's a McCarthy.' The bouncer

tipped an imaginary hat with as much sincerity as he could muster.

Making our way down a tunnelled tent, ah looked blankly at Eddie. Equally at home with football hooligans, he blended perfectly into this strange space. 'I suppose yer wondering what am doing here?' He beamed.

'The thought had crossed me mind. Thought you were away with the army.'

'Day release, and am home every night until we fly to Africa.'

'Aye, but why yer in this tent?'

'Am old buddies with Charlotte-Anne and her backing singer.'

'Rubbish. How do you know them?'

'Used to deliver Charlotte's milk, didn't ah. You didn't believe uz when ah said ah had all sorts of friends. Never underestimate Big Eddie.' Before joining the army, he'd worked for the milkman awarded with an OBE.

'Aye, but that means nowt.'

'Let's just say,' he tapped his nose twice, as the band ground on awfully, 'she's one of me biggest fans.'

'Yer full of it.'

Just then, mollycoddled by a squadron of male dancers with jawlines sharper than razorblades, Charlotte-Anne appeared. Her album *Schoolgirl Exuberance* and singles 'Famous Smile' and 'Fear in the Park' had created a superstar. 'Eddie!' she wailed at the top of her range. The stage manager looked as if he was about to yell quiet, but – in time to save his job – he realised who'd created the noise pollution. Grabbing me friend, Charlotte-Anne snuggled and guzzled. Behind her, a nymphet in a crop top and play-with-me shoes squealed whilst giving Eddie a "follow me" finger-wiggle.

'Here,' he said, before joining the popcorn explosion of Charlotte-Anne's entourage, 'something big might be happening Sunday, al keep in touch.'

Ah didn't move as the TV royalty kowtowed. 'Oh, ye of little faith. Never doubt Big Eddie.' And they were gone. The Wham! tribute band put the festival out of their misery. Ah nibbled me lip, unsure where to go, then Zoë appeared, looking more stunning than Eddie's mystery girl.

'Yer were brilliant. Me favourite song.'

With a passionless hug, she whined, 'You're welcome. I thought we did well.'

Pointing at the penguins, ah grinned. 'They think you'll win. Can we celebrate?'

She dipped her eyes. 'No, Carl. That was my parting gesture. I've loved you to bits, but it's over. You're not mended. I don't know if that'll ever happen. I can't be with someone who scares me. Don't do anything stupid. I'll miss you.' She stroked me hair before turning on her heels.

'Al change. Al never be violent again.' Her shoulders were slumped so deeply, I could no longer see her head.

Back in the sunlight ah thanked the penguins and saw Sophia's dad chumming-it with Mike Neville. Isaac had told uz about the van. In Zoë's absence, another obsession resurfaced. Less than a minute after renouncing violence, rage rumbled. It was the worst way to win her back. She'd told uz to do nothing stupid, but there were questions to answer about Mam. Zoë exited the tunnel with Fraternise and stopped uz in me tracks. Ah was torn.

Yin-Yang.

DC Carter

Unlike fiction, a case like Mrs. McCarthy's is a procedural nightmare. We read reports, interview, log, file, phone other forces, check for similar cases, get information from forensics, talk to the victim's family, colleagues and friends, check, check, and recheck. If films showed what it was really like, then Hollywood would ground to a halt. Writers love their protagonist to take a leap of faith, go rogue and follow their nose. Of the thousands of pathways, they usually choose the right one.

A cliché is that the lead detective becomes exposed during a lone-wolf investigation. No other police can reach a destination. Radios fail, rivers burst, roads close, planes fall, and pigs fly. It gets personal. Sometimes they've kidnapped one of the detective's family and have tied them up. In several fictional stories, the killer is a distant family member: a stepdad, cousin, in-law, estranged sibling, but whichever circumstance is explored, the killer is obsessed with the cop. The fictional cop places their life and others in jeopardy, as the killer waits for a one-on-one confrontation. Such foolishness in the real world would lead to instant dismissal for risking life. Stupidity, not braveness.

These same writers spend hours checking procedure, so it's technically correct – we had one in the station. Then, they throw it out of the window. Characters behave in wholly unrealistic ways and the procedural manual is ripped-up and flushed down the toilet – just like one of their victims. When this behaviour is real, people become a laughingstock. During the country's biggest case an idiot pretending to be the Yorkshire Ripper wrote letters and sent taped messages to the police. It led to Assistant Chief Constable George Oldfield following the wrong path. This vanity driven course of action was disastrous. Maybe he'd read too many crime novels. His foolishness meant other lines of enquiry weren't followed. Inadvertently, this led to more killings and the destruction of an otherwise great career.

Sat in our cubbyhole, there was no way we'd put anyone at risk. We were, once again, triangulating evidence. The lack of a prime suspect was the ultimate frustration. The hands-off DCI hadn't the appetite to wade through the tonnes of paperwork. Leaving us to take the strain with Quick up to his neck, the DCI was spending Sunday following his chosen path with the bible-bashers. We could have done with some divine intervention. 'Right, what have we got?' Quick asked. 'Let's not be rigid about routine.'

'I'm clearheaded,' I remarked. That was surprising after last night's bender celebrating Midsummer's Eve and England's qualification to the next round.

'Me, too,' said Pearson, who was moving like she had been riding her horse all day; she certainly smelled like it.

'With the risk of sounding like an old saddo, we need to go through the rigmarole. Why have we got list one? Why do we think it's people with a link to the Island who were in Geordie Pizza on the day of the reconstruction?' I asked, rhetorically.

Quick's head tilted, showing various tints of blond in the fluorescent light. 'Right. The ring was located that day, as well as the other regalia. Mrs. McCarthy was last known to be on the Island. The peninsula has one way in and out, people do not arrive by accident. Therefore, the perpetrator is either from the Island or nearby, certainly with links or local knowledge.' Despite his demeanour, he'd spoken without temper.

'So, to widen, it could be a delivery driver, ex-miner, or somebody brought up on the Island,' Pearson added.

'We can't have cast-iron certainty, but, in most realms of possibility, it would appear to be the case that who we're looking for is from the Island.'

We shuffled on, and Quick flipped over list two. 'Right, this is our leap of faith. Why do we think the perpetrator had links to the estate agents?'

'She was abducted whilst working. She paged to say she'd arrived. The only people who knew for certain were the agents and those linked to Mr. Patel, the subject of the meeting. Unfortunately, despite hundreds of interviews, we've failed to find any strong information. Back-tracking through her clients does provide some crossover on the lists. Due to the act occurring in broad daylight, we are assuming that Mrs. McCarthy knew her assailant, but we must treat this with caution, she may have been caught by surprise.'

'Caution certainly needs to be applied, as she may have been stalked – although we have no evidence of that, either. And we cannot totally disregard that this was opportunist.' Pearson said, flatly.

The triangulation continued. We moved onto list three. 'The crime scene was devoid of DNA and fingerprints. However, we did glean a solid tyre print from a van. We presume this is from the perpetrator, when he skidded off with Mrs. McCarthy inside. At first, we contacted van owners from list two but have widened it to all Island residents, as well as any vans entering the Island through stop-and-search – well, stop-and-scan.'

'Despite this intense, methodical approach,' Quick interjected, 'there has been no clear match. Yes, some vans have had the same make of tyre, but they have proven to have a different tread indentation, and the owners have bona fide alibis.'

'This leads us to believe that either we haven't located the correct van, or, if we have, the tyres have been changed,' I concluded. 'So, a prime suspect is non-existent. We do have people who appear on more than one list, but despite being reinterviewed, they're alibied for Good Friday. We've done more chat than Wogan and Jonathan Ross put together on this case. But I'm sure we've interviewed the killer.'

'Something must be written between the lines,' Quick added.

'We've searched every millimetre of the Island, so we believe the body was moved out of the area.' Peterson said.

Slouched down, we felt the mêlée of regret. 'What about the missing persons work on the computer?' I asked Quick.

He patted his hair. 'It's been difficult, the modem overheats, and the top brass seem reluctant to invest in IT.' He may as well have been speaking a foreign language. 'Have you any idea of how many people go missing?' We both nodded in reply. 'On the Island, the only missing person is your football hooligan. The only unsolved murders are the dead-babies.' As always, something in me fell on one side when I heard about those failures. 'I've created some algorithms.'

'Some what?'

'Algorithms. Its maths and helps create links. My first is about female abductions around the country where there is no kidnap-ransom or body. There's a few, but they're rare. On narrowing it down to those involving a van, we end up at zero. My second is unsolved murders. In the North East there are fourteen women. Unfortunately, none have the same MO as the McCarthy case. Maybe this is his first, but I doubt it. An abduction in broad daylight by a novice would've resulted in a forensic dream, as well as sightings.' I felt the same as Quick. Whoever had done this had done it before. Maybe

he'd changed his MO. But that was just a theory – a leap
of faith. Maybe we'd only know when he struck again.

Dan

A drug-crazed generation throbbed to a heart-pumping hammer of electronic music. The atmosphere was drizzled with chemical love. Hands made crazy patterns under strobe lighting. Punctuated dance beats, sweat, perfume, whistles, and grimy drugs made for a streak of insanity. I'd seen films about Woodstock and had witnessed the crazy dancing. Being repeated on the spot where Mam was taken was something I'd not considered.

As usual, partygoers had been moved all over the North East. Word had got out that there'd be a rave. After a wild goose chase, the posse had descended on the new industrial estate. Fortunately, we'd had a nod-and-a-wink about "something big" from Carl's friend, Big Eddie. Although the huge soldier scared the life out of me, it was nothing compared with his scuzzy friends. Even love-bombing our conversation with wide-eyed innocence couldn't hide their thuggery. These people were terrifying. One looked like he'd had his jaw wired together, and another had an eye patch emblazoned with a smiley face. From the warehouse's opened doors, cars were clustered around the padlocked gates which prevented police entry. Ravers had found access through the fence around the back, and the CCTV had, yet again, been disabled. Once Eddie's friends entered the misty dance floor, my mood eased.

'Look at those crazies taking drugs. You two not on the happy pills?' Eddie asked, with a hint of menace.

'Nah – don't fancy it,' Carl replied. Like me, this place meant only one thing to my brother, and we were uncomfortable. Mam's eyes were upon us.

'Think everyone else is out of their heads. Where's the third pea in yer pod?'

'Our Isaac? Building a scooter. It's nearly ready,' I replied. 'Don't you do drugs, Eddie?'

'Me? Never. Prefer the opposite sex. But ah don't even want to get off with a lass after the amount of fun av had over the last few days. Think al head home and watch a cop show. Listening to the lads wittering on will be too much.'

'Ah thought you might be out with Charlotte-Anne. Did you know he's bosom pals with her?'

My face was occupied with more than a seed of doubt.

'It's true. What can ah say? Some of us have it, some of us don't.' Eddie pontificated with his tongue placed firmly in his cheek.

'Massive cop show fan, aren't yer, Eddie?' Carl remarked.

'Aye, ah love them. Might join up when av finished with the army. Ad love to be a copper.'

'Ah bet Charlotte-Anne would say you'd look good in uniform,' Carl joked.

'Hey kid, not all of us have what it takes – as you know!' Eddie retorted. They continued to banter and wind each other up, but I'd faded out to the dream-thrum of hypnotic music. Lyrics came: *Dream with me / Dream with me / Close your eyes / Whatcha see? / Hunks and junks / Nerds and birds / Dream-thrum baby / Dream with me.*

At the elevated turntable, Sean – Fratenise's singer – was shirtless and in conversation with the DJ. We had won the Garden Festival competition and were presented with studio time in London; Zoë had finished third. Obviously, he was away with the fairies, and his face was triumphant with unpolluted delight. It wasn't thoughts of the band's success that had caused the euphoria, but chemicals. When he'd told me about The Stone Roses at Spike Island, he'd been disappointed. The sound just wasn't right. He said we'd performed better at the Garden Festival. Although the charts were full of cool bands – Inspiral Carpets, Soup Dragons, and my favourite James singing 'Come Home', which reminded me of Mam – Sean wanted to find something new. He'd cobbled together a DJ kit. Despite the impending London trip, we feared Sean would move on. The band had ripped it out of him about blokes only becoming DJs to sleep with younger women. He was less than impressed. Yet, as many girls were stripped down to their bras with taut stomachs and unyielding jaws, I thought the scene would prove too seductive.

Peering through the old pit gates were the officers who'd came to our house when Mam had gone missing. He looked gigantic, tall enough to step over the padlocked barricade. She looked like she'd be more at home on the dance floor. Their car's blue light flashed, and they hid their eyes from the sun. I walked to the recently tarmac'd spot where they had found the skid mark, hoping to absorb Mam's pain. Was she caught by surprise? I'd kept my suspicion about Coach Taylor to myself, but the doubts remained. I wondered whether I'd always feel the ache. I hoped so. Stroking the ground gave me a paper cut and I sucked away the blood. Hurting my fingers was unacceptable.

There were more blue lights and dogs barked. 'Do you know they name police dogs after guitarists?' Carl asked Eddie. 'One of thum's called Hendrix.'

'Class. Think it's time to go. Don't want Bo Diddley sniffing me balls. Leave the law to deal with the loved-up dancers.'

'Howay, Dolly Daydream!' Carl yelled.

'I'm not in their league,' I remarked, pointing at the rave where a relentless bassline made the silver walls throb like a boiling kettle.

Mary

The things I've done and the places I've been. Every weekend, gallivanting from town to town in search of the ultimate high. I've had the time of my life. Having a rave so near home was a Godsend. The sun shone. Of course, the warehouses were a fabulous venue. Pills were sorted by a dangerous looking girl, (the Island's very own oompa-loompa) but had delivered a fantastic vibe. My friends felt the same. Like living inside an oven, the walls dripped with sweat. Harmoniously, we leapt and swayed; the music and our heartbeats one. We popped with perfect passion. Streaking like a comet's tail, the sounds, lights, and atmosphere were unified.

Of course, it came to a juddering climax. The plug was pulled. A police raid spoiled the epitome of nights. They must've expected a battle. But boys and girls in bucket hats hugged the boys and girls in blue. Glow-sticks fell to the floor. I felt the softness of fur against bare legs as a dog weaved. A handler with a dog called Prince gave me a wink. Ravers skidded on discarded water bottles whilst the DJ attempted to pack away, unnoticed.

Funnelled outside, it took a good second to adjust to the gentle breeze. Although the night was muggy, it was like moving from a frying pan onto a warm plate. I became self-aware, not just a cog in the crowd. My Smurf T-shirt clung. My Nike trainers squelched. My underwear felt as though I'd wet myself. My hair belonged to someone else. And my brain was scrambled. I was a hot mess.

A policeman, about twenty-two to my seventeen, who looked like he'd spent the weekend being stretched on a rack, pointed to the exit around the back. 'My friends went through the front gates,' I smiled. Unfortunately, he looked like a boy who only laughed at his own jokes.

'Listen, twinkle toes,' he grunted. 'Out the back. You'll catch up.' There were people everywhere. 'I'm sorry. Rules are rules.' I'm sure he checked me out as I took off my shoes.

'I've got the blues for you. Blow me a kiss,' I sang. Joining the trundling throng heading towards fields, the music had lodged inside me.

For once, the love drug didn't allow me to be impressed by a boy's chat. On several occasions I'd met up with someone after a rave. Trying to relive a night is like revisiting a favourite holiday, expecting the people and feelings to be waiting but there's only bricks and mortar. I've spun that trick several times. When the vibe is lost, boys cast blame and destroy positivity. It's about living in the moment.

Police chopped up the crowd and I was directed through a fence. I knew that I'd catch my friends on the Wagon Way. A killing moon was murdering the day, creating an evanescent twilight on rapeseed fields. People soon doubled back to their transport and voices became whispers. Suddenly, I felt fatigued. Despite the quality of the ecstasy pills, the tiredness was psychosomatic because I was alone. Shortcuts and pathways were familiar, but blind spots dotted my brain. Awful childhood memories filled my head for a few seconds before being replaced: hiding shoeless in the fields; frightened and cold hearing the hate in their voices; locked in the dark with the spiders and bugs; why did they... I had to escape from those nightmares, there was no point going back.

When I entered a labyrinth of trees, I felt like the fool from the Hill. I couldn't blame my childhood for being scatty. It'd become colder now. Where was the Wagon Way? The twilight became night; the sun had given up. I dropped a shoe and thought about glass in the grass. There was friction, like someone brushing sandpaper against a tree. My situation wasn't good. Visions from my upbringing were back. I thought about the threats and secrets. I did that thing. Running a few steps, I'd stop and walk, turn my head... repeat. Sick to my heart, I wanted to dance again, hug a stranger and talk, talk, talk. I thought about screaming. Not so long ago and not so far away there were police everywhere. Surely other ravers must be skulking nearby, avoiding a chemical hangover. 'Is anyone there?' I called. Why had I said that? If someone replied, I'd pass out with paranoid fright. Then, ahead of me, there was a rattle of stones and someone humming a nursery rhyme.

Killer

As a teenager I had left a trail of unconscious girls. Hot summer nights and a continuous supply of football had dredged up so much. I had walked through fields with a soundless tread night after night. I'd broken Sally's skull on the beach, but she possessed me. Having her pin in my pocket didn't help. All I thought about was her. In comparison, the memory of Mrs. McCarthy was fading.

I liked my ladies to be a similar age to me. But, when I saw the girl, I couldn't believe it. Fresh from the dispersed rave, she was a bombshell. A vision in a kilt, barefoot, with nipples protruding from a Smurf T-shirt. But I was baffled. I'd seen Sally's head shatter. How had she come back?

A firework exploded in my mind. Day turned to night. I knew my thoughts were hazardously gratuitous. Stirring between my balls and buttocks was the echo of death, giving me the biggest hard-on. I loved to plan. The thrill of the hunt was part of my routine. But the luck of the devil had presenting her to me. Sally Two – the sequel. Could it ever feel that good, again?

There was only one way to find out.

Double-quick, I darted to the fishy van and wondered whether I should risk all I'd achieved by being caught red-handed? I'd watched the police raid the rave. They weren't far away. Near enough to hear a scream? I was unsure. Impulsivity wasn't my MO, but I felt a higher power. A magnetic pull. I had to take a chance. In disbelief at finding her, I had disregarded my better judgement. Damage and destruction were all that mattered.

The day I had introduced Sally to the purest hell was the greatest of my life. She'd danced in my dreams ever since. I could feel the supple muscles between her legs and my hand around her throat, crushing her trachea. Consumed by the pathos, I readied myself.

Inside the sports bag was a special kit: mask, sawn-off baseball bat, hairnet, and plastic gloves (from the kitchen). I thanked the Daily Mail for explaining how DNA was recovered from a scene. The bat and mask had been with me from the start, but the gloves and hairnet were recent additions. The bag had been in the van for a week. Deep down, I must've been hoping for an opportunity, because I'd only ever travel with it for an operation.

The mask hid a sneer. Moving quickly, I circled the periphery of trees to get ahead. Catching myself on needles and spines, I strode on with salty breath. Sensing her on the other side, I imagined her bones cracking. Her thoughts would be overcome with how she'd stupidly found herself exposed on a dusty path, with the smells of summer being the last thing she'd sense, wondering how one minute she'd been dancing with friends and the next she was alone. Would her family blame the police? Would the papers blame drugs? Would they blame youth culture and music? Would they invent something like Sally's promiscuity? Only time would tell. I thought about how I had dumped Sally and wished that I had kept her longer. Those shiny eyes were like tiny chips of glass.

Composure. I stopped, hummed, and sung. '*If you go down to the…. for a big surprise … better go in disguise.*' Twisting on stones, I stepped from the trees. The bat was by my side. Through the mask's slits, I watched her freeze. She opened her mouth, but, like the others, there was a soundless scream. Just as Sally had done, she dropped her shoes. Urine ran down her legs. Fight or flight? I expected her to flee. But no. Maybe it was the drugs, but she snarled and swung, fighting like a wildcat, scratching and kicking. But she was small and frail and going nowhere. The moon gazed over trees and there was a star-speckled sky. Henna designs on her hands and jumping azure beads contrasted Sally.

The bat obliterated her temple. Its blow rapid and, with her feet in the air and head on the ground, I observed the quality of impact. Eyes rolled and the coloured parts disappeared into her skull. Gristle and blood oozed from the wound. From experience, I knew how they'd moan and groan. Ripping off the T-shirt revealed that Sally Two was braless. With it stuffed inside her mouth, she gagged in reflex. Dragging her to the van, the sickly sweat rubbed on my clothes. On the rapeseed's pathway, her buckled feet left a ridge, but I was stunned to hear, 'Hey, man, what you doing?' Dropping Sally Two like a ragdoll, I turned to face a pair of dead-beats who'd sprung from nowhere. 'Hey, man!'

'I'm definitely giving up drugs,' the second boy remarked.

The ramifications of being caught brought two options. Giving up on an operation had happened once before and I'd been left in a terrible state. I had no desire to return there, and I was obliged to empty myself onto the lady's legs. Taking in the sticklike teenagers, I knew that I could eliminate them. Clubbing them to death would be easy; they were out of their minds. On the other hand, those who do what I do say that changing routine leads to a downfall which would seal my fate.

In a split-second I left the lady, knowing it'd crush me. Stinging nettles and tripping-weeds tried to slow me down. As predicted, the flimsy boys went to the girl. With no one in sight, I fired the ignition, berating myself. How could I have been stupid enough to break from the operation that'd served me so well?

I hadn't even taken her azure beads or looked at her feet.

Chapter 11: Owl

DC Carter

The pager buzzed through the intoxicating cloud of stale alcohol. Staggering downstairs, half-comatose, I hoped it'd be important. Providing the catalyst towards sobriety were a flask of black coffee, and ice cubes – the latter I applied to my eyes. Fighting the intoxication further, my old Sarge's information hit me with a shot of pure adrenaline.

Later, he told me the station had been engulfed with a mellow euphoria. Being the first rave to be broken up in our area, they had marked some cards with arrests. But the Sarge said that the body of revellers had been compliant. Their biggest crime had been drinking the water dispenser dry, like sweaty antelopes at an oasis.

He thought the stragglers were experiencing a bad trip. Arriving at the dead of night with darker news, they had been ignored. Sarge had sensed panic in the pair's ghostly stares whilst they wiped dew from their shoes. He had given them priority. 'The lunatic was in an owl's mask. We think she's dead.' Luckily his experience had told him to pursue their story. Within minutes he had called for an ambulance, the DCI, Quick, and me before setting off to the scene with uniforms and the spaced-out duo.

If I'd been pulled over, I would've been several realms over the limit, as my stinging eyes made driving perilous. I was only a few minutes on the empty roads but I was relieved to see the cordoned area. Emblazoned by flood lights, my fellow officers had made camp up the country lane. A shudder went through me. Drawing closer, the luminous yellow tape gave me the creeps. This unremarkable woodland should've been a place of peace, not one tainted with victims of men's crimes. An ambulance's flashing light blinded as it licked the Cortina's paintwork.

Bookending the cordon, two burly PCs gave me a nod as they lifted the tape. Stooped over the victim, the Sarge had secured the scene and had what looked like a T-shirt in an evidence bag. 'How is she?' I asked, and he made room for the paramedics.

'Breathing. I think she'll make it,' the Sarge replied. Only with the dead-babies had I seen him so grave. 'Fortunately, these two stumbled across the attack, or she would've been a stiff.' He'd pointed with his head. Slumped beneath an oak tree two teenagers were sucking cigarettes with lung busting drags.

'Can I speak to them?'

'You're the detective, young 'un. Get as much as you can, but we'll do it properly as soon as the cavalry arrive.'

I nodded. 'What sort of person could do this?' Not waiting for an answer, I approached the victim. 'Can I peek?'

'Nice and quick, detective. There's no time to waste with head wounds,' the medic said. It was bleak, the dent a crater. She was younger than I'd expected, and her mouth had drooped.

'Thanks, lads.' A PC escorted the victim in the ambulance.

Inside a spot-lit circle, the Sarge joined the revellers. Skyrocketing to the top of a hundred questions was a description. 'Hello, lads. I'm DC Carter. My old Sarge told me how brilliant you've been. Honestly, without your intervention, I think we would've had a murder on our hands.'

'We did nothing, really,' one of the lads said, lighting yet another cigarette.

'Did you manage to get a look at him? Sarge told me that he wore a mask.'

'An owl's mask, the freak!' one of the lads said. His hands were shaking so much, the cigarette couldn't find his mouth. 'The owl screeched off into the killing moon.' He laughed nervously at his own dramatic words. 'Just before that, we heard a shriek after a sound.' The raver looked to his friend to finish the sentence.

'Like a car hitting a wall.'

'So, you didn't see his face?' I asked, sticking to the task and helping him light up.

'No, nothing. He was quick, though. He wasn't tall, but strong – stocky, yer know? He flung the lass around as if she was made of straw.' The departing ambulance wobbled, avoiding approaching cars.

'Is there anything you remember? Did he speak?' They shook their heads. 'I think we should go to the Nick, get everything written down.'

'We were a bit off our heads,' one of the lads said with the sorriest tone, 'but can you remember the van?'

'Oh, aye,' his friend replied. Our eyes flickered and I sensed the Sarge tense.

'Van?'

'We were wandering for a while, but there was a white van, over there on the tracks.'

'White?'

'Yeah, but that's not it.' I heard Quick and the DCI's voices. 'There was something written on the side.' My chest swelled and I couldn't speak. 'Can't remember everything but one of the words was "*chips*".'

Isaac

We were used to the sepia air surrounding us. As I had polished the final piece of my scooter – a chrome exhaust – police sirens had soared. In bed, the tendrils of rants from the rave had gone on for hours. Blaming the hot night wasn't enough. The click from my metallic tongue had kept me awake. It had been a long night, and, in the morning, I was on hyper-alert.

For once, I didn't touch the third-from-last CD when a firm knock raised me. Answering to Carter wasn't unusual, he'd been like one of the family since Mam had disappeared. Yet, something in his facial expression had altered from the usual shabbiness. Even the heavy mix of coffee and booze couldn't hide the new spirit. My stomach ached and alarm bells rang. Within seconds, Auntie Suzie arrived with Carl and Dan in tow. Dad poked his head through the lounge door and Carter invited himself in.

'Morning,' the detective said, a few octaves lower than usual. In response, we found uncomfortable spaces in the front room and Dad folded his sleeping bag.

'You look like you've been up all night,' Aunt Suzie bustled, tightening the belt on her dressing gown.

'It's not far from the truth,' Carter croaked. 'Simon, can you remember what I once said? Investigating a case like Donna's is like waiting for a crack in the ice. Once that occurs, things move quickly.'

'Has something happened?' Dad asked. 'Has there been a breakthrough?' We squeezed onto the sofa. Unusually, I was glad to feel the closeness of my brothers. Carl felt clammy and his breath was seething, whilst Dan was cold. Stood in front of us, Carter ran his tongue over chapped lips.

'Last night a young woman from the local area was attacked. Mercifully, she's alive but unconscious at the RVI in Newcastle.'

Saucer-eyed, Aunt Suzie hugged herself. 'Oh my God. Oh, my good God.' Dan consoled her.

'Anyhow, there were eyewitnesses.'

'They saw him. Who it is? I'll cut his balls off!' Carl shrieked. As usual, his emotions were displayed in Hollywood-sized letters.

'Listen, son,' Dad soothed, compassionately. 'Listen to what Carter has to say.' The detective accepted Dad's therapeutic intervention, understanding the grieving process was different for us all.

'When we spoke to the witnesses, they said that they'd spotted a van with the word "*chips*" written on the side.'

Powerless, I was knocked off-balance. The whole room spun and closed in. Carl's eyes burned. The earworm I'd had for months about Sophia's dad exploded. Carl paced. I knew that we'd had the same thought: we'd let the monster elude us – hidden in plain sight. I'd come up with the slogan *Cheaper than Chips* for Geordie Pizza. How could he have invited me into his home and allowed his dad to open for the film crew during the reconstruction? I'd known all along. I should've trusted my instincts, but it hadn't fully connected because of Sophia. Her dad was the killer. How would I ever forgive myself? And I knew that he was planning another attack.

'We tracked down the vans in the local area known to display the words *chips*. This morning, at five a.m., we simultaneously approached three lock-ups on the Island.'

I couldn't hold it in any longer. 'Was the van from Geordie Pizza?'

'That property was searched, but no, it wasn't.'

My heart and head were blown to pieces. I struggled

to make sense of what was being said. Was I wrong?

Sophia's dad *was not* involved!

I listed pizza toppings from A-Z, but the guilt was too heavy that I only reached anchovies.

'Carter?' Carl groaned. 'Yer said there were eyewitnesses. Did they see the nutcase?'

'He was wearing a face-covering: an owl's mask.'

'Coach Taylor, who runs our football team, has a sandwich place called Owl and... something on the Island. He dressed as an owl when they did the Great North Run. His van's got the word chips on the side. Don't tell me that it was him. He was in our house.' I'd forgotten about Dan suspecting Coach Taylor. Was he having the same thought about pursuing his gut instinct? The coach had acted oddly around Mam. He swung her around when we scored and picked her up first for the fund-raisers. I wish I'd taken my brother more seriously. Was he right?

'Please, could you all sit down.' Carter moved wearily. 'Yes, our search centred on lock-ups connected to The Owl and the Pussycat Sandwich Bar and Geordie Pizza, but preliminary enquiries show that the owners of those vans were not involved in yesterday's attack.'

'If not them, then who?' Dad asked, his nails ripping through the sleeping bag.

Carter took a deep breath. 'The location of the van in which we're interested was in a lock-up belonging to the fish 'n chip shop.' We wilted, and I remembered the cockroaches from the chippy fighting in Geordie Pizza on the night that Mam's ring was discovered.

'Who is it?' Carl spoke for us all.

'Unfortunately, I'm not at liberty to divulge. We're gathering evidence and an arrest has been made, but as we speak there are no tangible connections to Donna's case; however, that's the major thrust of our investigation.' Looking Carl dead in the eye, he continued. 'I must ask you to remain calm and trust us.' Then his tone slipped from the official. 'If it is him, son, we'll nail him.'

Killer

They did come. I knew they would because I had heard the tolling bell. During the wait I had promised my ladies that I would allow the pigs to piece it all together. It was down to them to reveal what they knew. All those times that I'd waited for the knock... but this was different: I hadn't squeezed her throat until she'd turned green; I hadn't watched her tongue ground into sand; I hadn't greased her passage to the next world; I hadn't tasted her final breath.

Even above the night-time radio, I had heard their inefficiency. I had stacked the ginnel with bins and the pantomime fools had walked into them, blaming each other. With Aladdin's Cave open, my clothes burning in a barrel, and the grass-stained van sitting pride of place, I had waited. When the shutters had unfolded, I jittered with excitement, and they had splurged in like water from a broken dam. Of course, I had considered disabling them with my sewn-off baseball bat, which had proven to be a most effective weapon. What better way than doling out the damage to show how it's done? Instead, I had sat cross-legged. 'Can I help you, gentlemen?'

The black semi-circles beneath Carter's eyes failed to hide his surprise. Taking in the lock-up, I had half-expected him to go the whole hog and batter me, inflict the kind of justice that lived below the surface. How many times had I sold the Pigman fish and chips (with a pie on the side)? I had even discussed the McCarthy case with him.

A wide-eyed uniform scanned the cabinet. 'Jesus, he's a psycho killer.'

'Qu'est-ce que c'est?' I asked.

'Don't touch a thing. Everyone out. We need to

preserve the scene. Radio through for SOCO and forensics. Fredrick Anderson, I am arresting you for GBH and the attempted abduction of Mary Ryan…' He monosyllabically delivered the spiel spouted a thousand times on rubbish cop shows. It was weird to hear the young lady's name, because she was Sally Two to me. I had dispensed a razor smile which cut the detective.

*

The gravitas of what was happening wasn't lost when we had arrived at the station. Although they went through the usual rigmarole, the amount of police that appeared had been shocking. It was as if I was Elvis. They must've expected me to be scared beyond belief, yet what they hadn't figured was that I was a genius at reading human behaviour. How did they think I had walked around for years, been interviewed several times, and spoken casually to the family? Embarrassingly, they had lubed themselves up for a "go". I had visualised this experience a thousand times and was prepared for their blunt instruments.

*

It was late afternoon. I found myself in an interview room going over the events surrounding my arrest. A blade of light speared through a gap on the grime-covered window. Sterile and lacking in personality, the walls were white and the furniture black. A CCTV camera had been erected in the corner and an unplugged tape recorder sat on a shelf that had a screw missing. DS Pearson looked even more skitzy than when she'd studied my van. If I hadn't decided to stonewall them, I could've shouted, "BOO!" and she would've folded into a heap. Drummond – my solicitor – looked uncomfortably hot inside this shoebox of a room; it was no weather for a three-piece suit and heavy-duty brogues. I had told him that I knew nothing, and they were digging.

Pigman Carter was the ultimate blunt instrument. Thank goodness for my brief's Cuban cigars, otherwise Carter's aroma would've been unbearable. How dare they send a bath-dodger to interview? But deep down I'd hoped it'd be him. Watching him fall apart when he couldn't solve the Dead-Babies case was legendary. Crying in front of the media. What was that all about?

After pleasantries, Pearson bleated about the zonked-out lady. Finger wagging and expecting me to discover a bagful of remorse, it would've been easier to withstand an interview with a children's TV presenter. Theatrically, she placed down a plastic bag containing my sewn-off baseball bat, which I'd drowned in bleach before they'd arrived. She told me: 'Forensics are working on matching the bat with the wound inflicted on Mary Ryan.' I thought that they couldn't be working that hard if it was stretched out and suffocating in a bag. Shutting-out the conversation, I wondered who'd wiped the grubby window? There should've been more security.

From the Pandora's box where the bat had materialised, Carter took some paper. We made eye contact. He pulled a face and dry skin fell from a cold sore. 'When interviewed about the disappearance of Donna McCarthy,' he laid out my interview sheet, 'you said that you left to collect fish in the afternoon as stocks were running low. You said that this was around 2:00p.m., to attend the freezers at your lock-up, and you'd returned by 2:15p.m.' For the first time, I felt some turbulence, narrowed my eyes, and focused. 'Whilst attending an altercation on Good Friday, a PC stated that, on entering your premises, you were not present. The quarrel they were present for occurred due to a frustrated queue that had gathered on the terraces, as people were left waiting due to a shortage of fish. You – in your own words – were collecting haddock to relieve the backlog.

What the PC said corroborates your story.' I nodded. 'However, the time logged for the call to the station re: the customer's violent attack was at 2:24p.m, which means it would have been around 2:30p.m. when the arrests were made, and when the PCs entered the premises.'

'Excuse me, detective, we are here to discuss Mary Ryan, not Donna McCarthy,' Drummond interjected. The Pigman and I maintained eye contact.

Clever boy, I thought. *You have been busy*. But he knew as well as me that without a body, murder was much more difficult to prove.

'My client could have been preparing the fish, or simply at the toilet. Is there any evidence, such as information presented in a police logbook or a sighting of him in another location?'

'No. Following the arrest this morning, I recalled that a trustworthy Sergeant informed me of the incident at the fish shop on the day in question. I followed that up today with an interview with the PC who had been in attendance. We now know that your client's alibi has more holes than a string vest.'

'Hearsay!' my brief condescended. 'Now, please, can we stop these diversions? Do you have any other questions that are backed up with evidence, or should we call a halt to proceedings? My client was seen on Good Friday by literally hundreds of people.'

'Oh. We have much more.' The Pigman never once looked at my solicitor. We were locked in.

Carl

Noxious fumes created a smoke screen. Hordes of gossiping islanders watched the flames, whilst an ice cream van – playing 'Greensleeves' – offered relief from the fiery atmosphere. Dazzled eyes took uz in. But this had nothing to do with me. Ah had to admit that watching the chip shop aglow, showing how to treat murderers, made sense. Except ah couldn't help thinking that the plumes were a cloud of shame. Despite a full-scale manhunt, he'd walked among us.

Yesterday, Carter wouldn't reveal who'd been nicked. But within an hour the Island's drums were beating about Anderson being missing. The press had hovered on broomsticks, and lying hindsight mystics hacked up bile about knowing all along that it was the chip shop owner.

It was disturbing and disorientating. When Mam went missing, ah thought of many woeful scenarios that were difficult to control. Scabby Mary's face had alternated with Mam's, and nothing made sense. Ad convinced meself that the yeti from next door was involved. But earlier Isaac had remembered that Mam had found Anderson new shops with restaurants. Dad said it was easily overlooked, as it was her job; she'd found properties for hundreds of clients. Dan had reminded us that she'd discovered new locations for our football coach, and he had links to owls. It would've taken ten thousand police to fully investigate every client.

The morning papers were full of it. Like small-minded crime novel writers, they were coming up with names for him: The Owl, Freddie the Fish, and Mr. Chips were but a few. The red-tops were desperately trying to pick "the winner". Ah wouldn't have been surprised if they'd run a competition to find the nation's favourite label.

The photographs boiled me head. One hack had even climbed onto the police station roof, smeared the window, and snapped the interview room. Most pictures showed his lock-up that ad walked past a thousand times. Inside were huge fridges, a van, and a metal locker containing scrapbooks about me Mam and other women. There was even the middle page spread of us at the football, where a hazy picture showed Anderson stood near Dan. He'd kept them all. Probably touched himself whilst reading them.

Ad been aggro but had just wanted to get inside the lock-up, read what he'd kept, get an idea of his secret life; not burn down the chippy. Invisible from the road, ah had tried to find a way, climbing walls and scaling roofs, but there were so many coppers that there was no chance. Ah couldn't see why some hack could take pics, whilst the family weren't allowed in. Ah supposed the only time ad see what he'd collected would be when he published a book. Who'd want to read that? Weirdos.

Fire engines obscured the sound of 'Greensleeves'. They primed to dowse the flames. Sweating under a T-shirt and tripping over a kerb, Big Eddie gave uz a shout. 'We were heading to yours,' he called. 'Can't believe it was that little fishy-smelling f...'

'Alreet, Eddie.' Everyone else had given uz a wide berth. It was good to talk, if only to escape me thoughts. Hoses unwound and yellow-helmeted firefighters created a clearing. 'Why were yer coming to mine?'

'Yer kna' John, don't yer?' Lagging and paler than milk was a lad with a quiff.

'Okay, mate?' ah said. A far cry from the blokes Eddie met for the match, ah knew John was one of Eddie's childhood pals. A year above uz, he was a great footballer, but ah only knew him to nod to. Dan knew him better, as they were into the same music, and he said he was a great lad. Years ago, he'd been caught in a fire and ah thought that's why he looked subdued. Mam had helped his family move once their house had been repaired.

Eddie held uz with a crocodile stare. 'We thought you should be the first t'know,' Eddie began as bursts of water hit the building and John exchanged a thumbs-up with a firefighter. The crowd jeered.

'What?'

'You know ah used to deliver milk?'

'Aye.'

'Well, John still does.' Ah looked at him; he'd turned his back to the flames. 'When news broke about Anderson, we got talking. John said something about seeing his van a few weeks back.'

Steam, like the breath of the devil, shushed the firewatchers, but Eddie's conversation held me attention. 'What yer on about?'

'It was more than once. There's not much on the roads, first thing,' John added, looking ill-at-ease. 'When we were on the Hill, his van exited the copse. My boss, Adam, said that it was Anderson, and, like him, he was into birds.'

'A horny-cunch-u-list,' Eddie remarked with authority.

'An ornithologist,' corrected John. 'A birdwatcher. We thought nothing of it. Then, when news broke, we thought, well, Eddie reckoned we should report it.' Eddie gave a firm nod and looked ready to outmuscle uz; ah was unsure why. 'My girlfriend's parents are coppers, so I asked their advice. Her dad said he's your pseudo-FLO's old Sarge. They took it dead seriously. We've come straight from the Nick. They interviewed me, Eddie, and Adam.' As the chip shop frazzled, worry moved into John's eyes.

'Ah think they're going to search the area. After watching loads of cop shows, ah reckon they think…'

Ah interrupted. 'Hear you loud and clear. They think Mam's there.' The switch in me head snapped but, before all hell broke loose, Big Eddie secured uz in a bone-rattling bear hug.

'We'll get yer brothers and go together, kid.'

The flames slowly dissolved.

Dad

Hearing my name across the Tannoy brought back memories from that awful Wolves game when she'd gone missing. I met Mr. Tanako in the car park, and he provided permission to leave mid-shift. With the deepest bow and me repeating, 'Thank you, Tanako-san,' it took forever for him to raise his head, which meant the loss of valuable seconds.

Carter was right: apart from Mr. Tanako's respects, things were moving quickly. On the drive to the copse, I sensed Donna's rotting body and involuntary guttural noises left my body. I thought of her so near, yet so far away. The last thing she would've felt were his hands around her neck, the taste of bitter soil, or the dreadful smell of fish.

Parked next to TV vans on the main road, I made way up the tree-lined path running parallel to electricity pylons. Donna loved walking here with the boys; she admired the formation of trees. The irony wasn't lost on me, especially when an outstretched owl created a silhouette. Being so close to nature provided many learning opportunities, she had said. Picnics and foraging had ensued over the years, as well as tree-climbing and numerous outdoor games. Amongst the thick foliage, a stain of journalists – cheek-by-jowl – were rubbernecking. With a crush of cameras on mounted tripods, they were ready to witness the most despicable game of hide-and-seek.

'Mr. McCarthy, do you think they will find Donna's body?' asked Peter David from the local rag. I hadn't forgiven him for his disgraceful articles about Carter and the police.

'No comment,' I replied, brushing him aside. There

were so many of them. How had they landed so quickly? Attracted to disaster like paperclips to a magnet, they were prophets of doom.

'Do you think they'll unearth the truth?'

'Can you believe a killer serves chips?'

'Have you heard that he was once pulled in as a Peeping Tom?'

I fiddled with my wedding ring, which I'm sure a photographer would've picked up. They were only doing their job, but surely they must've spoken to other victims' families. We were in the public eye and at the rawest edge of grief. Many times, I had thought of ending it all and all they wanted was a snap or insignificant quote. I felt like yelling: 'My children will spend their lives fighting with the word "*why?*".' Had they not considered the boys' fragility?

A flimsy barricade of bollards, staffed by James and Smyth, housed my boys and their friends. Suzie's face was in her palms, and I took her in my arms. Behind us, cameras clicked like chattering teeth. Unlike the journalists, most islanders had shown their respects by staying away.

Across the field, a canvas tent, akin to those seen at a scout's fate, stood in a sterile sun-puddle. Carter's unmissable shape hovered around the edges, with others in plastic overalls. A group of uniforms – with dogs – had made a line and stood at-ease to one side. 'Do you think this is it?' I asked Suzie.

'Part of me wants it to be,' she whispered. Although the boys could hear, they stared forward, looking too frightened to speak. 'Apparently the dogs picked up something.'

'Good.' There was nausea in my throat, but I didn't want my wife down there a minute longer. 'I know she said that she wanted to be cremated, but I want to give her a proper burial.'

Suzie squeezed my hand. 'I agree. Do it right. He won't have the last laugh.'

'He's nothing. Absolutely nothing. I feel sick that I spoke to him and spent money in his shop.'

'The chippy's been burned down.' Suzie said. I looked at Carl. 'Nothing to do with the lads. Some islanders took the law into their own hands.'

There was movement from the tent. The whole thing happened in slow-motion: a dark transit juddered across the field, the line of police with dogs made a wall, and Carter trudged slowly towards us. Surgically removed, we caught a nano-second of a stretcher being slotted into the transit. A gasp rattled, and for once, even the press seemed human. Like *Doctor Who*'s Tardis, a mob trickled from the tiny tent. Removing hoods, some wiped brows whilst others looked above.

Suzie and I swept up the boys. Their friends backed off. The metallic swirl from the pylons was the only sound. Carter drew close. He stopped and swallowed. He took the last few steps. I expected to smell the stolid stench of death, but there were only fresh fields. The cameras clicked once more. 'Can we rendezvous at your house, Simon? I will provide feedback on what we have discovered.'

The boys huddled. 'Tell us now, Carter. We need to know. Did you find Donna?'

He ran his hands over his face. 'We found an empty grave, four-foot deep, covered in sticks and bramble. The dogs picked up something not a stone's throw away. When the forensics dug up earth, they found another grave containing a body with matted hair, and...'

'And what, Carter?'

The world stopped.

'A neckerchief in her mouth.'

Dan

Carter had told us that it wasn't like in books and films. Mam's body would have to go to a forensic pathologist for an autopsy, whilst the evidence taken from the lock-up would be examined to the nth-degree, and, furthermore, the area around the copse and ginnel would be swept with a fine toothcomb. The grisly process could take weeks so that everything would stand up in court and Fredrick Anderson would never see the light of day again. Carter said that most fictional stories wouldn't reach court because of a lack of evidence, lack of professional procedure, and the recklessness of the detective's behaviour.

Hanging around made my teeth itch. Idle chatter about football, crop circles, and raves were quickly terminated; they weren't even half-hearted distractions. What we'd witnessed had knocked out any remaining stuffing.

On the street, a few thorny reporters remained. The others had scuttled off to their hotel for England's game. Despite the guitar on my back, they were unable to distinguish between us. 'Triplet, how's the atmosphere in the house?'

'Is there word from the pathologist?'

'Did you suspect The Owl?'

I left the estate, passing through the graveyard where courting couples created steamy windows during tonsil-pleasing sessions. Consumed with pain, I wanted a release, and considered running into a wall or cutting myself on railings. My agony was heightened because I wondered whether Fredrick Anderson had somehow infiltrated my sub-conscious. My story about "The Crow" when I'd first met Laura was bizarre. Had Mam's killer had the same ideas about being an owl? Had he sprung to the next level and carried out the fantasy? Was I like him? If so, I thought I'd dig a hole and join Mam.

Guilt about Coach Taylor was also strong. He had spoken to Aunt Suzie and explained that he'd arranged a pre-season charity match for Cancer Research. His mother, after a lengthy stay in Sunderland Hospital, had moved to a hospice; she was palliative. Every night he had visited before drowning his sorrows in Pete's parents' pub. Hill Hotspur had refused to stage a charity match a few summers ago, so that was why he had joined the Canaries. To rub salt into the wound – something I hadn't tried – they raised funds for Britain in Bloom instead. I understood his rage. How could I have thought that he'd hurt Mam? It was repellent. For weeks I'd thought that he was a stalker and his goal celebrations with Mam had been unfitting. How wrong could I have been? I'd even questioned his motives when he'd rescued me after being beaten up.

I had to make amends.

I caught a bus. The driver was surprised to see me and wouldn't accept a fare. Upstairs was empty, and the streets were also deserted. The country wasn't hooked on Mam's case, but on football. It meant that, on arriving in town, I was able to dart through the streets unnoticed.

The hospital engulfed the skyline, sprouting a gigantic cigar-shaped cylinder. Is that where body parts were burned? I knew that Mam was somewhere in the building, but I also knew that she'd be guarded under lock-and-key. It seemed a bit late for that.

When I arrived at the ward, a policeman stopped me. 'Sorry, you can't go in. Only people listed can pass.' I removed my guitar, hoping he'd recognise me like the bus driver. Nothing.

'It's one of the McCarthy boys,' a nurse with cropped blond hair said, tapping the policeman's arm. Shuffling, he looked more than uncomfortable. 'Sorry. I've seen your picture in the paper. I'm so sorry to hear the news of your mother.'

'News of your mother,' the PC echoed.

'Which one are you?' she asked.

'Dan.'

'Hello, Dan, I'm Staff Nurse Campbell. Can I help?'

'I've come to see Mary.' They looked at each other and swallowed in unison. I knew that visiting the girl who'd been attacked by the same person who'd murdered Mam would seem odd. But it made sense to me.

'Okay. She's with her parents, now. I'll speak to them and find out if that is something they'd want.' She straightened her uniform and left the policeman with me.

'Are you watching the match?' he asked. 'Think this our best chance since '66.' Even as he spoke, I could feel him cringe.

'Not bothered,' I replied.

'We've rigged up a telly. You're more than welcome to join us.' I moved my mouth into a shape, and he glowed.

The nurse returned with a couple who looked more like grandparents. 'Hello, young man, I am so sorry for what you've been through, particularly today. Our hearts go out to you and your family.' He paused. 'The nurse tells me that you'd like to see Mary.' His wife clung to him; she had the kindest eyes.

'I'm sorry to bother you,' I said, resting on my guitar. 'I'm so glad that Mary is alive. I know it sounds weird, but I'd like to see her, maybe sing her a song.' The little posse exchanged confused glances.

'You know what?' Mary's mother cooed, taking my hand. 'That sounds like a wonderful idea.'

'I know her, you know. Well… we went to primary school together. She wasn't called Ryan then, that's why it took a while for people on the Island to work out who she was. When we were little, some of us were nasty and called her Scabby Mary. She used to fall down a lot and make daisy chains. She used to play hopscotch by herself. I'm sorry. I'm so sorry.'

'That was before we adopted her, and you've got nothing to be sorry for,' her mother reassured. 'She's brought so much to our lives. Come on, Alan, we'll have a coffee, and this charming man can see Mary.' They smiled; even the policeman didn't fluff his lines.

I approached but had no remedy for her shattered skull. Held together with glue and what looked like the flimsiest paper, her head had been patched up. I pitied her pain; she'd been lucky to survive. Mam was somewhere in there, too, their faces interchangeable. I tuned the guitar, unsure what to play and strummed until I found The Beatles. Of course, Mother Mary came to me. To my surprise, tramlines of salty tears ran down her face. I stopped.

'Sorry, Mary. I didn't mean to upset you.' Her skeletal fingers patted the bed. For the briefest moment, her eyelids fluttered and bronze sunlight sparkled in her eyes before they slid away. A soft groan escaped and soon she was sleeping. Lyrics of my own appeared like they often did. *Girls with looks like yours / Were born to open doors / No matter how much he tried to fright / He'd never remove your light.*

Chapter 12: Death

Isaac

It was a distinctive hum, like stoned hornets wakening inside a twenty-tog duvet. The scooter wasn't only buzzing, it looked immaculate, too. Gathered on the back lawn, my family gave a round of applause, as I – with Sophia's hands around my waist – piloted the gate. My brothers rapped like John Barnes: '*Get round the back.*' Helmets removed, we gave a salute and Sophia's smile reflected in the chrome. I'd hoped that the mystery surrounding Mam would've been solved by the scooter's maiden voyage. With Anderson due in court the following day, I'd been proved correct.

Thankfully, I'd never mentioned my suspicions to Sophia about her dad. Plus, the mystery of the photographs and conversation between him and Stefano had also been solved. Sophia was going to own a bistro! He had told her that when Sorella, her aunties' restaurant, opened, he had met with Mam about arranging a venue for Sophia's future. Of course, he had hated keeping it secret and had asked Mam to do the same. That week they had visited premises with one of Mam's old colleagues. An empty shell, they had planned a grand opening for Sophia's eighteenth. With pride, he wanted to name the place "Sophia's", but she had her own plans. With it being Italian, and in memory of Mam, she'd decided on "Bella Donna" – "Beautiful Woman" in English. Tears had streamed from Mam's colleague. When Sophia told me, I was speechless; we decided not to enlighten the family until after the funeral.

England were semi-finalists, which meant that we'd cruised through empty streets. Sophia said that every television donned the suave TV presenter Des Lynam. Unfortunately, the World Cup had been background noise due to everything that'd happened. We'd been gripped by our own hysteria. My brothers had let Dad down when they hadn't turned up for the Holland game – and every match since had coincided with dreadful news – but we were all present for the showdown with Germany.

I used one of Mam's phrases when my brothers approached the brilliant bike. 'Eyes are for looking, not hands. Keep your distance.' They couldn't help themselves and offered congratulations, saying it was amazing. I couldn't have agreed more.

'Lovely bike, son. It's the dog's,' came a voice like sandpaper as a cigarette butt landed. Arriving with a dossier was DC Carter. Gathering evidence must've taken its toll as his skin was even more sallow and his eyes haggard. It'd been over a week since the arrest, and the police had been piecing together the life of Mr. Chips; the press wanted his heart on a platter. Monsters come in disguise, and he'd picked up victims through vague acquaintance. According to Carl's Criminology course, Mam's killer was a typically unimpressive sociopath who'd used his persona as a small businessman to catch prey.

'Drink?' Aunt Suzie asked the detective as I kicked away the fizzing cigarette.

'No, I'm on duty and I want to get back for the match. The girls are at my Mam's. It's cost a fortune getting them kitted out in England kits.'

'You want to try having triplet boys!' Dad laughed. 'The amount we've spent on football, me and the missus could've been holidaying in Barbados.' The mention of Mam was met warmly.

'Simon, I've got the testimony we've assembled. It'll be a while before any court case, as tomorrow's simply a formality, but it's important that you get your head around what'll be revealed.' Moving to the kitchen, a sheen of sweat covered Carter's face. 'Are you sure that you want everyone to see? It's not pleasant.' Carter's voice was on its last legs. He'd looked at Carl, well-aware of how combustible he could be. Dan and Aunt Suzie were more subdued, whilst Sophia had stayed outside, knowing it wasn't her place. Being the eldest, I stayed next to Dad at the table.

'Yes, we're in it together.'

'Right, we're far from done and dusted,' the detective began. 'Bearing in mind that we've had nine days, you can see the chunkiness of the document.' He held it up. 'This isn't a brief résumé: it's an unexpurgated account of everything we've gathered so far. Firstly, Fredrick Anderson hasn't said much, the shutters came down. What isn't in this report – as this all relates to Donna – is that since his arrest several women have come forward recounting attacks, sightings, and confrontations linked to a man in an owl's mask. Many are previously unreported historic crimes from as far back as the mid '70s. Obviously, the team is investigating each one. Also, since taking his DNA and sampling evidence in the lock-up, we are much more confident about how many, where, and when. The times and dates of these suspected incidents will be presented to court tomorrow, including a geographical pattern. Due to how long it takes to analyse DNA, we are blocking up the system; however, this is proving fruitful.'

'So, it's true what we've heard in the press? He's done this before?' Carl asked with fiery eyes.

'We believe so. We knew this wasn't an entry crime, due to the lack of evidence.'

Dad was flicking through the document but closed it when a harsh close-up made me wince: a skull fracture with colouring around the neck, and I was shocked at the preservation of Mam's body.

'We're dealing with an unpleasantly sour individual,' Carter continued, 'who has been totally focussed on his own satisfaction, carrying out the cruellest crimes. If I were you, I wouldn't get bogged down in the detail, but I must give you the opportunity to do so. It is filled with a sense of evil. I think that he's enjoying being thrust into the limelight.'

'Really?' Carl groaned.

'One thing he did say when we uncovered undeniable evidence about him digging the grave near the forensic site was that it was to observe birds. He's a keen ornithologist and tried to resemble a normal person. But, being a cold and calculated liar is easy when you've done what he's done. Rest assured; we've got him with bells-on.'

'Thank you, Carter. I'll come to the station to read this properly.' Dad handed back the report.

'Of course. When it goes to crown, your solicitor will arrange a synopsis.'

'Thank you. I'll view it in full, but not tonight.'

Dan

When Carter left, Dad did something unusual. He'd acted differently since the discovery of Mam's body. It was as if he'd walked out of a dark cloud. He was more like his old self, encouraging Isaac to finish the scooter, washing the Cosworth, and even repeating some of his old stories beginning with, 'When I was a lad…'

'I think the house has been too quiet.' He took Bowie's *Hunky Dory* CD from the pile. 'I think it's time we listened to a few tracks.' We breathed together. The house used to blare out music, but it had been too much of a reminder since she'd gone.

'Great idea,' sang Aunt Suzie. The weird opening to 'Changes' – funky, funny, sexy, and completely original – blasted away cobwebs. I can't speak for the others, but I felt Mam dancing, bringing us together. It was marvellous. Not only sound but light returned to our lives. By the time 'Kooks' had finished, we made our way to the front room for the National Anthem.

England's team looked formidable. Bobby Robson stood proudly in a grey suit, and, for once the Germans didn't have the upper hand. We had more than a chance. 'You boys relax; Sophia and I will get drinks,' Suzie said. Surprisingly, Carl said that he didn't want alcohol.

England were the better team. Gascoigne had a great drive saved early doors, and we stayed on top for the majority of the first half with the Germans forced into shots from a distance. Dad had been right about watching the football together. It was something we did. Yes, it was where we'd first heard the terrible news, but shouting and being with each other was cathartic. It was like being stuck back together. *We're joined by something strong / Something brewed in song / Something that hurt but bound / Something lost and found.*

At half time, Carl wandered around whilst the rest of us admired Isaac's dream-machine. At the start of the second half, the Germans were stronger, forcing errors. Not long after, they scored when a wicked deflection sent the ball looping over Shilton. Instead of their head's dropping, Robson's men raised their game. There were a few great chances, and a penalty shout for a foul on Waddle saw us hit the ceiling. With ten minutes to go, Lineker notched. The game was heading to extra time. Inevitably, penalties arrived, but not before Gascoigne was booked, Waddle hit the post, and Platt had a goal disallowed for a dubious off-side. Carl said that he couldn't watch and went into the garden. The tension was unbelievable, especially for us, as for once it didn't centre around Mam. I told Carl that I'd give him a shout – one way or the other – when it was over. The Germans were ruthless, and when Waddle missed, England were out. Bobby Robson had the same resigned look as Dad's when Mam's body was exhumed.

Sophia hugged Isaac and they cried with Gascoigne; Aunt Suzie and Dad did the same. I left to break the news to Carl. Outside, he was nowhere to be seen. The gate was open, and I thought he may have headed onto the street. Then, I stopped. Froze. Tendons tightened. My tongue went sour. I closed my eyes. Had I dreamt that? He couldn't have. No. I turned on my heels. I was right.

Isaac's scooter was missing.

What was he playing at?

Back inside, preparing themselves for the post-match interviews, Dad and Aunt Suzie were captivated. 'Carl's gone to Zoë's to drown his sorrows,' I lied.

'I hope she'll see him. I'm sure she will,' Aunt Suzie said with a smile. I signalled to Isaac to join me outside.

'What is it?' I held my hands open and widened my

eyes. 'What! What in God's name!' Isaac circled the spot where the scooter had been. 'Has he really gone to Zoë's? Did you see him leave?'

'No, I just made it up because he's gone with the scooter.' We headed onto the street, looking around, hoping he'd miraculously reappear.

'I didn't hear the revving engine. How did he slink away?' Isaac said through gritted teeth.

'I thought it was strange when he didn't want a drink,' Sophia added.

'And him not watching the penalties. I put it down to the pressure we've been under, but in the past he would've called someone soft for not being able to look. He's been odder than usual,' I concluded.

'If he messes up my bike, I'll deck him. He knows it's taken months.'

We went into the garden. 'Oh, no,' Isaac groaned, as if he'd walked into an invisible wall. 'I didn't think it could get worse.' Following his eyeline, I saw that one of the paving stones had been removed; it was skewed at a peculiar angle.

'What is it?' Sophia asked.

'That's where I hid the gun. He's got the gun, Dan.'

Blue fog filled my head; we were back on the helter-skelter. And Isaac had blurted our deepest secret in front of Sophia.

'Gun! What are you talking about... gun?' Sophia's voice was filled with trepidation.

I didn't have a sixth sense, but I knew what Carl was like when the madness kicked in. 'Look, I'll go to Sophia's,' Isaac said, entering planning-mode. 'It'll explain the missing scooter. Tell Dad I've let her have a first ride, as I've been drinking. We'll have to be first at court tomorrow to stop him.'

'You need to inform the police, tell Carter!' Sophia

blurted.

'We can't dob our brother in it,' Isaac scolded with conviction. 'But I'll tell you everything, Sophia. I promise,' his voice grew softer.

Once they'd left, I fed the lie to Dad and Aunt Suzie, who were crying at Pavarotti's 'Nessun Dorma'. I hoped they wouldn't be crying about something more serious the following day.

Carl

The cobbled alleyway was quiet. There was no one around. With the scooter hidden for a quick getaway, ah enjoyed the peace. Cold against me thigh, the gun's metal was in sharp contrast to the warm breeze. Ad spent all night fantasising about a bullet going through his head or balls; it'd be a lovely day for him to die. What he'd done had filled uz with hate. Was revenge the answer, or was revenge for mugs? There was only one way to find out.

Up the alleyway, outside the corner shop, the newspaper stands shouted: 'England out; Gazza's Tears,' and, 'Exclusive with: Girl battered by Mr Chips.' Dan had told us that he had been visiting Scabby Mary, and the press had taken their photo. What a scoop: the son of a murdered woman with the one who'd got away. Dan spoke about Mary as his new squeeze. With that phoney Laura out of the way, he'd gone from someone more damaged than a broken window to someone more damaged than a bombed house.

Ah hadn't told anyone that ad thought about Mary and Mam, their faces interchangeable, like they were the same person. Only after she'd become the next victim did ah see it as a premonition. How else would ah have known? Ah had the same vividness when ah thought about the bullet going into Anderson. It'd be too difficult to get near enough to kill him with me bare hands. That was me real fantasy. Up close and personal, just me and him, me face being the last thing he'd see. Ah wish ad had time to practise, but ad known that gunshots would've drawn the police like alcoholics to a free bar, so ah gave it a miss.

Ah heard the throng before ah saw it. When ah stepped from the cobbles onto asphalt, ah realised there was little distance between isolation and a seething mass. Me heart sunk. Outside the court were hundreds more people than ad imagined. Not only was there a congregation for Mam, but there was a crowd for the first of the Poll Tax cases – loony lefties, extreme right-wingers, and everything in between – pocketed into islands by criss-crossing police tape.

Big Eddie was there, moving his head like a searchlight. It made uz duck behind a group of women who had flasks and a Tupperware box of sandwiches, ready for the day's entertainment. Little did they know they'd get more than their monies worth. A scrum of Geordie peacocks and thuggish blokes gathered around Eddie, many holding anti-Poll Tax slogans. Amongst the mix, ah saw me brothers. Me anger blazed. They must've headed to me mate when they'd noticed the gun was missing. Ah guessed it was there when ah stood in the garden. Why would Isaac have a wobbly flagstone unless something was buried below? Near the court steps, running the gauntlet of reporters, Dad and Aunt Suzie looked pensive.

Ah knew ad only get one shot at salvation.

In me head, ah saw another premonition of a news report about a shooting; the sweet smell of cordite would soon fill the air. There was no turning back. Suddenly, the knot of Poll Tax protesters hugging the court began to loosen whilst the overrun police worked doubly hard to create a channel. That's when the van door opened to a chorus of boos. Leaving the women behind, ah ran towards the courthouse shrieking, 'Die. Die. Die!' just like ad heard on the television when the Yorkshire Ripper had been taken into court. Anderson had sawn our lives in two, and when ah saw him, ah yanked the gun from me waistband.

'Gun. Gun!' The shout was as loud as a bullet. The

press broke from their trance. Dad gawped. Anderson was smothered by the police. Me chance was gone. For less than a second, me eyes met the bottomless swampy holes in his head. Ah hadn't been quick enough.

The day was one notch away from chaos. Big Eddie was almost on top of uz. Ah gave him a don't mess with me face, but he looked bigger than the Canaries' new changing rooms. He secured me in a chokehold, and we wormed to the floor. The gun slithered through me fingers. Surrounded by expensive trainers and a forest of legs, ah was drowned into the masses. Instantly, Dan and Isaac's faces were next to mine. 'Stop, Carl, the police are coming!' Like a skyrocket, the fuel leaked, leaving nothing but embers of regret. Then there were a pair of familiar legs. Gazing up, Zoë was looking down, her tears dripping onto my face. I tried to speak, to say something, to make everything better, but there was nothing.

Dragged to me feet, ah was stunned. The police were smiling. What was going on? Then ah saw the football hooligan come anti-Poll Taxers squirting water-pistols into the air, shouting: 'Gun, Gun, shoot down the tax!' The chant changed when Anderson belatedly made way into court: 'Chop him up, cut him up, and stick him in the freezer.' The officers' expression changed, but their eyes displayed their true feelings. Zoë shuddered and couldn't look at uz. Ad blown it and knew that revenge was indeed for mugs. Over her head, ah saw Blind-Boy Bob hotfooting with his sister in her wheelchair towards the backstreets.

Then, there was a shout from the police: 'Man down!'

DC Carter

I hadn't slept since we'd caught Anderson. Interviewing a murder suspect is the ultimate game of cat-and-mouse. The pressure is immeasurable.

I had felt old and wheezy.

I had felt the ache in my chest.

I had felt the shooting pain through my arm.

I had bathed in the waterfall of sweat.

I had felt light-headed.

I'd just put it down to the stress of the game. The more evidence that Quick and the overworked lab technicians exposed should've eased any stinging doubt about Anderson. But I was desperate to nail him and not to leave any legal loopholes. Unable to gather clues on the Dead-Babies case and losing the missing football hooligan had taken its toll. I had to get this one right. Had I put myself under too much pressure?

I had an eye on Dan and Isaac, who were amongst some unscrupulous looking specimens, with little Zoë looking racked with worry. When the call of 'GUN!' went up, something snapped. I dropped my cigarette and orange sparks scattered like fireflies before resurfacing behind my eyes. Already drowsy, my chin dropped to my chest. As I viewed my overhanging belly, it felt as though an electric razor was pressed on full speed inside my breast pocket. Terror-stricken, I watched water squirting from toy pistols. The calls about a gun had been bogus. Clint Eastwood would've pulled his .44 Magnum, but I was no hero, and it was too late for me; the horse had bolted.

I became a fallen tree. Wobbling and waiting for the final shout of timber, I – without protest – felt dark asphalt cushion my collapse. Stunned by pain, I cursed the bone-deep fatigue.

From nowhere, my old Sarge was there. Through the fogginess I felt him carrying out our training – checking ABC – telling me that I was going nowhere and there'd soon be an ambulance. One second, I felt colder than a snowstorm, the next red-hot irons nipped my skin. Despite Sarge creating space, it was like a foot had pinned my chest.

The severity of the situation was impossible to ignore. I felt one heartbeat away from never seeing Sammy and Caz again. Thoughts of feeding them in their highchair, pushing them on swings, and watching a frenzied dance routine caused fluctuations. Sarge was stroking my brow and telling me to be calm, but everything squealed towards an inevitable end. 'Come on, Neil. Come on, son. Don't be a total cliché and die on the job. We need you, lad.'

I saw myself in a shallow pit with Mrs. McCarthy, my mouth drought dry as the ambulance's siren squawked its final whine. I watched the sun's inefficiency as its light lolled and grew colder.

Killer

The stupid names that they called me: Mr. Chips, The Owl, Freddie the Fish. It was a travesty and showed no respect. I saw myself as Ah Puch – the Mayan God of Death – who was depicted as an owl. Whenever the Mayans heard a hoot, they knew that death was near. When I'd write my memoirs, that's what I'd call them: Ah Puch – God of Death.

The courtroom was a fiasco. When there'd been a shout of 'Gun!' the police had chucked me back into the van with sadistic glee. Providing unnecessary digs on the metal floor, they had offered no apology and claimed that it was for my own safety. Of course, the catcalls had been delivered by idiots. The protesters should've been taking direct action instead of acting up, squirting water pistols and singing silly songs. That's the problem with this world; not enough people stand by their actions with conviction. Having said that, I had pleaded "not guilty". But I had shocked the court. I can just imagine what the press made of my speech: *Owls with dark brown or black eyes prefer to hunt at night; owls with orange eyes are active at low light, such as dusk and dawn; whilst owls with yellow eyes hunt during the day.* It was a shimmy of gold dust that would add to my legend.

My solicitor had told me that there'd been a problem with Pigman Carter. With his expertise for ballsing things up, I was surprised at how accurate he had been during interviews. Sometimes he had tried to humiliate and others he had been friendlier, with tales from the Island. In my head, I could hear the exit music and knew there'd be no new ladies, so I had no idea why he had been so visibly distressed. Some people just don't know when they're winning.

Sure as ever, the freakish Pearson was present, flapping panicked eyelashes. When Quick arrived – carved from plastic like a gameshow host – I couldn't have been happier. Easier to intimidate than Carter, I looked forward to reminiscing. 'Good morning, Mr. Anderson,' he began. 'The accused is joined by his solicitor, Mr. Drummond, and he will be interviewed today by myself, DI Quick, and DS Pearson.'

'How's Carter? He mustn't be good if he isn't here. I think the only enjoyment he has in life is talking to me,' I said, and Pearson almost fell from her chair. In all the hours that we'd spent together, I'd uttered less than fifty words. Drummond was in my ear recommending that I say nothing.

'DC Carter is fine, thank you. I'm sure you'll see him soon,' Quick replied. Whilst shuffling paper, a stray hair fell onto his forehead. 'I don't think he'll stay away for long,' he concluded with a disingenuous grin.

'Okay,' Quick continued, 'I will outline the five murders to which you've pleaded "not guilty". The evidence gathered from your lock-up exposed newspaper cuttings and videos linked directly to these crimes. We have, therefore, employed forensics to investigate. With advancements in scientific research, we have been able to link you to these women through evidence preserved from the scenes. Shall we begin?'

I nodded and Drummond adjusted his tie.

'Sally Dixon aged seventeen at Seahouses, Northumberland, on June the sixteenth, 1982. As you're aware, we have re-examined clothing from the scenes belonging to all victims. We have found your DNA – in the form of semen – at scene one on Miss Dixon's kilt, and the pin found on your person is a perfect match with the afore mentioned garment.' Images of that bewitching little sprite forever played on my mind. 'We found that you collected fish from the harbour, which is adjacent to the petrol station where she worked.'

His words were turning up some ghosts.

'Louise Jones aged twenty-one at Craster, Northumberland, on July thirteenth, 1985. Once again, a semen DNA match to yourself was found on her clothing, this time on her underwear, and, in your lock-up, we found an engagement ring that her fiancé – from that date – confirmed as belonging to her.' I'd made her special with my treatment, and she'd looked more frightened than any other. 'She was a barmaid in a pub less than one-hundred-yards from a campsite where you frequent.'

I remembered watching her pulling my pint of Guinness, good grip on the pump, nice and steady.

'Sarah Church aged twenty-five from Cramlington, found burned at Blyth, Northumberland, on June fifteenth, 1988. Although no DNA was recovered, the head wounds are consistent with Dixon and Jones. Once again, in your lock-up we found one of her possessions: a pair of emerald earrings given to her by her mother. She worked at a supermarket check-out where your elder sisters are employed.'

Burn baby, burn. The stench had made me retch; I remembered being mesmerised by the flames and crackling skin.

'Kelly Swan aged thirty from Cullercoats, Tyne and Wear, and found in North Shields with the same MO as Sarah Church on April sixteenth, 1989. A bracelet belonging to her was found in your lock-up.' That was my last burning. It brought too much attention, and I hated smelling a lady in flames; fires weren't right. I preferred Sally and Louise's glassy eyes. 'She taught at Whitley Bay High School and arranged career opportunities for pupils, allocating placements at the fishmongers where you have a contract.'

I recalled recording the school-children's vigil on the television, the tape was kept in Aladdin's Cave.

'Donna McCarthy aged thirty-eight from the Island, Tyne and Wear, found in a shallow grave. Her DNA was recovered from an unused freezer at your lock-up. The autopsy also revealed a major skull fracture and a snapped hyoid bone. The examiner states that it is wholly consistent with the other murders, and wooden shards from the victim correspond with those taken from a weapon in your lock-up.' Donna: what a chase! I loved watching her family fall apart afterwards; it showed the brilliance of my work. 'She located premises for your company in her role as an estate agent.'

I glowered at the detectives, dreaming of throttling Pearson. They had no right to have my property. I'd earned it, and they'd given me so much pleasure. What would happen to them? Stuffed on a shelf in a darkened room when they could be with me. But I knew how to wear a mask, and they had no clue what I was thinking.

'What we can't understand is the change in MO: why did you break the pattern? We found several different panels to hide the words on your van. Why weren't they attached? We presume that these would be assembled prior to an assault. Did you forget on Sunday? As you know from the library of books about other killers from your lock-up, murderers feel more confident the more they get away with it,' Pearson interjected. 'What we don't get is how someone as cold and calculating could reveal himself in such an open way as you did with the sloppy attempted abduction of Mary Ryan.'

'My client denies any involvement in that crime – in all of these crimes.' The truth was that I'd taken the bait. Seeing Sally again had been too much. Unfortunately, she did not receive my coup de grâce, but I knew that the "Son of Sam" and Ted Bundy had been caught stupidly, so I was in good company.

'Miss Ryan's head wound is the same as all five murders. And the tyre prints from the field match your van. Wooden fibres from Mary Ryan's wound match the aforementioned weapon. There's much to discuss.'

'The thrust of today's interview,' Quick said with a little too much relish, 'is looking back, starting from Mary Ryan, at thirty-six different assaults between 1973 and 1990, and discovering the journey of your MO.'

I belted in, ready to listen to my greatest hits, some of which had annihilated skulls.

DI Quick

What were their names? I recognised them from the newspaper and the picture on his desk. Pammy and Cat... that didn't sound right. Being a DI who's been interviewing a murder suspect affects memory. Anyhow, Carter's kids looked happy as they danced by, which meant that Carter was on the mend. I didn't know his ex-wife's name, so smiled silently as our paths crossed. She looked stumped and drawn.

Anyone meeting Carter would know that he was precisely the kind of officer who'd collapse with a cardiac arrest in the line of duty. To be fair, he had that old twinkle in his eye, but the hippo-like body didn't require wires going in-and-out to let me know that he needed a lifestyle overhaul. There were many things I'd grown to admire about Carter, but I promised that I'd never let myself "go" to such an extent. To begin with there'd been no love lost, but he'd worked tirelessly for the McCarthys. I had once been on a course on how to recall personal details. Carter could do that in his sleep. The way the McCarthys trusted him was commendable, whilst I couldn't even remember his children's names.

'To what do I owe the pleasure?' he asked with the thrill of an amateur dramatist.

'Your girls look chipper.'

'Sammy and Caz?' I registered his words. 'They were scared to begin with, but I tickled them and told them a few tales. Can't wait to take them on holiday.'

'Was that your ex?'

'By, you never stop being a detective, Quick – great deduction skills!' I preferred how we were now. I'd been wrong about him and had told him on several occasions. To be honest, I trusted him more than anyone else on the force, including Pearson. 'What's in the bag?'

I emptied a load of procedural crime novels. 'The lads gathered these. They say you need to read them to become a better detective.'

'Think their bull might see me off for good. By the way, if our case had been a crime novel, it'd now flap open onto a page which would solve the Dead-Babies case,' he sniggered, picking up a book as if it were diseased. 'Stories are stuffed with death, serial killers, and police being murdered, but in the real world they're still as rare as hen's teeth. This might be the only multiple case you work on, Quick.'

'I hope so.'

'Has he said anything... The Owl?'

'Not a dicky-bird.'

'Some of these sickos sing like canaries, whilst others' mouths are shut tighter than a penguin's backside.' It was great to hear his humour return. A few days earlier, I thought he was going the way of the dodo. 'Listen, you've done an amazing job with the DNA. You were the one who used your algorithms to work out that he could've been responsible for those unsolved murders. Then hey presto, they're in his infamous scrapbook. Checking back on DNA evidence from years ago was a master stroke; it proves his guilt. More families will get some peace. And you'll go down as the one who uncovered a serial killer.' He held up his palms and bowed like he was not worthy.

'I just wish we could've caught him sooner. He was in plain sight, on the Island. A juvenile record for being a Peeping Tom, and Donna McCarthy finding his premises on the Hill when he'd bought his new shop.'

'Look,' he said, growing more philosophical, 'most of a murder investigation is spent looking in the wrong place, and we didn't exactly have a truckload of witnesses queueing up. In fact, he had half of the Island as an alibi. Walking up and down the terraces offering free mushy peas just after he'd taken her.'

'Mrs. McCarthy's DNA was inside an unused chest freezer.' I felt a chill in my spine. 'I reckon he must've taken her, whizzed around to the lock-up and dumped her, gone back to work, and returned later and moved her to the burial site. What a great alibi, though. Everyone saw him. But how could he behave normally?'

Carter nodded. 'We wouldn't be able to surmise if we didn't have proof that she'd been in there. He'll never see the light of day again. He put those women through the most dreadful things imaginable. It proves his callousness to even think of an alibi.' I toppled over the books and sat down. 'How's the young lass?'

'Doing well. They've patched her up.' I shuffled free from the final book and handed it to Carter.

'This writer,' he said holding up the book, 'would have made sure that the victim wasn't Mary, but one of the McCarthy boys' girlfriends. Probably the one who deserved it most, so it wasn't as bad as the mother dying.'

'I wish I knew why he'd done it.'

'It's a who-dunnit, not a why-dunnit,' Carter croaked, which coloured his doomed complexion.

'Calm down, Neil,' I replied, feeling a groan in my gut.

'Pass me a drink, would you?' he asked. I poured a glass of water, and he took a sip. 'Look, academics will come out of the woodwork with a multitude of reasons, like the devil drove him or something, when it's just some nutter doing it for fun. He's a woman hating bully. I couldn't give a monkey's whether someone abused him, or if he was forced to live in a cage. There's nothing to say. People will want quotes so they can stick them in a book like he's a street poet. They'll look for the excuses for his depraved acts. Him simply being a cold-blooded murderer won't fit their sick narrative. Face it, children who survived the Concentration Camps haven't gone on to become serial killers, and they saw the worst things imaginable. What could be his excuse?' I considered what he'd said, but something must have driven Anderson to murder. 'Look, I've smoked a suicidal number of cigarettes and have had a heart attack. I had a choice, just like he did. We've got him and he'll say nothing. But he'll wax lyrical to a journalist, like that troublemaker Peter David, with the switch stuck on self-absorbed repeat. Remember, Anderson had a choice that he gave to none of his victims. He didn't have to murder those women and wreck those families' lives.'

I memorised that for the next interview.

Carl

Ah decided to walk through the sun-infected air. The rest of me family would arrive in shiny black cars, and ad be there to greet them. The congregation drooped like their muscles had withered in the heat. Ah debated whether they would've turned up if she hadn't been murdered. Carter was propped up by his old Sarge who wore the smartest police uniform ad ever seen. Ah exchanged nods with the copper ad chinned – his hair was like whipped cream. 'How are yer, Carter?'

'I'm fine, kid. Thanks for asking. How are you?' He took my hand.

'Dunno.' Me heart pounded. 'There's so many people here.' It looked like one of those Lowry paintings: small, faceless groups shuffling at the cemetery gates. Dan's band, kids from school, blokes from the car factory, the Italians and scooter-boys from the pizzeria, the football lads, loads of coppers, old miners, Mam's colleagues (some wearing neckerchiefs), folks from the caravan site, and even Wild Bill. No one had gone through.

'Anything you need, just ask.'

'Thanks for everything, Carter.' Ah moved from his grip and looked at the chapel door where the undertakers' suits contrasted with the Minister's white. Ah swallowed hard, knowing that ad soon be following a coffin.

From the Wagon Way, Big Eddie approached. Freshly cut grass filled me senses, and bees hovered around the bluebells and wildflowers. He hugged uz with all his might and was already blubbering. 'This is terrible, mate. Ah dunno what to say.'

'Thought you were away on duty.'

'Army says it could be Belfast instead of Africa. They've given uz the jabs, so ah hope it'll be the big continent. Would love to see a tiger in the wild. People keep talking about The Gulf, though – whatever that is.'

Some lights flashed and ah realised that the gentlemen of the press were showing their usual decorum. Of course, ad met some serious journalists – those who'd reported Mam's death in-depth, with the human suffering at its heart – the opposite to what passed as news for these sensationalist soundbite merchants. Eddie must've noticed uz flinch.

'Do you want thum sorting?'

'No, Eddie,' ah said sullenly. 'Nee bother today.'

'Of course, mate.' But he gave them a lens-breaking stare.

'It would've been different if yer hadn't stopped uz at the court.'

Eddie checked that no one could overhear. 'Ah get it. But there were hundreds of people around and loads of police. Yer not like Hotshot Hesla at the barracks. On his way to being a sniper that one. Even he would've found it hard to hit that little fishy chipper from where you were. Imagine if you'd shot someone else's mam?'

Ah straightened me tie. 'Ah know. It was crazy. Still wish he was dead, though. Can't imagine that'll ever change.' Eddie's hand was on me shoulder. 'You watch loads of cop shows, don't yer?'

'Aye,' he replied, questioningly.

'Ah keep thinking about those scenes from a thousand films when someone inside comes to a relative's funeral handcuffed to a guard. That could've been me for prancing about like a movie star with a shooter.' He nodded in recognition. 'That would've taken all the emphasis off Mam.'

'Always consequences, always.'

'Where's the gun now? Thought ah saw Blind-Boy Bob away with his sister when it went missing.'

'As if ad tell yer! Anyhow, Bob and the boys have been locked up. Got caught causing criminal damage during the Poll Tax protest in town. They tried to nick a police horse and were tooled-up. Not with your gun, though. With their records, they were banged up straight away on remand.'

'Bloody hell.'

Without warning, the congregation moved as if in a trance, allowing the hearse to funnel through. Taking a lead, ah joined the head undertaker as he slow-marched – silver-tipped cane in hand – through the gates, leaving Eddie behind. Each step, ah fought against the imminent inner collapse, but somehow made it. Inside me suit it was hotter than an oven.

There'd been a debate whether we should carry Mam's coffin, but, in the end, we left it to the professionals. I walked between Isaac and Sophia, who held me hands as we followed Dad and Aunt Suzie. Fortunately, me brother hadn't given uz the hard time ah deserved for taking the scooter. Later that week, Isaac and Sophia were going on a coffee-date.

Behind uz, Dan was with Mary. She wore a hat to hide the scars. She'd been lucky with a cerebral-edema and a subdural-hematoma, and was in long-term recovery for the mental injuries. Ah found it difficult to speak to her. Ah couldn't explain why ad thought of her as a victim after Mam had gone missing. It was too weird, the whole scenario messed with me brain. Was it really a premonition? However, the best thing had happened the day before. Laura had turned up to ask if she could join Dan at the funeral. Stood with Mary at the front door, he casually shut it on the star-screwer's face, kissed his new girlfriend, and asked for an update on her pain score.

At the graveside, the Minister preached about God, forgiveness, resurrection, and redemption. But me Dad's words, a broken man who had been buried in depression, were what struck a chord. He talked about the song 'Nessun Dorma', the theme-tune for the World Cup, and how the lyrics were for us. He explained that Nessun Dorma meant "*none shall sleep*". He clarified how difficult it is to close your eyes when love is demolished, and described how the words about the princess in her cold room related to Mam in her temporary grave. He closed with how love would win, and how the darkness (the night in the song) departed when we brought her home to a safe place. It was beautifully healing. Ad never listen to that song without me heart being lodged in me throat.

Through misted eyes, ah noticed Zoë framed between her parents, tears streaming. Ah wanted to feel her pressing shoulder blades and cradle her. She attempted a smile which broke her in two. That's when ah saw the light: love is more important than hate.

Always.

Ah needed her more than ah wanted to hurt Anderson.

Ah wanted to soothe her, despite me own pain.

Ah hoped our relationship had a little life in it yet.

As they lowered the coffin, ah focussed on Mam's graveside picture. She smiled in a way which showed that all that mattered was you. Desperately, ah wished she was alive. The hole that was left was larger than a thousand graves. I imagined her telling me how to win back Zoë.

Suddenly, a scream louder than a parliament of owls screeched, as if the flock had showed up in support of Anderson. But it was just Dan adjusting the speaker. It settled to the opening bars of 'Nessun Dorma'. Me heart shattered. Me brothers and I stopped each other from falling. Three peas in a pod, Mam would've said, always there for each other.

Killer

I'm an artist, not an artisan. Those around me in the canteen obviously realised that they had accomplished nothing compared to me. My achievements had surpassed all with their proficiency and precision. But the comedown of being inside was worse than a post-operation lull. My brief – Drummond – reckoned that we could claim that the evidence was contaminated, as most of it had been stored before DNA was even a thing. There was a glimmer of hope, especially with so few of my DNA components being identified.

I remembered the evenings when I had tracked Sally amongst the sand dunes, watching her pout as her boyfriends climaxed. Everyone who'd gone before me had said: 'the past is a place you cannot revisit (but we all try).' Being a dogmatic planner had served me well, yet I'd ripped up the rule book. I cursed how I had become an opportunist because of Mary's resemblance to Sally (unfortunately not a dead-ringer due to a hesitant deathblow).

Reading the faces of row upon row of skeletal and porky caged animals, the grapevine remained fanatic. Despite the overcrowding, all eyes were on me. Fortuitously, the screws were no different. I'd have made the perfect prize for a violent wannabe. Being the star of the show was a role that I grudgingly accepted.

A fine balance of bubbling acid and flammable fumes was the only way to describe the atmosphere. The already gluttonous prison had been filled to bursting with Thatcher's Poll Tax protesters. All that was needed was a match up its gaseous backside to blow the place to Kingdom Come. And, like an owl attack, there was no warning. Taking a tray, a big ponytailed bloke whacked someone on the back of the head. The screws scattered with hands on their keys, the posse leapt onto tables yanking wires from CCTV, all to the accompaniment of literal and metaphoric alarm. Chair legs and masonry magically appeared. Prisoners banged balconies, with – judging by the tone – a variety of implements. It was difficult to say which was worse: the racket or lawlessness? As the crew smashed everything in sight, utensils and cups were hurled. From the kitchens emerged the stench of burning fat. Violent or fearful herds concealed themselves amongst the shadowy edge of the concrete jungle. My principal thought was to get out. The whole prison was in lockdown: the lunatics had taken over the asylum. I liked being in control, and this was far from it.

Darkness.

All lights were out. They say the jungle comes alive at night. Without doubt, the noise was animalistic. A Tannoy shrilled with no answer and the first random scream was heard – soon followed by the second and then third as scores were settled. The inmate next to me was caked in fetid horror, whilst anxious breaths heaved nearby.

My long-term plan was to use my culinary skills in the prison's kitchen. Luckily, I'd done a recce and had scanned the area when collecting food. Uppermost in my mind was to get through the trial unscathed, keep my head down, and lure them into a false sense of security before arming myself to the teeth.

Flames from the kitchen provided hazy light. Like forest animals, prisoners scattered from the blaze. Sensing an opening, I headed into the smoke. If any of those chancers fancied a ruck, this would be the time to find a weapon.

The sprinklers erupted, creating a blur of steam. I had

a feeling that I was not the predator but prey and gathered a rolling pin from a work surface. All senses were ready to react. There were no rattling keys and I'd die before running from another prisoner, so I chose to fight. The warm wood in my hand felt like my old sawn-off baseball bat. They wouldn't know what'd hit them; I'd batter their confidence into submission. They'd feel the fear. Rooted to the spot, I tried to locate the direction of attack.

From behind, a shackle wrapped around my neck. Wrenched to the floor, I swung my weapon until I had to drop it to tug the chain. It wouldn't slacken, and my eyes bulged from their sockets. On the floor, a succession of kicks and punches teemed-in, and the metal was tossed into the embers of a burning bin. Skin flapped from my face, and I wondered what sort of disfigurement I'd inherit if they didn't pummel me to death. They were bloodthirsty and committed, and my teeth whittled on a metal cabinet, skittling to the floor.

They spun me over and sprinkling water stung my exposed cheekbone. Trying to make eye contact for a revenge mission, I stayed conscious. Unsure whether it was real, a pirate in an eye-patch looked down. On his hands were Yin-Yang tattoos which made me think that I was dreaming. Harmony. Karma. Reap what you sow. Hilarity. 'We're going to chop you up, cut you up, and stick you in the freezer!' Creating a snail's trail of blood, they dragged me over wet tiles; there must've been three or four of them. Still, I felt no fear, my heartbeat consistent.

Abruptly there was a huge clunk and the Tannoy told everyone to stand still. The bang of shields let me know that the screws were attempting a raid, but, judging by the commotion, the criminals were in for the long haul. 'Bloody hell,' said one of my abductors, 'we need to be quick.' I spat out a wedge of blood. Taking my limbs, they picked me up. 'We need to cut his balls off.' The last thing I saw were flames and the bin's melted plastic before they stuck my face into it, a boot on the back of my head.

Strengthening in colour and definition from the bonfire of my own private hell, a handful of ladies' faces beckoned before their beauty distorted and decomposed. From within stemmed an appalling scream.

Then she was there.

She was always there, with huge owl-eyes.

My trousers slackened and I heard the scrape of sandpaper.

Epilogue

Peter

The whole congregation had stayed tight-lipped. Their reluctance to discuss anything had been shocking, no doubt instigated by that fool Carter. Having the temerity to claim success for catching Anderson, I had written a double-paged spread about police inadequacy. The editor had held it back until after the funeral. I would be on his case to print. Reminding people of Carter's dereliction of duty on the Dead-Babies case, and his recent heart attack, might force a removal from the force – now, that would be a scoop!

Following the funeral, I'd spent the day in the field where Donna McCarthy's body had been found. Sending a crime correspondent to look at crop circles was a first. The editor had thought it was ironic that they should appear on the day of the funeral. I hoped we'd find a parked UFO. It'd be as likely as council house associated vermin carving artistic designs. Anyhow, I thought it'd curry favour for the article, so I had delivered three-hundred words, but the aerial photos told the real story.

Arriving home, the phone was ringing. I ignored it and made a cuppa, but I couldn't unwind; the thing drummed off the hinges. 'Hello, Peter David.'

'Pete, it's Leo. Where've you been? You need to get to the prison. There's a riot going on. All hell's broken loose.' It took a few seconds to digest his words. 'There's fires, and the anti-riot officers were beaten back.'

'Bloody hell,' I said, spilling tea.

'Two bodies of Section-45 prisoners have been chucked out. They're alive but the paramedics can't get near them. The inmates are burning clothes, running around semi-naked. The governor reckons it's to get rid of evidence. They've learned from Strangeways.'

'Two bodies? Any prison officers hurt?'

'Oh, it beats that. There's another one.' As a crime correspondent, I couldn't imagine anything better. 'It's unconfirmed, but they reckon there's a body inside a chest freezer. Word is that it's Fredrick Anderson, and you should see what they've done to him.'

'I'm on my way.'

Acknowledgements

This book could not have been written without the love and support of my wife, Nikie, my fabulous children, Cerys and Siân, and my stepchildren, Jacob and Isabella. They are my protective factors, without whose unstinting presence, none of these words would have been written.

A special thanks to my siblings and parents. Being brought up in a household filled with such fabulous storytellers has proven to be the best grounding for writing.

A huge thank you to Cath for her unwavering support and encouragement. Likewise, to Adam and the gang at South Shields Fiction Writers (a very talented group, indeed), there is a heartfelt thank you.

Thanks to all at Blossom Spring Publishing for this opportunity – Claire for her advice and guidance; Isabel for her editing suggestions and humour; and Laura for her fabulous artwork in the cover design. I can't thank you enough.

David John Peat

About the Author

David was born in Newcastle-upon-Tyne and lives in the North East of England with his wife and stepchildren; his own children live nearby. He has an MA in Creative Writing from Northumbria University and a degree in Psychology.

He is a teacher who has worked as a Learning Mentor, Residential Child Care Officer, and Youth Worker. He is passionate about children's rights and the opportunity for children to read. His love is writing, and he immerses into words during his spare time.

As a child, David did not have his head in a book. His interests were around sport, music, and politics, and although the sporting prowess and attention to politics may have waned, he constantly listens to music. He creates a soundtrack connected to what he is writing to act as an inspiration. The tap of the keyboard is drowned by beating basslines!

David's favourite authors are John Irving, Irvine Welsh, John Niven, and Alex Wheatle as they mix reality, crime, and social conscience with humour, wit, and mystery. He self-published his debut novel, *Flaming Adolescent*, in 2020, and *Nessun Dorma* is his first published novel through Blossom Spring Publishing.

www.blossomspringpublishing.com

Printed in Great Britain
by Amazon

22333562R00182